The Unforgettable Mr. Darcy

A Pride and Prejudice Variation

Victoria Kincaid

ISBN: 978-0-9997333-2-5

Chapter One

"What shall I do if Miss Bennet will not speak with me?" Bingley asked. "If she cuts me?"

The carriage rattled over a bump in the road, causing Darcy to lurch as he considered how to respond to this latest inquiry. This subject had occupied Bingley's entire conversation for the length of their journey to Hertfordshire. Darcy considered new ways to offer reassurances. "It is highly doubtful that Miss Bennet has ever cut anyone in her life."

"No, no. She is an angel." With a small sigh, Bingley fell back against the squabs. Within a few minutes he would no doubt find a fresh cause for concern, which Darcy would need to assuage.

Darcy gritted his teeth, wishing he could be as sanguine about his welcome as he was about Bingley's. Miss Jane Bennet would assuredly receive his friend with tolerable composure and a warm smile, but Darcy could not be as certain about his own reception. Miss Elizabeth Bennet was unlikely to cut Darcy publicly, but her reception of him might be cool. Even disdainful. She might even refuse to speak with him in private, thus depriving him of the opportunity to apologize for his behavior in Kent. The words he had uttered during his proposal at Hunsford Parsonage continued to haunt him; only a heartfelt and abject apology could possibly exorcise them.

Bingley need only apologize to Jane Bennet for his precipitous departure from Netherfield in November. In contrast, Darcy sought Elizabeth's forgiveness for having offended and insulted her—and her family—while making her an offer of marriage. Not for the first time he wondered if there had ever been such a maladroit proposal in the history of the world.

Darcy's fingers drummed restlessly on the seat beside his leg. Perhaps this was a fool's errand. Upon waking that morning, Darcy had nearly convinced himself of its futility; were it not for his obligation to Bingley, he might have begged off the whole venture.

Darcy's regret over his role in separating Bingley and Miss Bennet had been increasing for some time. As had, he admitted to himself, his desire to see Elizabeth Bennet once more. Two days ago, Darcy had finally confessed to his friend that he had concealed Miss Bennet's presence in London the previous winter. He also had unburdened himself of the entire sad tale of his proposal to Elizabeth at Hunsford. While rejecting Darcy, Elizabeth had suggested that her older sister had been anything but indifferent to Bingley and actually had mourned the loss of his company.

Bingley's fitting anger at Darcy's duplicity had quickly given way to eagerness to see the woman again and seek her forgiveness. When Darcy offered to make amends for his deceit, Bingley demanded that Darcy accompany him to Netherfield as his penance. Darcy had agreed with alacrity. Over the long months of May and June, he had harbored delightful fantasies of encountering Elizabeth, begging her forgiveness, and demonstrating the amiable side of his nature. Perhaps there was hope he could change her opinion of him.

But the nearer the horses brought them to Longbourn, the more Darcy's doubts increased. While Bingley had every reason to anticipate a warm reception, Darcy did not. After all, Jane Bennet had never declared Bingley to be the last man in the world she would ever be tempted to marry.

"Darcy?"

Bingley's voice roused Darcy from his reverie and the sight of both his fists clenched on his thighs. Deliberately relaxing his stiff hands, he nodded at Bingley. A smile was beyond his capacity at the moment.

But his friend was not concerned with Darcy's state of mind. "What if she is engaged to somebody else?"

"Surely not in so short a span of time," Darcy said even as his mind seized the possibility. *Elizabeth* might have accepted an offer from another man! Nausea roiled his stomach as Darcy silently urged the carriage to greater swiftness—as if arriving half an hour earlier could thwart such an event.

Dear Lord, there were so many possibilities with which he could torment himself.

Momentarily appeased, Bingley glanced idly out of the window. In relaying the story of the disastrous proposal in Kent, Darcy had deliberately avoided details. His friend did not know of the vehemence of Elizabeth's rejection or how badly he had botched the proposal. If Bingley understood on what terms they had parted, he never would have suggested that Darcy face her again. He would not have understood why Darcy leapt at the opportunity to visit Longbourn.

Darcy did not understand it himself, save that he had no choice.

Darcy had tried for the better part of three months to forget his feelings for Elizabeth, but she had haunted his waking thoughts and inhabited his dreams. His stubborn heart insisted that only Elizabeth would make an acceptable wife. Every other woman he met paled in comparison.

Bingley noted the angle of the sun. "We are in good time. Perhaps we might visit Longbourn before arriving at Netherfield?"

"Of course," Darcy said, simultaneously anticipating and dreading the inevitable.

***

Darcy stretched his stiff legs as he alighted from the carriage, hoping that the Bennets would offer them some refreshments. Hours in a closed coach had made for a stifling journey.

The late afternoon sun was still bright, and Darcy squinted as he surveyed the front of Longbourn. There was none of the activity he associated with the house—no servants bustling about or chickens pecking along the drive. The sounds of giggling Bennet daughters did not float in from the garden. Was the family from home? No, there was no reason for alarm; everyone simply must have sought refuge from the heat in the relative coolness of the house.

The two men strode to the front door, and Darcy reached out to knock—only to withdraw his hand with an oath. A length of black crepe had been secured to the knocker.

Bingley sucked in a breath. "They are in mourning."

The two friends exchanged a swift glance. If only Darcy knew the family well enough to have maintained a correspondence with Mr. Bennet! Or indeed anyone in the neighborhood. But he had been too proud then to forge the ties that would provide him with valuable information now.

What if they mourned Elizabeth's father? The Longbourn property was entailed away upon the odious Collins, placing the Bennets in distressing circumstances. Or perhaps it was Elizabeth's mother—or one of her sisters. Darcy's heart clenched painfully in his chest. What had Elizabeth endured these past few months? He should have visited earlier.

Bracing himself for distressing news, Darcy banged the head of his walking stick on the door.

The ensuing wait stretched several minutes, tempting Darcy to knock again, but finally the door was opened by a craggy faced housekeeper. She stared dully at the two men, only coming alive when they gave their names and produced cards.

She ushered them into a cramped drawing room, mumbling that the family would soon join them. Darcy's eye was caught by a fraying sofa arm and several chairs at least thirty years out of fashion, but he dismissed such observations as uncharitable. The housekeeper eventually returned with a tea service that she set on a low table, but they still saw nobody from the family.

After several minutes, the door opened to admit Mr. Bennet, moving slowly and with a heavy tread. At least he was not the one who had perished, Darcy thought with relief. Still, he might have aged ten years since their last meeting; Bennet's face was drawn and pale as he shook his visitors' hands. They had exchanged only a few pleasantries before Mrs. Bennet and Miss Jane Bennet—both wearing black mourning clothes—slipped into the room. Darcy had hoped the deceased was some distant relative, but their demeanor and dress suggested otherwise.

Mrs. Bennet gave Darcy a cursory curtsey but hurried to Bingley, embracing him warmly. "Mr. Bingley, I am so glad you are come, even under these circumstances!"

"I am very glad to be back in Hertfordshire, madam," Bingley responded.

Surprisingly, the normally voluble Mrs. Bennet did not follow up on the subject but merely invited them to sit. Darcy took a chair opposite the three Bennets while Bingley and Jane had somehow managed to sit beside each other. A long, uncomfortable silence followed.

"I am afraid we are behind the news," Bingley said finally, his face solemn. "I see that your family is in mourning…?"

Jane Bennet's hand flew to her mouth, her eyes wide with horror.

"You do not know?" Mrs. Bennet exclaimed. "I thought you called to offer your condolences."

"I am afraid we have had no recent word from Meryton," Bingley responded.

Tears rolled down Jane's cheeks. Darcy found himself holding his breath. All evidence suggested a grave loss. Had one of the younger daughters perished?

"Our darling Lizzy is gone!" Mrs. Bennet sobbed. "Gone! A full fortnight now."

Chapter Two

Darcy's mind spun. He heard the words but was unable to comprehend them. *Who was Lizzy? Oh yes, that was what the Bennet family called Elizabeth.* But that meant…

The room swung alarmingly, causing Darcy to grab the edge of his chair.

"Elizabeth has passed away?" Bingley echoed incredulously.

No. No.

Darcy's head shook in denial even as Mr. Bennet nodded solemnly. Darcy staggered to his feet. "No…" The word was intended to be a forceful denial, but it emerged as a single strangled syllable. The world reeled again, and Darcy grabbed the back of his chair to keep his balance.

The eyes which had been fixed on Bingley now turned to Darcy. Mr. Bennet blinked rapidly at him while Mrs. Bennet's mouth hung open with an imitation of a fish that would have been humorous under other circumstances. Jane Bennet's eyes were soft with understanding even as she blinked back her own tears. Darcy could only conclude that only Jane knew the story of his disastrous proposal to her sister.

Darcy's mind scrambled about like a frenzied animal in a cage, seeking relief from a horror that could not be escaped. The words could not possibly be true. He conceived and immediately dismissed several explanations. He had misheard. Or there was a mistake. Perhaps they lied. Or they meant some other Lizzy.

Of course, his Elizabeth could not have perished. Not just before he had realized how badly he needed her in his life. Not when happiness had seemed within his grasp. At any moment she would walk through the door and take her place on the settee beside her sister.

But the rational part of Darcy's mind reasserted itself. No other explanation was possible. At the very moment he had recognized that he would do anything—give anything—if she would accept his hand, she was lost to him. His resolutions to improve his behavior…his rehearsed apologies…his plans for the future… It was all for naught.

Bingley's eyes darted to Darcy's face as he realized that choking noise was emerging from the back of his own throat. This reaction must necessarily betray his feelings for Elizabeth, but it hardly signified. Nothing mattered now.

Elizabeth…

Darcy's shock and horror were reflected in Bingley's face. As Jane sobbed softly into a handkerchief that already was quite damp, Bingley's hand hesitantly reached out to hers where it lay on the arm of the settee. Jane glanced up at Bingley in surprise. Then her fingers curled around his.

Darcy averted his eyes.

"How—" Bingley cleared his throat. "How did such a melancholy event come to pass?"

Knowing the particulars would change nothing, Darcy thought dully. Still unsteady on his feet, he toppled back onto the chair, allowing the words of the conversation to wash over him. Their meaning registered only in a distant part of his mind.

"Oh, it was the most dreadful thing!" Despite her evident grief, Mrs. Bennet's voice was strong, as if she relished relaying the bad news. "I had presentiments of danger. I did. I told my sister Phillips that no good would come of the trip, but nobody would listen to me."

Mr. Bennet rolled his eyes.

"Lizzy had planned on visiting the Lake District with her aunt and uncle, but they had to alter the plans at the last minute. Would that they had undertaken that journey! Then my beloved Lizzy would still be with us." Mrs. Bennet dabbed her eyes dramatically with her handkerchief. "Instead the Gardiners took Lizzy to Brighton where she could visit her sister Lydia. Lydia is a particular friend of Mrs. Forster's you see, and such a favorite with all the officers."

Mr. Bennet appeared to be grinding his teeth.

Oblivious, Mrs. Bennet rattled on. "While at Brighton, Lizzy thought to visit her friend, Anna Wilson, who married a man from the isle of Jersey. The Gardiners' friend captained the cutter that takes supplies to the garrison on Jersey; he offered to take Lizzy so she could call upon her friend. She was the only woman aboard, but the captain said he would watch over her…."

Here Mrs. Bennet paused and glanced at Darcy uncertainly, although Bingley had asked the question. Darcy nodded for her to continue. He had never been to Jersey, or any of the Channel Islands, but he knew they were heavily fortified since they lay so close to the French coast.

"Well," Mrs. Bennet continued with a flourish of her handkerchief, "the boat had almost reached Jersey when it exploded!" Her eyes were wide with excitement. "Just blasted to pieces!"

In the ensuing silence, Mr. Bennet stood and strode swiftly from the room, blinking furiously. His wife paid him no heed. As Jane sobbed anew, Bingley handed her his handkerchief.

"There was quite a lot of gunpowder in the hold, you see," Mrs. Bennet explained after a moment. "Somehow it ignited."

Now Darcy recalled reading of the incident in the paper, but he had taken little notice of it. How blissfully ignorant had he been, unaware that such a distant incident had ruined all his chances for happiness!

Mrs. Bennet was sniffing dramatically and dabbing her eyes.

Bingley released a shaky breath. "Did anyone survive the mishap?"

The older woman shook her head vigorously. "It was very deep water. They were not even able to recover m-most of the b-b-bodies..." Her tears flowed more freely, affected grief giving way to genuine emotion. "My L-Lizzy at the bottom of the ocean!" The last word dissolved into a sob.

Bingley's eyes sought Darcy's in wide-eyed alarm as they listened to the quiet sobs of the two women. A distant part of Darcy's mind supposed he should attempt to provide words of comfort, but grief paralyzed his tongue.

Eventually, Jane stumbled to her mother, sitting beside her on the sofa and embracing her.

I should give my condolences. It is only proper under the circumstances. But the moment seemed beyond any possible speech, the events too enormous for words. If he so much as opened his mouth, Darcy would shatter into shards—like a glass vase dropped on the floor, never to be reassembled. *I will never see Elizabeth again.*

How paltry and petty his objections to Elizabeth were revealed to be. Her family's lack of propriety, her connections shriveled to insignificance. He had allowed these trivial considerations to blind himself to her truth worth. In other words, he had been an unpardonable fool. He would happily accept an entire town's worth of inappropriate relations if he could have another hour's conversation with her.

A thick, uncomfortable silence had fallen over the room. Finally, Bingley coughed. "Is there to be a service?"

Darcy's heart gave a tiny leap. He could make one more gesture to honor Elizabeth; he could attend her funeral.

But Jane dashed the hope to pieces in the next moment. "The funeral was a week ago," she responded in a low voice. "There is a headstone in the churchyard, although we had nothing to bury." Fresh tears welled in her eyes.

Darcy pictured Mr. Bennet standing solemn and solitary by the graveside of his second eldest daughter. No wonder the man had aged so considerably.

As another heavy silence closed in, Darcy conjured up words of sympathy, but the huge obstruction in his throat made speech impossible. He breathed too quickly but could not seem to slow the strangled gasps, even as the lack of air made him lightheaded. The walls of the room were bearing down on him, slowly and inexorably, and he needed to escape.

Darcy lurched to his feet. "I fear you have long been desiring our absence at such a time."

Appearing a bit shocked, Bingley also struggled to stand.

Jane regarded Darcy sympathetically. "Your visit was a welcome distraction. I hope you will come again." Her gaze slid to Bingley.

He nodded earnestly. "If you would like."

"I pray you do return," Jane responded, regarding him shyly. "It is good to have the comfort of friends."

Darcy shuffled toward the door but paused beside Mrs. Bennet's chair. "My condolences on your loss, madam."

She inclined her head but averted her eyes, obviously finding his manners wanting. But Darcy's heart had lodged in his throat, and he could say no more.

Without having made a conscious decision to leave, Darcy found himself sweeping over the threshold and into the corridor, where his feet carried him to the door. He could not escape Longbourn quickly enough.

***

She is dead. She is dead. She is dead. The rhythm of the horses' hooves seemed to pound out the words again and again until he could hear nothing else. When he closed his eyes, he saw Elizabeth's face: the pert smile and fine eyes that he would only ever glimpse in memory. How long until the details of her features faded in his mind?

He had no likeness of Elizabeth, no miniature or silhouette. No lock of hair. No letters. With time, would he forget the curve of her cheek? The sparkle in her eyes as she teased him?

He had remained only one night at Netherfield, visiting Elizabeth's grave in the morning before boarding the carriage for London. The sight of the gravestone had compounded the weight upon his chest. Its very existence was akin to a death knell.

Darcy's father often had spoken to his mother at her gravesite in Kympton churchyard, and Darcy had been tempted to address Elizabeth at hers. But Anne Darcy's body rested quietly in the bucolic country churchyard while Elizabeth's was in some unknown watery grave. He would be casting his words into an empty hole in the ground.

Bingley had remained behind at Netherfield, gladdening Darcy's heart. Now might not be the time for Bingley to resume his courtship of Miss Jane Bennet, but she—and her family—had obviously welcomed his presence. Before his departure, Darcy had begged his friend for any word should the Bennet family want for anything. He should have been a better friend to them before Elizabeth's death, but he would do what he could for them now.

Bingley had agreed, although Darcy suspected that his friend intended to address any of the family's needs himself. Darcy had no doubt that one day he would attend Bingley's wedding to the eldest Bennet daughter.

Perhaps sufficient quantities of brandy might help Darcy survive the ceremony.

Bingley's besotted stares at Jane were one of many reasons Hertfordshire could not be endured. Every sight in Meryton, every room in Netherfield, every word spoken at Longbourn recalled Darcy's loss.

He drew in a ragged breath and released it slowly, willing himself to calm. Outside the carriage window, heavy clouds hung over endless fields of wheat. For hours rain had seemed imminent, but the day remained gray and arid.

Darcy tried to slow his thoughts, achieve a state of numbness. But he was unable to prevent himself from cataloging the missteps that had led to this melancholy place. *If I had been less proud and difficult when making my proposal, perhaps Elizabeth would now be my wife, safely ensconced at Pemberley. If I had visited Longbourn earlier, she might have been persuaded to change her mind. If I had not allowed my damned sense of superiority to interfere with Jane and Bingley's romance...*

He had assumed he had all the time in the world to make Elizabeth love him. Even after his disastrous proposal, he had expected to have a second opportunity.

If she had accepted him—if he had made it possible for her to accept him—she never would have been on a ship bound for Jersey.

Darcy's hands curled into fists, nails biting into his palms. He was so damnably *useless*. During her life, he had caused Elizabeth only anger and grief. And now she was beyond the reach of any benevolence.

Furthermore, he had encouraged the Bingley sisters to disparage the Bennets—a family now sunk low into grief. And Darcy could do nothing to rectify the situation or assist the family. Perhaps someday he might be of a small service to them, but otherwise he was useless. Even Bingley did not need Darcy; he could easily conduct a courtship on his own.

Now Darcy would return to London—to balls and card parties and dinners. Every activity more empty and useless than the next. Each place populated by people who did not know his devastation. He had not been engaged to her nor had he formally courted her. His grief would be invisible to everyone, compounding the pain.

Women would talk and flirt with him. Men would joke and converse about horse racing and the latest legislation in Parliament. Nobody would realize that they were speaking with a hollow man; he would appear normal, but inside he would be empty.

How could he endure one day—let alone months, years—of balls and dinners?

Darcy's walking stick rested across his legs. It trembled violently under his hands. Was the shaking a manifestation of his fear—or anxiety?

No. He was shaking with…anger. Elizabeth had been torn from his life. Torn away from her family. It was grossly unfair…

Perhaps anger made no sense in the situation, but with every beat of his heart, it pulsed through Darcy's veins, demanding action. Foolish heart. What action could he possibly take?

He could not save Elizabeth. Her family did not require saving. What was left? Vengeance?

Elizabeth had drowned; he could hardly take revenge upon the sea. But something had caused the ship to explode. The Bennets had possessed few details about the accident, and the newspaper accounts had been vague about a cause. He had assumed it was an accident caused by large stores of gunpowder and a careless match. But Britain was at war.

Was it possibly a deliberate act? Had a specific person robbed him of his beloved?

Darcy's breath quickened. If someone had taken Elizabeth from the world—and from him—Darcy wanted him punished. But how could he possibly learn what had happened to the ship?

Fortunately, Darcy knew just the person to answer that question.

***

Darcy found the object of his quest the moment he stepped into White's. In the first room he entered, Darcy's cousin, Richard Fitzwilliam, was lazily perusing the day's paper, a glass of port at his elbow. Unsurprisingly, given the time of year, they were the room's only occupants.

"William!" Richard stood and shook his cousin's hand heartily. "I thought you were gone to Netherfield with Bingley. What brought you back to town?"

An unobtrusive servant arrived with a glass of brandy for Darcy; they knew his tastes at White's. Darcy dismissed the man with the assurance that he would need nothing else. "Nothing good." He sank into the upholstered chair opposite Richard's.

Eager to delay his story, Darcy took a sip of the brandy, relishing the burn as the liquid slid down his throat. He would need every drop to endure the conversation.

Alerted to his mood, Richard leaned forward in his chair. "Good God, man, what is it?"

Darcy stared at his brandy. "Do you recall my confession the night of the Fairchild ball?"

"Of course. We were in our cups, but I was not too foxed." Richard shook his head. "I still cannot believe Miss Bennet refused your offer, although it did explain your foul temper."

Darcy took another sip, holding his glass in trembling hands.

"Did you visit Hertfordshire with the purpose of calling upon Miss Bennet?" Richard arched a brow at him.

"I hoped to apologize and win a chance to court her properly."

"Your countenance tells me your effort was not successful. Did she refuse to see you?"

Darcy opened his mouth, but no sound emerged. He swallowed and tried again. "She is gone… Elizabeth is dead." The words emerged as a harsh whisper.

Starting, Richard nearly dropped his glass. "Good God, Darcy! Hell and damnation!" After taking a moment to collect himself, his hand reached out to touch Darcy's forearm. "I am so sorry." He gave a slight shake of the head. "I do not have the words…"

Darcy inclined his head. There were no words for such an occasion.

Richard sighed. "She was such a…lovely lady. Beautiful, lively…clever…"

Both of Darcy's hands squeezed the brandy glass. "Yes."

"How did it come to pass? Was it an illness?"

"She was a passenger on the cutter that exploded near Jersey."

Richard's mouth dropped open. "Elizabeth Bennet was aboard that ship?"

"She was visiting a friend who lives on the island."

Richard's abstracted look and the way he rubbed his chin suggested his cousin was considering what to say. Employed by the War Office for nearly a year, Richard had dropped enough hints that Darcy had no doubt his cousin was involved in espionage of some kind.

"What can you tell me?" Darcy fixed his cousin with a stare. "The War Office must have investigated the disaster. They could not ignore it."

"I should not tell you anything," Richard said slowly.

Should not was not the same as *would not*. "So they are investigating it."

Richard sighed. "Of course. But with the ship itself at the bottom of the Channel, they can discover very little. Nonetheless, the incident is very suspicious. Captain Briggs was not a careless man and would not have stored his gunpowder recklessly."

"The War Office suspects sabotage?"

Richard tossed back some more port. "We believe someone aboard the ship ignited the gunpowder."

"Do you know who?"

"There is a French spy who has sabotaged other ships and ruined cargo, but he has never killed before." Richard was holding his glass so tightly Darcy was surprised it did not shatter. "Major Bellows fears Napoleon is considering an invasion of the Channel Islands."

Darcy nodded. It made sense to deplete the islands' supplies of gunpowder and kill replacement troops before an invasion. "Do they know the spy's name?"

"He goes by the code name Black Cobra."

"What is a cobra?"

Richard waved one hand. "A kind of snake found in India—very poisonous. I do not know how the man acquired the name. One suspects he bestowed it upon himself."

Darcy leaned forward in his seat, eying Richard intently. "How does the War Office plan to apprehend him?"

"We cannot." Richard's shoulders slumped. "We do not know his true name or the first thing about his appearance. One cannot capture a ghost."

Darcy set his glass on the table with a thump. "But he is not a ghost. He is a man—who must have left some trace of his presence."

"He would be in France now." Richard grimaced. "Chances are he set a fuse and escaped the ship in a rowing boat. They were not far from the French shore."

"Does the crown have any agents in that part of France?" Darcy asked.

Richard blew out a breath. "We have a few, but the Black Cobra covers his tracks well. We know nothing about him, save his code name. The bastard is likely to escape any punishment."

Darcy launched himself from his chair and stalked to the window, where he stared without interest at the London street below. "Elizabeth deserves better than that." Darcy slammed his palm against the wall. "Her death should not be unavenged."

"I do not disagree. But the War Office is overextended as it is. We do not have enough men to track the movements of Napoleon's troops or sufficient funds to attract more agents. And vengeance is not a high priority."

"Surely there is something to be done…" Darcy said slowly, an idea forming in his head. "You could send me to France. I will find him and bring him to London for justice."

Richard's shock would have been comical under other circumstances. "What are you about, Darcy?"

"I can visit the area in disguise and make contact with your agents. They can help me find the man." The more he spoke, the more he warmed to the idea.

"No, it is too risky. The moment you open your mouth—"

"I speak fluent French, as you well know. Adele served as my governess until I was ten and Georgiana's after that; she and I spoke nothing but French."

Richard waved his hand in acknowledgement of this fact. "Still, it is too dangerous. You have responsibilities—"

"I had a responsibility to Elizabeth!" Darcy roared, startling his cousin. He took a deep breath, trying to regulate his tumultuous feelings; Richard did not deserve his ire. "If I had courted her properly, this would not have happened," he said in a hoarse voice.

"You are not a gypsy fortune teller. You could not have foreseen what would happen."

Darcy scowled. "If I had not proposed in such an offensive manner, she might have accepted my offer and would now be living safely at Pemberley."

Richard snorted. "You can find a reason to take responsibility for anything. Tell me, how is the Peninsular War your fault?"

"Richard, I must do something." Darcy paced the length of the room. "I need employment—a purpose. I am not fit for civilized company as I am. I must do something before I run mad." He stopped and stared at his cousin. "I may do nothing for Elizabeth now, but if I can bring her murderer to justice, it would mean something to her family." Darcy ran both hands through his hair. "And perhaps I might gain some measure of peace."

His arms crossed over his chest, Richard regarded Darcy skeptically.

"Send me to France," Darcy pleaded. "I may help the crown—at no cost."

"No, merely at the risk of my dearest friend's life." Richard's tone was scathing.

His cousin's skepticism would not deter him. From the moment Richard had mentioned the Black Cobra, Darcy's course had been clear.

"You hope to find her body." Richard's words were a statement, not a question.

The thought had occurred to Darcy. If he could bring her remains home to Hertfordshire, it would salvage a little solace from the tragedy. But Richard would never see it that way, and Darcy had no desire to argue the point.

Instead he leaned across the table, holding Richard's eyes. "I can travel to France with the blessings of the War Office, or I can go on my own. You cannot stop me."

Richard glared. "Damnation, Darcy!"

Finally, Richard looked away with a heavy sigh. "Very well, I will discuss your offer with my superiors, but they may not agree to send you."

Darcy shrugged. Their disapprobation would present only a small obstacle. One way or another, he would go to France.

Chapter Three

Two days later, a small boat rowed into the surf near a beach on the French coast. With a nod to the sailor manning the oars, Darcy jumped over the side and waded to shore, thankful it was summer. He could let his feet dry on the beach before donning his stockings and boots. The journey would have been far more unpleasant in January. Soft splashes behind Darcy warned him that the rowing boat was returning to the fishing vessel that had brought him across the Channel. With its departure went any opportunity for Darcy to change his mind. He was quite alone in enemy territory. *This was what I wanted. I have a mission to complete,* he reminded himself. Still, he could not completely suppress a shiver of unease.

After the War Office approved his plan, Darcy had consulted the navy's best sailors, as well as a few fishermen who regularly navigated the Channel. Considering the weather, the time of day, and the currents, the experts had agreed that a small boat escaping from a Jersey-bound cutter in the late afternoon most likely would land in Brittany, particularly the Saint-Malo area.

The office had several agents in Brittany; one lived near Saint-Malo, and Darcy's first task would be to contact him. "If the Black Cobra is in Brittany, Pierre Dreyfus will know about it," Richard had said confidently. Darcy had strict instructions not to apprehend any suspected spies himself; any attempts to capture and punish the man should be left to the War Office. But Richard had relayed the instructions with an air of weary resignation; he knew it was unlikely that Darcy could prevent himself from meting out justice.

Darcy waded on to the beach, sand crunching under his feet. Although a wispy cloud concealed the moon, there was sufficient illumination to prove the beach was fortuitously empty. A midnight stroll in the surf would be suspicious.

Glancing up, Darcy saw the ancient citadel of Saint-Malo—with its lone church steeple—silhouetted against the sky. That was his destination; Dreyfus's house lay just outside the walls at the city's southern edge.

Trudging across the beach, he found a path snaking up the cliffs and into the town. He sat on a boulder as he brushed sand from his feet and donned his hose and boots, wincing as he pulled the latter on. The leather was far stiffer than what Darcy was accustomed to; likewise, his clothing was coarser than anything ever worn by the master of Pemberley. Greeves, Darcy's valet, would be appalled. But he was to pass himself off as a wandering laborer, and the master of Pemberley's clothing would not suffice.

Darcy rolled down his trousers and tucked them into his boots. They were still damp at the edges where they had touched the water, but the warm night air was drying them quickly. All his clothing in place, Darcy swung his satchel over his shoulder and started up the side of the cliff. Hopefully he would reach Dreyfus's house by the time the sun arose.

***

The sun was just peeking over the horizon as Darcy laid eyes on the house he sought. It was set back from the road, screened from view by trees and undergrowth and accessed by a short drive that branched off from the main road.

The house was constructed of the same wood and warm yellow stone as the other houses in the area. Not terribly large but well maintained, it was the sort of abode a prosperous merchant or solicitor would own in England.

A short, round-faced housekeeper answered the door when Darcy knocked.

"Bonjour," Darcy addressed the woman in French. "I am calling for Monsieur Dreyfus. I am a friend of his uncle's." This lie was the code he had been given by the Home Office. Richard had assured Darcy that Dreyfus had been notified of his arrival and would be prepared to render all possible assistance.

The housekeeper gave him a sour look. "Mr. Dreyfus is not at home."

Darcy strove to keep his face impassive. This was a blow to his plans.

"But he did expect you," his housekeeper hastened to add. "You are welcome to stay and rest. I can supply a bit of breakfast, and he will return by mid-afternoon." Her attempt at a welcoming smile more closely resembled a smirk.

Mid-afternoon! Darcy was loath to lose so much time. During those hours he could question a good number of people in Saint-Malo for evidence of the Black Cobra. "Very well. I will return at mid-afternoon."

The woman finally showed some animation. "No, no. Mr. Dreyfus was quite adamant that you must remain. He will be offended if you refuse his hospitality."

Darcy did not respond well when others gave him orders. "I have other tasks to complete and little time," he said curtly. "I do not wish to spend half the day sitting in Mr. Dreyfus's drawing room."

She blinked. "But I can give you breakfast…and luncheon…!"

"I will purchase both in town. Please give Mr. Dreyfus my compliments and tell him I will return later in the day."

"But, monsieur—!"

Accommodating others had never been Darcy's greatest talent, and grief had made him even less inclined to please. He felt no obligation to debate his plans with the woman. "Good day." Darcy spun on his heel and stalked away, leaving the housekeeper sputtering in his wake. He did not understand the reason for her insistence, and he did not care.

***

Saint-Malo was a large town in comparison to Lambton or Meryton but tiny compared to London. A stranger would be conspicuous, but not extraordinary. Darcy had a ready tale about why he had ventured into Brittany. A half hour later, he was passing through the ancient and unmanned city gates just as the sun was burning off the last of the early morning haze. The streets were alive with activity: laborers hurrying to work, shopkeepers opening their doors, children playing and yelling, women gathered on street corners to chat.

Originally a medieval fortress, Saint-Malo had been built right on the coast, with many of its ramparts sitting on rocks that jutted out into the water. Newer homes like Dreyfus's had been constructed outside the city walls, but it was obvious that the true hustle and bustle of the neighborhood lay within the walls. Darcy made his way into the older part of the city, which boasted narrow cobblestoned streets lined with rows of identical sand-colored rowhouses of four or five stories.

Darcy wandered and learned the plan of the streets until he came upon a market square where vendors had set up tables to display their wares. A few people spared him glances, but the sight of a stranger excited little notice. Darcy breathed a sigh of relief. His height always made him remarkable, but wading through the sea and journeying along the dusty roads had added an authentic layer of grime to his simple clothing that apparently served well as a disguise.

As he wandered among the stalls of breads, cheeses, and vegetables, a loud growl from his stomach reminded him that it had been hours since he had eaten. A bit of apple with some cheese and bread would not go amiss. But he wanted to select his vendor strategically; the right merchant also would be a good source of local gossip.

He selected a plump, matronly merchant with dark hair and spectacles. She had an open smile and spent as much time chatting with her customers as she did selling them food. Her stall held a promising array of breads and fruits from which he could make a breakfast.

Adopting the shy smile of a stranger, Darcy approached her table, but before he reached it, he was bumped by a passing man. He felt fingers fumbling at the money pouch at his waist. *The man is trying to rob me. I need that money to complete my mission.* Panic gave Darcy strength. Grabbing the man's wrist, Darcy shouted in French, "Thief! Thief!"

Every eye in the square turned toward the altercation, and a few people hurried in Darcy's direction. The thief's eyes went wild with panic as he twisted his hand in Darcy's grasp, but Darcy would not let go. Before he could blink, the would-be thief produced a knife and sliced into the skin on the back of Darcy's hand.

The shock of pain loosened Darcy's grip, and the man pulled his wrist free with a wrenching twist. With amazing speed and dexterity, the thief dodged around an approaching merchant and disappeared down a narrow alley. Darcy considered giving chase, but his hand required immediate attention. The gash was long and shallow, and it bled profusely. Bright red drops splashed the cobblestones at his feet. Darcy swore—being careful to do so in French—and pulled his handkerchief from a pocket, wrapping it around his injured hand, where it immediately became drenched in blood.

The plump fruit seller hurried to his side, tutting in disapproval. "I have seen that scoundrel before, but I do not know him. He is not from Saint-Malo, that much is certain!" Several of the other merchants nodded in agreement. "This war is no good for the youth of France. It corrupts their morals and turns them into criminals. Trying to steal the purse of a good hardworking man. He should be ashamed!" Several of the bystanders muttered about Napoleon under their breath.

She offered a length of linen—clean enough for the purpose—and bound up his hand while maintaining a soliloquy on the state of Saint-

Malo, France, and the world in general. "It is all the fault of that man who calls himself our emperor!" People in the growing crowd grumbled agreement, and several uttered Napoleon's name scornfully before spitting on the ground. Richard had said Brittany and Normandy tended to be more sympathetic to the royalist cause than Napoleon's, and here was proof. But Darcy was a bit mystified as to how his encounter with a thief was Napoleon's responsibility.

"You do not support the emperor?" Darcy asked, surprised she offered her opinion so freely to a stranger.

"Bah!" She rejected the idea with a flip of her hand. "Since Napoleon, the youth have no morals, every Sunday the pews are emptier, drought makes the crops wither, and cows give half as much milk." Again, many onlookers nodded.

Darcy suppressed a smile.

She scowled at him. "I hope you are not a supporter of the 'emperor.'"

"Not at all." Darcy managed to keep a straight face.

Someone in the crowd murmured words about reporting the attempted theft to the gendarmes, and Darcy stiffened; he had no desire to attract the attention of the police.

A burly man beside Darcy laughed bitterly. "The gendarmes are worse than useless."

"Yes, there is no point in filing a report," his shorter companion agreed.

The fruit seller knotted the linen tightly around Darcy's hand. "That will do for the moment, but you must have it stitched up."

Darcy cursed inwardly, but he knew she was right. Such a long wound was unlikely to stop bleeding on its own accord. "I am new in town," he said. "Where is there a doctor?"

By now the small crowd contained at least thirty people. Most likely this was the most interesting event Saint-Malo had witnessed in weeks. *I have been in the country for a handful of hours, and already I am the center of attention*, Darcy mused. *I am indeed fortunate that I do not rely on my talents at espionage for my livelihood.*

"You'll be wanting Mr. Martin," the fruit seller said without hesitation.

"Is he the best doctor in town?"

Her brows rose. "He is the *only* doctor in town. But he will fix you up right, and he won't charge too much either. Just tell him Celeste sent you."

After receiving directions, Darcy hurried from the square, uninterested in creating additional spectacle. With the fingers of his right hand pressing on the wounded left, he twisted his way through narrow cobblestoned streets.

Each step took him closer to the seaside and homes that were notably older and larger than those he had seen earlier. Finally, he arrived at his destination: King Street. While many houses were four- and five-story townhouses, Mr. Martin's house was detached, although it crowded quite close to its neighbors. It was built of stone; two stories of windows were ornamented by blindingly white shutters, and a third story boasted dormer windows. Given its location in the older quarter of the city and its appearance, Darcy guessed it was at least three hundred years old.

He regarded it from across the street. Would it be a mistake to visit the doctor? He might ask questions that Darcy could not adequately answer. Or something about Darcy's demeanor might alert his suspicions—even his accent. It was good, but Darcy had not planned to converse at length with anyone, particularly not a wealthy and educated citizen who might be on friendlier terms with the gendarmes than the merchants.

However, the linen wrapped around his hand was turning red at an alarming rate, and the wound ached abominably. Darcy was unlikely to find someone else trustworthy to stitch it, and the doctor might have valuable information. Darcy would only need to be careful in the man's presence.

With a sigh, Darcy crossed the street and knocked on the door. It was opened quickly by a thin, ruddy-faced woman who admitted him and bade him wait after he explained his errand. As he waited, Darcy admired the furnishings. The front hall was decorated with an intricate inlaid wood floor, and a gleaming mahogany staircase led to the second floor. The house was not spacious compared to a Mayfair townhouse, but everything suggested the doctor was prosperous and meticulous.

Within a few minutes the man himself descended the stairs. He was tall and slender with a craggy face and gray, thinning hair. He gave Darcy an amiable smile. "I am Robert Martin. What is the problem?"

Some of the tension in Darcy's shoulders unwound at this friendly greeting. As Darcy explained the problem, all the doctor's attention focused on his hand. He led Darcy to an examining room where he gently unwrapped the linen, shaking his head at the sight of the wound. "This will require some stitches, I am afraid."

Darcy nodded. "Whatever is necessary."

The doctor busied himself pulling supplies out of the copious drawers in a wide white cabinet against one wall. The door opened, and a tall woman with a severe hairstyle and careworn face slipped into the room. Without looking up, Martin gestured to her. "This is my wife, Marguerite. And this is—" He peered closely at Darcy. "I am afraid I do not know your name, monsieur."

"D'Arcy," Darcy replied. "Guillaume D'Arcy."

"Very good, Mr. D'Arcy. Rest your hand here," the doctor instructed, inviting Darcy to sit at a small table. He began the delicate process of closing the gash in Darcy's hand while his wife handed him supplies as needed.

The process was painful. Darcy gritted his teeth, hoping the doctor would be quick. Martin gave him a sympathetic smile. "Where are you from, my friend? Your accent is difficult to place."

The man was trying to distract him from the pain but unknowingly provoked greater anxiety. Fortunately, Darcy was prepared for such questions. "Near Dunkirk." He winced as the doctor tugged on the stitches.

"What brings you to Saint-Malo?" his wife asked, her smile bright and curious.

"I am seeking work. I came to visit a friend who said he might be able to help me, but he is not at home."

"Yes, many young men find it advantageous to be away from home these days," the doctor murmured, his eyes focused on his work. There seemed to be a hidden meaning in the words, but it eluded Darcy. However, there was no suspicion in the doctor's eyes.

"What kind of work do you seek?" his wife asked. "We may be in a position to help you."

"That is very kind, madame," Darcy responded. "I will do anything. I had worked on a farm before."

"Hmm." The doctor frowned, and Darcy resisted the urge to flinch. Did the man suspect something? But Martin merely stood after tying the end of the thread. The row of neat stitches had closed the gash completely, and the bleeding had ceased. "I am finished, but I should inspect it again tomorrow. We must be careful of infection." The man wound a clean cloth around Darcy's hand and tied it tightly.

"Thank you, sir. What do I owe you?"

Martin named a price; however, when Darcy rose to retrieve the coins from his waist pouch, the world blurred and darkened around the edges of his vision. His head seemed ready to detach itself from his shoulders. Darcy quickly dropped back into the chair. What was wrong with him? He had been injured before, but he never had swooned like some maiden in a novel!

Mrs. Martin gave her husband a meaningful look. "Have you eaten yet today?" the doctor asked.

"No, I— It is still early."

Martin nodded sympathetically. No doubt he thought Darcy was husbanding his money. "Blood loss with an empty stomach will make you lightheaded. Why do you not join us for breakfast?"

Darcy hated to take advantage of the man's hospitality when he was completely capable of paying for his own meals. "That is not necessary."

Martin waved his hand in the air. "You will be doing us a favor, friend. We do not often travel from Saint-Malo. You may tell us stories about the rest of the world, hmm?"

It was an appealing offer. Darcy knew not when he would have another opportunity for a good meal, and he could ask the Martins for clues about the Black Cobra. "Very well, if it is not an imposition."

Husband and wife smiled as if he had given them a great gift. "I will get the breakfast parlor ready," his wife said as she hurried out of the door. The doctor stowed supplies in various drawers, chatting idly about the weather.

Breakfast was delicious. Over thick slices of bread and cheese, eggs and fruit, the Martins questioned him about his "home" in Dunkirk and his family. Darcy answered vaguely, inventing some details. But he quickly turned the conversation to recent events in Saint-Malo. After some roundabout questioning, they revealed no knowledge of strangers recently arriving in the town by rowing boat. Darcy sighed inwardly, hoping Dreyfus would have better news for him that afternoon.

At the end of the meal, Mrs. Martin excused herself, but the doctor invited Darcy to linger over coffee as he discussed possible places where Darcy might find work.

His attention wandering, Darcy's eye was caught by a bookcase opposite his chair. There were several volumes of poetry, plays of Shakespeare's, and books about English history. The doctor and his wife were well read.

The doctor's eye followed Darcy's. "You read English?" he asked. Only then did Darcy realize that every title on the bookshelf was in English. He flinched. *I am a truly terrible spy.*

Martin chuckled softly. "Do not worry, my friend. Many of us have studied English, even if it is not fashionable these days."

Darcy covered his confusion with a sip of coffee. What could he possibly say in response? A simple laborer like Guillaume D'Arcy should not be able to read English. Many men of that class would not read at all. Richard would laugh at Darcy's ineptitude.

"My mother was English," he mumbled. That was true enough.

"I say, do you speak English?" Martin's eyes widened.

Nothing to do but continue the charade. "Yes," he admitted.

"I have a patient who speaks only English, and I cannot understand her. I read English well, but my conversation leaves much to be desired."

Darcy hesitated. Revealing anything more about himself was dangerous, and he should return to Dreyfus's house, but the doctor had been very hospitable. Darcy could spare a few minutes to repay the man's kindness.

"I would be glad to be of assistance." Only belatedly did the request strike him as odd. "How did you acquire a patient who speaks only English?"

"She is a bit of a mystery. She washed up on the beach some time ago, half drowned. She has been quite ill, and we have been unable to communicate with her. We do not even have her name."

Darcy froze. Was it possible the doctor had found the Black Cobra? No, surely the spy would be a native French speaker—and male. "She could not even tell you her name?" Perhaps the woman was touched in some way.

"When one of the fishermen found her on the beach, she had suffered a blow to the head and nearly drowned. She wavered in and out of consciousness for many days; I feared for her life. Then, just as she seemed to improve, she contracted a lung fever. Her moments of consciousness have been brief, and she does not seem to understand where she is."

"Understandable," Darcy murmured. Poor woman. Now Darcy wanted to lend assistance for her sake as well as the doctor's.

"Indeed," the doctor said. "She is often feverish and incoherent. But perhaps she will say enough that you may ascertain her identity."

Darcy stood. "Take me to her." He would not allow his mission to stand in the way of assisting someone so unfortunate.

The doctor led Darcy up the polished staircase and down a corridor to a room at the back of the house. Mrs. Martin met them at the door.

"How does she fare?" the doctor asked.

His wife's expression was grave. "Feverish again. Sleeping or unconscious, I do not know which."

Darcy felt a pang of regret. If he could not speak with the woman, he could not be of much help to her. "Perhaps I should return another time," he said.

Martin considered. "At least come into the room for a minute. Sometimes she speaks in her delirium." He opened the door.

The room was dim, illuminated only by the sunshine peeking around the edges of the heavy curtains. Closed up as it was, the chamber was airless and quite warm.

On the bed, the woman lay very still, her hair a dark tangle over her face. Even from a distance Darcy could discern that her complexion was not good—pale and waxy. The covers were pulled up to her chin so that only her face was visible.

She moaned and shifted slightly as they entered, but her eyes remained closed. "Come closer." The doctor gestured to the bedside. "Perhaps she will say something."

Darcy joined the doctor reluctantly. It was the height of impropriety to be in *any* woman's bedchamber, particularly that of a stranger. Of course, Darcy had no intention of taking advantage of the situation, and nobody need ever hear about it.

This close, Darcy could see that the woman was quite young; her skin was smooth and unmarked.

She moaned again, turning her head toward Darcy. A shaft of midday light struck her face, and he instinctively reached out to brush the hair from her cheek.

Darcy froze, unable to do anything but stare.

Briefly he catalogued what he could see of the woman. Her hair was a jumble of dark brown curls, and her skin was slightly tanned under the pallor. The nose...the sprinkling of freckles on her cheeks...was achingly familiar. If she opened her eyes, he knew they would be a bright forest green.

Elizabeth was lying in the bed.

Chapter Four

Darcy blinked, trying to clear his vision. Was this a dream? A hallucination? Had he finally lost his grip on reality? His eyes scrutinized her features, looking for subtle differences that would declare him to be in error. Over the past months, his wishful mind had perceived "Elizabeths" in any number of places.

No, even after a second and third glance, the woman in the bed was still unmistakably Elizabeth.

He gasped and lurched forward, his body moving of its own accord. "Elizabeth!"

Her face was slack, her lips parted slightly, and sweat beaded on her forehead, but Darcy had never seen a more beautiful sight. He had to touch her, ensure for himself that she was real. His arms encircled her slight frame—she had lost weight—and he clutched her to his body, cradling her against his chest. She stirred but did not awaken, a warm and frail weight in his arms. Under his hands, her chest moved with shallow inhalations and exhalations. Nothing had ever felt so good. "Oh, thank God, Elizabeth!"

Tears welled up in his eyes and trickled down his cheeks, but he did not care. He held Elizabeth, and she was alive. It was a miracle. Divine providence must have brought him to this place; no other explanation would suit.

After a long silence, Mr. Martin cleared his throat. "I take it you know this woman?"

Darcy froze, recalled to himself. He was clutching a woman, naked save for her nightrail, in her *bed*. Gently, he released Elizabeth, laying her ever so carefully back on the pillows. He considered and discarded many possible explanations for such inappropriate behavior.

"Mr. D'Arcy?" the doctor prompted.

He could not help stroking a wayward lock of hair lying on the pillow. "I thought she was dead," he whispered. "In a shipwreck."

"And what is she to you?" Martin's question was tinged with disapproval at Darcy's untoward behavior.

"She is my wife." The words sprang from his lips without conscious thought. "My Elizabeth."

"Your wife?" The suspicion in the doctor's voice was no surprise. The coincidence was nearly too great to be believed. "Can you identify her in some way?"

Damnation! Darcy did not know her body as a husband would, but he had viewed her in a ball gown that revealed more than the nightrail. The image was branded on his mind. "She has a birthmark…here." He touched a place on his left shoulder.

The expression on the doctor's face suggested that he had noticed the birthmark, but he remained suspicious. Darcy wracked his brain for other things that might identify her. "She usually wears a little amber cross on a chain. Did she have it upon her?"

The suspicious lines on Martin's face smoothed. "Marguerite removed it for safekeeping." He opened the drawer in the table beside the bed and removed the necklace. A piece of jewelry had never before had such a profound effect on Darcy's heart.

"Why, this is marvelous!" the doctor exclaimed. "You believed her to be dead?"

"For…these past weeks. The ship exploded; everyone perished." Darcy brushed loose strands of hair from her face, desperate to touch her and prove that she was warm and breathing—wondrously alive.

Yet…her face was as pale as the sheet, and none of the activity in the room had disturbed her. "Why does she not awaken?"

The doctor's face turned grave. "She has contracted a lung fever, no doubt from the sea water she swallowed."

Darcy's heart beat a ragged, frantic rhythm. "Will—" His voice faltered. "Will she survive?"

The doctor's sharp eyes regarded her clinically. "Her fever has abated in the past few days, and she has awakened more frequently. She has a strong constitution. I am…hopeful."

Martin had not really answered the question. "I will do anything, pay anything," Darcy entreated the doctor.

The other man waved this offer away. "I would care for this woman for nothing. We have grown quite fond of her over the past weeks. I am pleased to have a name for her." He smiled down at the unconscious woman. "Elizabeth."

The doctor grasped her wrist to take her pulse, provoking irrational jealousy in Darcy. *He has saved her life*, Darcy reminded himself. Martin nodded and carefully placed Elizabeth's arm under the covers. "Her pulse is stronger."

Darcy was pleased at this news, but at the same time, he worried that perhaps he should be doing more. Surely he could provide some help.

In the next minute, a fit of coughing convulsed her body; her chest heaved as she wheezed and gasped for breath. Darcy clung to her hand, utterly incapable of rendering any assistance. Once the coughing eased, the doctor smoothed the covers over Elizabeth's shoulders once more, saying, "The coughing has improved." *If that is better, thank God I did not witness the worst*, Darcy mused.

The gaunt appearance of her face was rather alarming. "She is so thin. Cannot you persuade her to eat?"

"We coax her to drink water whenever she awakens." The man gestured to a glass and pitcher by the bed. "And occasionally she eats some soup."

Darcy could not draw his eyes from her face. "I cannot lose her. I cannot lose her…again."

"I will do my best." The doctor's voice was gentle. "I hope you will remain here as our guest. The room adjacent to this one is unoccupied."

The thought of putting a wall between him and Elizabeth provoked a cold shiver. "I will stay here." The words burst from him with no forethought. *Oh, Good Lord, what am I saying?*

"That is not necessary. We will take good care of your wife."

Darcy had forgotten for a moment that he was "married" to Elizabeth; that gave him the right to stay in her room. "It is necessary."

Martin chuckled. "You have not been married long, have you?"

"No." That was a true statement. "Why?"

"You act like a newly married man," the doctor said with a smile.

Darcy saw no humor in the situation. "How would *you* behave if you believed your wife to be dead?" he asked with a growl.

Martin sobered. "Of course. It would be pain beyond imagining."

Darcy returned his attention to Elizabeth's still form, aware that the doctor's eyes were upon him. After a long moment the other man spoke. "You are not a laborer searching for work." It was a statement, not a question.

Darcy stiffened. "No?"

"Your hands are too soft, with callouses only from a horse's reins." The doctor's voice was matter-of-fact, not accusatory. "A farm laborer's hands are calloused everywhere."

Darcy cursed himself silently for not having anticipated that detail.

"And you have an English wife." No doubt myriad explanations occurred to the doctor: spies, expatriate nobles, smugglers.

Darcy readied himself to fight. Were he alone he could simply flee, but he could not leave Elizabeth behind—and traveling might kill her.

But Martin spread his hands, giving Darcy a gentle smile. "I am not your enemy. To me, you and your wife are simply patients in need of care, and I have taken an oath to care for all who need it." Darcy regarded the doctor steadily. Did he dare take the other man's word? Did he dare put his life—and Elizabeth's—into this man's trust?

Darcy sighed, and his shoulders slumped. In truth, he had no choice.

"I swear I will not give you up to the authorities. I have no love for them. I would not give a rabid dog into their keeping." For a moment Martin's expression was quite fierce.

Darcy nodded, somewhat reassured.

Martin looked at him sidelong. "But will you tell me how an English gentleman and his wife came to be in Saint-Malo in the midst of a war?"

An English gentleman. Darcy rubbed his face with both hands. Despite his clothing, Darcy apparently might as well be wearing a sign proclaiming his name and rank. Very well. The doctor had guessed enough of the truth; Darcy might as well tell more. "Elizabeth was on a ship that exploded near the Channel Islands. It was reported that everyone on the ship was lost. I am seeking the man responsible for the explosion, but I did not expect to find..." He gestured to Elizabeth's still form.

"Yes, I remember hearing word of that. An explosion would explain the blow to the head, but her survival is wonderful indeed. I know of no other survivors."

The rise and fall of Elizabeth's chest fascinated Darcy, and he allowed himself to revel in the simple fact of her breathing. Although he did not like the soft rattle in her exhales or the convulsive coughs. "It is a miracle. I had no hope."

Martin clasped Darcy's shoulder. "If someone killed Marguerite, I would hunt him down as well. I wish I knew this man so I could help you seek revenge."

Darcy continued to regard the other man warily.

Martin chuckled. "Our countries may be at war, but I have no quarrel with you, sir. Your secret is safe with me."

Did Darcy even dare to trust the man? "I cannot ask you to take such risks…"

"The risk is not so great. Bretagne only grudgingly supported the revolution or the emperor. My sentiments are very common."

Darcy was humbled by the man's generosity and trust. "I thank you, sir. I will be forever in your debt."

The man took the necklace from the table and poured it into Darcy's hand. "You must keep this safe until your wife may wear it once more." Darcy stared dumbly at the pendant in his hand. "I am afraid the chain broke when we removed it from her neck."

Darcy threaded the chain of his watch fob through the loop at the top of the pendant. He had chosen his plainest, cheapest watch and fob for the journey, but the doctor's sharp look suggested it was still out of place. Hopefully the future of Britain did not rest on Darcy's abilities to pass as a common Frenchman.

Darcy heard a knock sounding on the front door. Martin looked toward the source of the noise. "Ah, I have a patient for a return visit." With a nod to Darcy, the doctor slipped through the door and closed it behind him with a quiet click.

Darcy was alone in the room with Elizabeth—his sleeping miracle. His eyes sought out her face once more, savoring the features he had never thought to see again in this lifetime. His heart was so full that it felt ready to burst from his chest. Yes, Elizabeth was ill, and they were trapped in a country at war with an unknown enemy threatening them. But Elizabeth was alive, and for the moment that was more than enough.

***

Darcy spent the remainder of the day and the following night in Elizabeth's room. An armchair beside the bed allowed him to gain a few hours of sleep. He only left the room to take dinner with the Martins— and only then with the proviso that their housekeeper would watch over his beloved.

The discovery of Darcy's "wife" caused a sensation in the Martin household. At dinner, Mrs. Martin demanded details of their courtship and marriage. Uncomfortable with the deception, Darcy kept his account brief and stayed close to the truth, describing their meeting in Hertfordshire and encounter at Rosings Park. He explained that he had proposed to Elizabeth at Hunsford, without revealing the actual conclusion of the event, and gave no account of the "wedding." Enchanted by the story, Mrs. Martin did not appear to notice his omission.

Only late into the night did Darcy recall his promise to return to Dreyfus's house, but he had no regrets. The search for the Black Cobra was no longer of much consequence. There was no reason to believe the Cobra knew or cared that Elizabeth was alive. While Darcy would still like to bring the man to justice, nothing took precedence over Elizabeth's convalescence and eventual return to England.

Darcy wanted to do everything possible to hasten her recovery. He could not look away lest he miss the slightest sign she was about to awaken or—God forbid—grow worse. He felt compelled to chronicle every twitch of an eyebrow or spasm in her hand. The coughing fits continued, but each was milder than the previous one, and the gasping in her breath improved.

Under other circumstances he might have been bored, but the simple sight of Elizabeth's chest rising and falling was mesmerizing. Only days ago, his world had ended, but now he had been given a second opportunity. *This time I will not waste it*, he vowed. *I will do whatever I can to win her love.*

Elizabeth did not awaken to full consciousness, although twice Mrs. Martin was able to rouse her to drink some water. However, she did grow more active in her sleep, moving with greater animation, moaning, or muttering incoherently. Visiting to check her pulse before retiring for the night, Martin was greatly encouraged by her progress. "She will awaken soon," he predicted.

These words provoked a fresh wave of agitation in Darcy. Naturally he longed for her recovery more than anything in the world, but he feared it as well. The Martins might be fooled, but *Elizabeth* knew they were not married. As they had not parted on amicable terms, she would not look kindly on his spousal claims.

Could he persuade her to continue the act? Or would she immediately denounce him as "the last man in the world whom she could ever be prevailed upon to marry?" Throughout the night, Darcy prayed she would awaken at a time when he might discuss the situation with her before she spoke to the Martins. If she denounced him immediately, it would complicate the situation considerably.

The next morning, he awoke early as beams of light crept around the edges of the curtains. He hastily checked on Elizabeth. Her color was better, and her breathing was less labored. He was not imagining it. Her complexion was closer to that of a woman enjoying a night's rest than a patient on a sickbed. Progress prompted joy but also unease. It was still highly improper for him to be in her room.

Shortly after sunrise, the doctor arrived to examine his patient. He pronounced her greatly improved and predicted she would soon awaken—an eventuality that Darcy both yearned for and feared. How displeased would she be to hear the news that she had acquired a "husband?"

Could he forestall her revelation of the truth to the Martins? Could he prevent her from banishing him from her life once she discovered his falsehoods? Determined as she was, Elizabeth was quite capable of deciding to find her own way back to England without speaking another word to Darcy. This thought alone was enough to cause his stomach to roil unpleasantly.

The Martins prevailed upon him to join them for breakfast. Although loath to leave Elizabeth, Darcy experienced an obligation to the Martins, who took a great risk by providing shelter to someone who could easily be accused of being an English spy. The food was delicious and the conversation pleasant, but Darcy had difficulty relaxing, wondering at every moment how Elizabeth fared. Just as they were finishing, the housekeeper called down to notify the doctor that the patient was awakening.

Since Martin reached Elizabeth's room first, Darcy lingered in the doorway, unsure how welcome he would be by her bed. Elizabeth's eyes ranged about the room with a growing look of panic, and her hands clutched the counterpane in agitation. She recoiled when she saw Martin looming over her bed.

He gave her a friendly smile. "Do not be so…scared, madame," he said to her in heavily accented English. "I am doctor. I am taking care for you." He gestured to Darcy. "And here is your husband."

Darcy held his breath, waiting for Elizabeth to reveal his falsehood, but she merely regarded him with a small frown. Knowing full well that Fitzwilliam Darcy was the last person she expected at her bedside, he attempted a reassuring smile and prayed she would not blurt out anything he could not explain away.

However, she looked away from him without any apparent recognition. Her eyes darted wildly about the room with an increasingly panicked rhythm, taking in the windows, the bed, the pictures on the walls, and the doctor, while her hands clutched the covers in a death grip. She made no sound.

"Elizabeth?" She returned his regard with blank incomprehension. Alarmed, Darcy crossed the floor in two long strides, daring to put his hand on her forearm. Perhaps she was simply too bewildered by the unfamiliar surroundings. "Elizabeth, you are safe. There is nothing to fear."

She squinted at him. "Who—" Her voice emerged as a strangled gasp. She cleared her throat and started anew. "W-Who are you?"

Perhaps her eyesight is not good. Or she is still confused from the illness. "It is I, Fitzwilliam Darcy." He kept his tone soft and unthreatening.

"Who are you?" she repeated with greater agitation.

Darcy staggered as if he were on the rolling, pitching deck of a ship in a violent storm and grabbed the bedpost for stability. "Elizabeth?"

Martin's eyes darted from Elizabeth to Darcy, no doubt wondering anew if Darcy had lied about their relationship. Darcy bent over her so she could see his face more clearly. "It is I, William."

Her brows knitted together. "Do I know you?" Her lost expression sent shivers down Darcy's spine. That blank lack of recognition was so wrong. Such confusion had no place on her countenance.

He had been prepared for denial of their relationship, not denial of his identity. Nor did she seem to be pretending her confusion.

"Is this your...husband?" Martin asked in halting English, taking his self-appointed role of her guardian very seriously.

Her deep green eyes met Darcy's searchingly. "I am married?"

Guilt stabbed him like a knife. His impulsive lie was confusing Elizabeth; perhaps the truth would be best. Darcy took her cold fingers in his, squeezing them reassuringly. "Elizabeth—"

"Is that my name?" With her free hand, she rubbed her forehead as if it pained her.

Darcy shot a wide-eyed look at Martin, who returned his expression of concern.

"Indeed. You are Elizabeth," he murmured soothingly. "Sometimes your family calls you Lizzy."

She shook her head, sitting up straighter in the bed as her breathing came in faster gasps. "That does not sound familiar. Are you sure?"

Although their problems had just become much larger than he had feared, Darcy could not help chuckling. "Yes, I am certain."

"Are you having the pain?" Martin's question drew her attention to him. She nodded and then flinched as if the movement hurt. The doctor leaned forward to examine the back of Elizabeth's head. She winced at his gentle touch. "What are you remembering?" he asked. "Can you tell me the last memory?"

Her eyes glazed over as she considered for a moment. "Nothing. I remember nothing."

"Not to worry." The doctor's voice continued low and soothing. "Can you say the name of where you grew up? Or your parents?"

She hesitated before replying. "No." Her voice climbed in pitch. "This is wrong. So wrong. What has happened to me?"

"Shh. Shh." The doctor laid her head back gently on the pillows. "You had a hurt to your head. Sometimes that causes forgetfulness." He glanced up at Darcy, speaking in French. "I have read about such cases. The condition is called amnesia."

"But the wound was weeks ago," Darcy protested. "Why is she not recovered?"

The doctor peered deeply into Elizabeth's eyes. "The blow was severe; there is still some swelling. And sometimes the effects linger even after the wound is healed."

"Her brain was damaged?" Darcy asked in a horrified whisper.

Elizabeth watched them both with sharp eyes that suggested she understood some of the conversation.

"I do not believe so," Martin said. "She seems quite rational. Her wits are intact."

"I am rational!" Elizabeth declared in English, proving that she spoke enough French to understand them.

Darcy could not suppress a laugh. "It appears her character is intact as well."

One corner of Martin's mouth curved upward. "It may be that only her memory was affected. There have been similar cases."

"Will the memories return?" Darcy asked.

The doctor shrugged. "Sometimes they do, and sometimes they do not. Researchers do not know why."

Elizabeth appealed to Darcy with a horrified expression. "Is he saying sometimes the memories do not return?" Darcy instinctively tightened his grip on her hand.

"It is too soon that we know for certain," Martin reassured her in English. "But, you are safe. Your husband is here—together with you."

She regarded Darcy in wonder. "You are my husband?"

"Yes. Fitzwilliam Darcy." He said a silent prayer of forgiveness for the falsehood.

The corners of her eyes crinkled. "That is quite a lot of syllables. Surely I do not call you Fitzwilliam." A little tension ebbed from Darcy. Forgetful or not, she was still his Elizabeth.

But what *should* she call him? He had never considered the question before. His friends simply used his last name. His parents had called him Will. The staff addressed him as Mr. Darcy. Only Georgiana called him William. Suddenly Darcy experienced a fierce yearning to hear that name on Elizabeth's lips. "No…er…you address me as William."

She nodded slowly, her eyelids lowering. "William," she murmured, her mouth lingering over each syllable as he savored the sound. Then her eyes snapped open. "Wait! What is my name? My full name?"

"You are Elizabeth Anne Bennet."

"Darcy," Martin corrected with a grin.

Damnation! He had forgotten already. How would he ever pull off this charade? "Yes, yes. Elizabeth Darcy," he agreed quickly. "We are recently wed."

She gave him a long, searching look. "I am married to you?"

"Yes," Darcy said, hating the necessity of the falsehood.

Elizabeth's eyes blearily examined him from the top of his head to the toes of his boots. "Hmm…" she mumbled sleepily as her eyelids dropped. "I may not know my name, but I know I have excellent taste in men."

Darcy had never blushed more furiously in his life.

Chapter Five

Elizabeth was deeply asleep, but Darcy could not bring himself to leave her bedside. Already her countenance had lost some of its grayish pallor and taken on a rosier hue. Her perfectly pink lips parted slightly as she inhaled and exhaled in a steady rhythm. Dark lashes brushed her cheeks. He often had envisioned how Elizabeth would look when asleep, and now he could look to his heart's content. But that was not why Darcy had difficulty tearing his eyes from her. Instead his scrutiny was borne of an almost superstitious fear that some ill would befall her if he left her presence.

The silent vigil afforded him plenty of time to think. Guilt nagged at him. He should not have told Martin that she was his wife—and should not have compounded that sin by repeating the lie to Elizabeth. Yet he could not regret it. Her eyes had gone wide with fear when she realized how she had forgotten her life. However, the presence of a "husband" seemed to be reassuring; at least she could sleep.

Still, he experienced a compulsion to confess everything when she awoke. Darcy abhorred falsehoods, and the confession would relieve his conscience. He would simply explain that he was not a husband or even a fiancé, but an acquaintance she disliked and whose proposal she had rejected.

But try as he might, Darcy could not imagine how such a confession would go well. She trusted him...now. If she knew the truth, she might believe she had nobody to trust. It would be disastrous to her peace of mind—and would perhaps slow her recovery. Surely placing her trust in Darcy was preferable. He would protect her with his life and would never do anything to hurt her. *Except lie to her*, a voice in the back of his head reminded him.

Darcy ignored it. There would be time enough for the truth later. Most likely she would remember on her own and then they could discuss it—hopefully before she ran screaming from the room.

Decision made, Darcy stood and called Mrs. Martin to watch Elizabeth. Loath though he was to leave her side, he needed to take other steps to secure her safety. Mr. Martin's promise of discretion was reassuring, but he needed to know more. Why would the man take such a risk with his family's safety?

Darcy found the doctor in his study, a dark-paneled, comfortable room with books lining two walls—exactly what Darcy would expect from such a learned man. The fireplace stood empty, but above it was a portrait of a young, blond man. He bore a striking resemblance to Mrs. Martin. A son perhaps?

The doctor was working at his desk but stood when Darcy entered. "Mr. D'Arcy, how is your wife?"

"She is sleeping now."

"Good." He nodded. "I would like to take this opportunity to examine your hand."

Darcy stared at the bandage; he had completely forgotten the wound. "It is of no matter."

Martin eyed him severely. "What will become of your wife if you die of an infected wound?"

Darcy sighed. *Damn the man for making sense!* "Very well," he grumbled, thrusting his hand forward. Martin took it in both of his hands, turning it toward the lamp on his desk as he unwound the bandage.

The stitches were small and even, and the area around the wound looked red to Darcy's inexperienced eyes. However, the doctor seemed unconcerned. "It is healing well," Martin said as he re-bound the wound. "But you must heal for several more days before I may remove the stitches."

Darcy nodded. "There is another matter I would discuss with you."

"Of course." Martin gestured to the seat before his desk, and Darcy sat. "Would you like some brandy?"

Real French brandy. Darcy's mouth watered at the thought. "Please."

The doctor went to the sideboard and poured from a glass decanter into two glasses. "What is on your mind, hmm?" Seating himself behind the desk, he handed a glass to Darcy. The brandy was as smooth and flavorful as he had imagined.

Darcy stared at the amber liquid, considering how to broach the delicate subject. "I am...surprised that you are so willing to conceal us from the authorities. They may not care about Elizabeth, but if they discover an Englishman in your home, they might arrest you..." He allowed his words to peter out, hoping the man would explain himself.

Martin set down his glass. "You are wondering if I secretly plan to present you to the gendarmes as an early Christmas present?"

Darcy would not have phrased it in such a way, but…
"Essentially."

The doctor waved a dismissive hand. "You have nothing to fear, my friend."

"To be blunt, how can I be sure? I am risking my wife's life."

The other man took a long, thoughtful gulp from his glass. "I do not know how familiar you are with the history of Bretagne, but the Chouan were very popular here, particularly in Saint-Malo."

The English newspapers had published many stories about the Chouan, French bourgeoisie who had opposed the revolution, leading to many violent clashes with republican soldiers. "I thought the movement had been crushed."

Martin's lips pressed tightly together. "It was. I myself was not a member, but…I lost friends…." He sighed. "However, the spirit of the Chouan was not completely crushed. Not here and not elsewhere in Bretagne."

Darcy indulged in another sip of brandy. He would have been more reassured if Martin had admitted to being part of the Chouan.

The doctor must have guessed Darcy's reservations; he gave a mirthless laugh. "If the Chouan still existed today, I would be the first to sign my name."

Darcy's eyebrows lifted in inquiry. What had changed?

Martin gestured to the painting over the mantel. "My son, Charles." The man could not have been more than twenty when the likeness was taken. "He was an ardent supporter of Napoleon when he was First Counsel—before the man styled himself *Emperor*." He uttered the last word with a sneer. "Napoleon claimed it was necessary to raise a Grand Army to defend France from its enemies. I doubted the necessity, but Charles—a true patriot—believed. He did not wait to be conscripted; he volunteered." Martin paused for a gulp of brandy. Darcy had a dark premonition about the ending of the story.

The doctor set his glass on the desk with trembling hands. "He was a soldier for two years, but he grew less and less content with Napoleon's cause. In his last letter to me, Charles expressed doubts about the Peninsular War. 'Why,' he asked, 'were we fighting in Spain? It does nothing to defend our borders. Spain does not threaten France.'" Martin stared into the middle distance as if seeing things not in the room. "He was not the only one with such questions."

Martin fell silent, lost in his reverie. After a long pause, Darcy cleared his throat. "Your son was sent to the Peninsula?"

Martin grimaced. "Yes. He fell in the very first battle. My friends said I should be pleased he died in battle and not of disease, as so many soldiers do." A cynical snort expressed what the doctor thought of that idea.

Darcy winced. Richard had fought on the Peninsula. Was it possible that Richard had cut down Martin's son? Unlikely, but still his stomach knotted with tension. Of course, Darcy had known that war was a horrible business, but the thought of Richard and Charles meeting in battle provoked a new awareness of the horror. Richard was a good man, and no doubt Charles had been a good man as well. Thank God Richard was now involved in espionage rather than fighting on the front lines.

"My condolences," Darcy said, aware that the words were horribly inadequate.

Martin appeared not to hear. "And now our *glorious leader* has taken the flower of France's youth to Russia. Russia! Where the cold and snow will kill them if the Russian army does not."

Darcy winced. British newspapers suggested that the French casualties from the Russian offensive were devastating.

"Why, I ask you, must we go to Russia at all?" Martin finished the rest of his brandy in a long swallow. "Everyone in Saint-Malo is sick of the war. We do not care if the 'emperor' wins or loses. We only want peace."

Darcy gaped. Such words were treasonous, dangerous to utter.

Martin gave another bitter laugh. "Do not worry, my friend. Everyone in Saint-Malo thinks the same. The war has been long and costly. Many here have lost sons, brothers, husbands—and everyone has felt the pinch of increased taxation and scarce resources. Even many of the gendarmes hate the war. They conscript too many of the youth. Young men often ask that I declare them unfit for combat. I can always find something wrong: weak lungs or flat feet. It is preferable to having them mutilate themselves to avoid conscription."

Darcy drew in a long breath. What a terrible price these people were paying for their leader's war.

"Naturally I would not vocalize such sentiments to the colonel who commands the town's garrison," Martin conceded. "But even he knows they are not popular here. Everyone speaks openly about hopes for the end of the war and the restoration of the monarchy."

Did Darcy dare trust the doctor's words? More, did he dare trust Elizabeth's life to this man? On the other hand, what was the alternative? Ferrying her to England in her present state would be nigh impossible. And the doctor's sentiments agreed with what Darcy had observed in the marketplace.

Trust did not come easily, however. Darcy stroked his chin. "How long will it be before Elizabeth can travel?"

The doctor pursed his lips as he thought. "It is difficult to predict, but at least a week. Her lungs need to recover, or you risk a relapse."

"How long until she recovers her memory?" Darcy refused to contemplate the possibility that she might never recover it.

He shrugged. "I cannot give you an estimate. The phenomenon of amnesia has not been extensively studied, and we know very little."

Darcy nodded. It was the answer he expected. He could only hope Elizabeth would be ready to travel soon. Every day increased the danger of discovery.

***

When she awoke again, she was alone. The room's emptiness made her heart beat a little faster. Although it had been disconcerting to awaken to two strange men, being alone with her own thoughts was nearly worse. Her head ached, and her throat was parched. The room was brightly lit; she was grateful for the curtains that kept out the worst of the summer sun.

Elizabeth. The darkly handsome man had said her name was Elizabeth, but it brought no sense of familiarity, no stirrings in her memory. Nor had the man himself—her husband—provoked any recollections. That was wrong, she knew. She should remember her name, her husband's name, and all manner of other things—her childhood, her parents, her home. She strained to remember even the smallest thing, but it was like reaching into a void: there was nothing she could grasp. This was wrong, all wrong. Who was she if she could not remember even the most basic information about her life? Did she even really exist?

I am in a bed. The sunshine is yellow and bright. The armchair has green and gold embroidery. She perfectly recalled words, objects, descriptions. But she could not recall even the tiniest detail about herself. *Do I prefer beef or mutton? Do I dance or sing? Do I have brothers and sisters?* Even the smallest details remained stubbornly out of reach. It was like trying to grasp clouds.

Her breath quickened, and her legs twitched as if readying themselves to flee, but she could not outrun this threat. Her panting triggered a coughing fit; she fought for breath, each gasp causing her lungs to ache.

Clutching the counterpane in both hands, Elizabeth willed her muscles to relax, her breathing to slow. *I am safe for the moment*, she assured herself. *My husband is here. I am alive.* Concentrating ferociously, she slowed her breaths until they evened out and her heart ceased its frantic pounding.

Seeking to avoid the yawning absences inside herself, Elizabeth turned her mind to other thoughts, such as discerning her location. The room was small, decorated in bright wallpaper with yellow flowers. It was sparsely furnished, with an armchair and a table by the side of the bed and a dresser against the far wall. *Is this my home? My home with William?* None of the furnishings tugged at her memory, but that meant little.

If only her head would not pound as though someone beat it like a drum!

Shakily, her fingers kneaded the hem of the sheet. The world was vast and complicated, and Elizabeth was small—tiny—and easily crushed. How could she hope to survive with no memories to rely upon? It was an impossible task. She would be lost. Utterly lost. A boat adrift in the middle of a lake with no oars and no way to reach the shore.

She fought back the black grip of panic. *I have a husband. I am not completely alone and unmoored.* What was his name? She cringed inwardly at the idea that she had forgotten such a basic fact. *William. Yes, his name is William.* As she pictured his face, her heartbeat instantly slowed. *William. The name suits him.*

Yet she recalled nothing about him or their relationship. How could she have forgotten a man so handsome, so tender? It seemed particularly unfair that she could not remember kissing him. Kisses from such a man would surely be worth remembering. No doubt she had kissed him many times. *I would kiss him now if he walked into the room.* The very brazenness of the thought made her blush.

And the wedding night! What had happened on the wedding night? She was wild to know, but her mind remained stubbornly blank.

It was part of a long list of things she did not know. "Upon my word," she exclaimed to the empty room, "I would not even recognize my own countenance!"

Suddenly it was very important to know her own appearance. Her hair was a dark mahogany, and her hands appeared young—unlined and unspotted—but she knew little else. Was she pretty? Was she tall? What was her age? A mirror hung on the far wall, but Elizabeth's position in the bed did not allow her to see it.

Climbing from the bed would not be condoned by doctor or husband, but neither was present. *Hmm....apparently I do not bow easily to the will of others. Good for me.*

If she were to make the effort, it would be best to do so now while she was still alone in the room. Sitting up provoked a wave of dizziness; Elizabeth paused for a moment to allow the room to stop spinning around her. Feeling steadier, she slid to the edge of the bed and dangled her legs over the side. They did not reach the floor. *Perhaps that answers my question about my height.* Fortunately, the dizziness remained at bay despite her movements.

Slowly, she slid off the bed, gingerly resting her weight on her feet. Her knees immediately buckled, compelling her to grab the edge of the bed. The next few minutes were occupied with steadying herself.

Holding the bed with one hand, she took a step and then another, pleased that she remained upright. Reaching the end of the bed, she was at the point where she needed to place all her trust in her legs. She took a minute to ensure her balance and then released her grip on the carved wooden bedpost, holding her breath as she stepped into the middle of the room.

Her body wobbled a bit, but she did not fall. She took another quick step, which brought her to the mirror. Steadying herself with a hand against the wall, she stared into it with rapt fascination.

The face that stared back at her might have been pretty were it not so pale and gaunt. Dark circles shadowed Elizabeth's eyes, and her cheeks had hollowed out. *How long was I sick? I might have been raised from the dead!*

At least her hair was dark and thick, curling around her face. And her eyes were bright, a startling green. *I have a few good features despite my complete want of complexion.* Under the linen nightrail, her frame was slender to the point of being thin. *I resemble a plague victim. What if my countenance never recovers?* Her stomach clenched. *Would William put me aside if I am never in good looks again?*

Without any warning, the room dimmed, her legs collapsed, and Elizabeth sank to the floor. *I am fainting. How odd, I have never fainted before. Actually, how would I know? This is so frustrating...*

The world went black, but briefly. After only a few seconds, she recovered consciousness. Her arms had broken her fall, but her legs were awkwardly twisted underneath her.

She did not try to arise immediately but remained on the floor, panting while her heart rate returned to normal. *I should call for help, but they will only chastise me for leaving my bed.*

Evidently I also am stubborn.

Once she had regained a modicum of strength, Elizabeth crawled to the end of the bed and pulled herself to standing with the help of the wooden bedpost. She needed another minute to rest before she could lift herself onto the bed. It required another rest before she had the energy to crawl up to the head of the bed, where she collapsed with her head upon the pillows, unable to muster the energy to crawl under the covers.

Elizabeth dozed, but when she awoke, nothing had changed except the angle of the sun in the window.

She considered what she had learned. The face in the mirror held no familiarity, and no memories had appeared in her head as she slept. She was a stranger even to herself. Was it possible for a person to be more alone?

Her hands clenched into fists. *I must not give way to panic. There must be other ways to learn about my situation.* Perhaps she could make deductions from her own observations. Earlier she had ignored the sounds of the household, but now she strained her ears to hear them.

A conversation between two women was taking place near the closed door to her room. Elizabeth understood only about a quarter of their words—enough to guess that the conversation concerned that evening's dinner menu.

Why did she comprehend so little of it? Was that an effect of the blow to her head? But she had understood William quite easily—every word. And the doctor had been comprehensible despite his accent. Because they had spoken...English. Her mind supplied the right word. Yes, he had spoken proper English while the doctor had spoken with a French accent. And the conversation outside her door was entirely in French—the reason she understood so little.

This amnesia was a strange thing. She could not remember anything of her childhood, but she was completely certain that she had accurately identified French and English. Had she taken French lessons as a child?

Why were the women speaking in French? And why did the doctor have an accent? She peered around the room: the furniture, curtains, paintings. Everything had felt subtly alien, although she was only now recognizing the sensation. This was not her home; there was nothing English about it.

Her heart beat an agitated rhythm, and her palms grew moist. *I must be in France.* For a moment she did not recall why the thought quickened her breathing. *This place feels safe, but I know France is not safe. Why?* But the reason eluded her. *I should be in England; I know it.* However, try as she might, Elizabeth could not picture where she lived. Did she live in a London townhouse? Or on a farm in the country? Or in an apartment over a shop?

At least if I live in the country, I may take long walks. I dearly love long walks.

How do I know that?

The strain of remembering was like trying to grab for handfuls of clouds. Her head throbbed, and her eyes drifted closed, as if the very act of trying to remember had taken more effort than her body could sustain. She fought sleep, wanting to learn more about the place, but soon her eyelids closed, and she fell deeply asleep.

***

When she next awakened, William sat in the armchair reading a book. He sprang to his feet the moment she stirred.

"How do you feel? Should I get the doctor? What do you need? Whatever you want, I shall obtain it for you."

Sitting up in the bed, Elizabeth tapped her lips thoughtfully. "Whatever I want? Hmm…I would like a strawberry and apple tart."

William took a step toward the door and then stopped, turning to her with a crestfallen expression. "I do not believe strawberries and apples are in season."

Elizabeth placed her hands on her hips indignantly. "No strawberries?" William's eyes widened with near panic until Elizabeth ruined the effect by laughing.

A slow smile broke out over William's face. "I should have known that even a blow to the head and lung fever would not quell your mischievous sense of humor."

Elizabeth grimaced. "At this moment I would happily trade it for a lifetime's memories."

Her husband's expression darkened. "Do not say so. I would not alter one thing about you."

She suppressed a shudder. Such sentiments were disconcerting when spoken by someone who essentially was a stranger. Elizabeth cleared her throat. "Would you pour me some water?"

"Of course." William poured a glass from which she drank greedily. "Have you remembered anything at all?"

"No." Trying to remember anything was like visiting a house that should be full of people and activity, only to find nothing but empty echoing chambers. Something of what she was feeling must have shown on her face. William took the glass gently from her hand. "It is early yet. You have barely started to recover."

Elizabeth wished she shared his optimism. William poured more water into the glass. "The doctor wishes you to drink. You have not drunk nearly enough over the past days."

Finding she was quite thirsty, Elizabeth eagerly drank and then held out her glass for more "Would you like some soup?" William asked. "You have not eaten a proper meal in days."

At the mention of food, Elizabeth's stomach rumbled. "I believe that is your answer," she said with a smile. "Soup would be welcome— and bread if they have it. And tea. Tea would be lovely." She could focus her attention on food and forget the agitation over her missing memories.

He left the room briefly to speak with the maid. Upon his return he hovered about the bed, observing her intently. "What else do you need?"

"I do not require such scrutiny, sir. I suspect my most interesting activity today will be falling asleep. And I am unlikely to injure myself doing so."

He shook his head. "You can always make me laugh at myself."

Was she indeed this sort of person? How strange not to even be aware of her own nature. William knew her better than she knew herself. A tight panicked feeling fluttered in her chest. What would she do if she never recovered those memories? Would she be trapped forever in a foreign country with a man who called himself her husband?

The room seemed suddenly too small, too close, with not nearly enough air. Sweat trickled from her temples as she tried to slow her breathing, but she could hear it come in harsh gasps.

"Elizabeth." William hastily clasped one of her hands. "I am here, and I will care for you. Do not fear."

How shameful that he recognized her fear! "It is only…the situation is so odd. I am a stranger to myself. You are a stranger to me."

He squeezed her hand gently. "You may trust me, Elizabeth."

Her breathing evened out. Of course, she could trust him; he was her husband. He cared about her. "Perhaps you could answer some questions?" Any information would feel like an anchor, preventing her from drifting in a vast sea of nothingness.

"Of course."

A timid scratch at the door announced the arrival of the maid with a tray of food. As she set Elizabeth's soup and tea before her, William opened the windows, allowing a fresh breeze to waft in. The soup—thick and creamy—smelled wonderful, and Elizabeth swallowed several spoonfuls as she considered what to ask.

William rolled up the sleeve of his shirt, revealing a muscular forearm, tanned from days in the sun. She knew nothing of his profession or family—or hers for that matter. His clothing was not the best quality; the weave was rather rough, and the trousers fit him loosely. He must be a farmer or other kind of worker. Perhaps she should be disappointed he did not command a greater fortune, but he had watched her with such earnest concern. Such caring was its own kind of wealth.

Thoughts of wealth gave her pause. She was unlikely to have a higher station in life than her husband, so they must be struggling. How were they in France? She bit her lip. Where would they have obtained the money for such an expensive voyage? She longed to know, but it did not seem an auspicious first question.

Instead she asked one of the first questions that had occurred to her. "Why are we in France?"

His eyebrows rose. "Figured that out, did you? You were on a ship which…met with an accident. Somehow, by divine providence, you washed up on shore here."

"And you came to France in search of me?"

He hesitated a moment. "Yes." *There is something he is not telling me.* But she had far too many other questions to linger over one inconsistency.

"Where in France are we?"

"Brittany. The town of Saint-Malo."

The town's name meant nothing to her. Her memory did supply a rough map of France and a vague recollection of Brittany's location.

Her hands moved fretfully over the counterpane. "We should not be here. I know that for certain, although I cannot say why. When can we return to England?"

He hesitated again. "We are safe for the moment. The doctor and his wife are providing us with shelter."

A memory returned in a rush. "Oh, England is at war with France! That is why it is dangerous." William nodded solemnly. "How is that I can recall that England is at war, but I cannot remember my own parents?" She rubbed her forehead fretfully.

"Mr. Martin said it often is thus with amnesia." William shifted in his chair. "The sufferers forget the details of their own lives, but factual memories remain intact."

Elizabeth swallowed a bite of bread. "Just as well. I would not relish learning to read or do sums again."

"Indeed."

He leaned forward in the chair. "Do you know how well you speak French?"

"You do not know?"

He avoided her gaze by staring down at his hands. "Our marriage was recent. We have known one another for less than a year."

Again, he was concealing something from her.

Was it possible that theirs was an arranged marriage? The thought struck her with horror. She was not the sort of woman who would want an arranged marriage. Or was she? In truth, Elizabeth knew nothing except that she was the sort of woman who took ships that met with accidents near the coast of France.

How disconcerting. She might stare into her own soul and find…nothing. What if Elizabeth discovered that she was not a good person? Not a moral person? Or that she had married William for the wrong reasons?

For that matter, how did she know that William was a good person? She had put her trust in him. Indeed, she had little choice. But she was sure he was concealing things. Might he hurt her?

She did not know how to navigate the town—or even the house. She knew nobody in this place. She must take William's word for everything. The thought made her shiver despite the warm summer air. She stared into his eyes, full of anxiety on her behalf. He had given her no cause to distrust him.

The soup bowl was empty, and the bread reduced to crumbs on the plate. As Elizabeth took a last sip of tea, a familiar lassitude crept over her limbs.

William noticed as well. "You should rest."

"But I have more questions."

He chuckled. "I am sure you do, but I will be here when you awaken."

She considered protesting, but her eyelids were so very heavy. Perhaps he was right. Elizabeth settled back on her pillows and gave him one sleepy nod before her eyes closed.

Chapter Six

The sounds of marching feet awakened Darcy.

Mrs. Martin had offered to give Darcy his own room, but he feared that Elizabeth might need him during the night, so the Martins' housekeeper had arranged a pallet on the floor for him. It was not the most comfortable bed, but it was infinitely superior to the armchair.

Only semi-awake, Darcy brushed the curtain aside and peered down at the street below the window. The rising sun was just beginning to cast a harsh summer light, touching everything with fierce radiance.

Wave after wave of French soldiers marched along the avenue in precise lines, their feet thumping in such a steady rhythm that the house's walls seemed to shake in time. Light glinted off the rifles on their shoulders and splashed over the blue of their uniforms.

Other than the cadence of the marchers, the scene was eerily silent. A few people lined the street, standing in doorways or peering out of windows—and even fewer waved flags or shouted, "Long live the emperor!" Most of the villagers were silent, observing the passing soldiers with baleful glares.

Hastily, Darcy drew back his head, twitching the curtain into place. His anxiety over being noticed was irrational; the curtain shielded him from view. However, the relentless sounds of tromping feet provoked an unease that crawled up his spine. *I am in a foreign country, a country at war. How can I hope to protect Elizabeth from the entire French army? I am a fool to even try. Yet I have no alternative.*

The sounds of rustling sheets interrupted his musings. Darcy quickly smoothed the anxious lines of his face so he could face Elizabeth with a tolerable attempt at a smile. Her eyes fluttered open. "Good morning, Mis—Elizabeth." She did not notice how he stumbled over her name, but Darcy silently chastised himself for the error.

"Good morning." She gave him a cautious smile.

"How do you feel?"

She stretched her arms over her head, a very appealing sight. "Ravenous. I suppose I have many days' worth of food to make up."

Darcy stepped out of the room to inquire about breakfast, and when he returned she regarded him shyly from under her lashes. "I am hungry for something else as well."

Darcy's heart skipped a beat, but she could not possibly mean what he thought. "Oh?"

"I am hungry for knowledge," she said. "Will you tell me about my life?" She laughed self-consciously. "Although that does sound ridiculous!"

Suppressing his more inappropriate reactions, Darcy seated himself on the edge of the bed. "Not at all ridiculous, but Mr. Martin thinks it is best if I do not tell you everything. He thinks your memories should return naturally."

Elizabeth made a sour face. He could just imagine the questions piling up inside such a naturally inquisitive person. "I can certainly answer the basic questions. Please ask," he invited her.

"Where am I from? Who are my parents? Do I have brothers and sisters? How did we meet? What—?"

Chuckling, Darcy held up a hand to stanch the torrent of words. "I can only answer them one at a time, if you please." She bounced with impatience, as eager as a young lady before her first ball.

He settled closer to her on the bed and took her hand. "Your family is from Hertfordshire. Your father owns an estate known as Longbourn."

She frowned, screwing up her face. "An estate? Is it large?"

Why would such news distress her? "Of moderate size and prosperous, I believe."

"Then…how did we meet?"

"We met at an assembly in a nearby town. I am not from Hertfordshire; I was visiting a friend."

Her hands clutched at the edge of the covers. "An assembly? Did we dance?"

He glanced away as she unknowingly touched on a sore subject. "Not that evening, though we did upon a later occasion." Perhaps she recalled something from their inauspicious first meeting that could cause her agitation. "Does this sound familiar?"

Her hands grasped the counterpane so tightly she was creating fine wrinkles. "No, not at all."

Perhaps the past was simply too fraught for Elizabeth to learn of it with equanimity. "Maybe you should rest until breakfast arrives."

She smirked at him. "I assure you that a quarter hour of sitting in bed has not fatigued me excessively. But I thank you for your concern."

Darcy snorted. She had not forgotten how to be Elizabeth. "This subject seems to agitate you; perhaps we should discuss another."

She gave him a level stare. "Did my parents approve of our match?"

Darcy hesitated. Embellishing his initial falsehood with yet more lies was so distasteful.

"They did not!" Her voice was harsh with anguish. "I see the truth in your face."

Darcy gaped, at a loss of how to respond. He had every reason to believe the Bennets would support his desire to marry their daughter if he ever had occasion to ask them.

Elizabeth continued, wringing her hands. "They disapproved of the inequality in our stations, did they not?" How had she guessed about the disparities in their fortunes? "Did we elope?"

"Elope?" Darcy felt as if he had arrived halfway through a play. "Why would we elope?"

Elizabeth gestured to his clothing. "Well, you are obviously not from an estate. Are you a farmer? A laborer?" She swallowed thickly. "A servant?"

It took a moment to catch her meaning, but then Darcy could not stifle a laugh. Once the laughter had started, it was difficult to stop. He owed Elizabeth an explanation, but the idea that he was unacceptable because his station in life was too *low*... This provoked a new bout of laughter.

When he finally gained control of himself, he apologized. "These garments are but a disguise. My clothing is usually of a better quality, but it would be too conspicuous here."

"Oh!" She sank back against the pillows in evident relief. "So what is your profession, then? A clergyman? A solicitor? Are you in the army?"

"I am of no profession. I am a gentleman."

"Oh." She exhaled slowly. "So coming to France did not bankrupt you?"

"Why would you—?" He stopped himself. It did not matter; he only needed to reassure her. "No, not at all."

"Is your property large?"

"Yes."

"And prosperous?"

"Extremely."

"So I was a complete fool to think you were a common laborer," she said with a self-mocking smile. "Your accent should have told me. In my own defense I can only say that I am recovering from a blow to the head."

"I am doing my utmost to avoid resembling an English gentleman and have utterly failed to fool the Martins, so I am pleased at least one person believed the disguise."

She rolled her eyes. "Yes, you fooled the woman who cannot remember her own name. Quite a feat." He laughed. "My family did not disapprove of our marriage?"

"No." Darcy feared lightning would strike him down, but it was a reasonable falsehood. No doubt Mr. Bennet would be quite pleased to have his daughter marry the master of Pemberley—particularly after he discovered Darcy had spent the past two nights sleeping in Elizabeth's bedchamber.

She considered for a moment, her head tilted to the side. It was such an appealing expression that Darcy wanted to kiss her. "Are my parents living? Do I have brothers and sisters?"

Resisting temptation, Darcy sat back in his chair, happy to address less fraught subjects. "You have no brothers, but four sisters. The oldest is Jane. You are second eldest. The others are... Mary..." Darcy strained to recall the names of the two younger girls; he had done his best to avoid them, but a husband would know that sort of information. "Katherine...and Lydia."

"Longbourn...Bennet...Jane...Lydia..." she repeated to herself. "Nothing. I thought that surely the names would provoke some memories."

Tears sparkled in her eyes. Darcy wanted to reach out and gather her into his arms. Blast it! He would if she were his wife in truth.

"You have been conscious for less than a full day. Give yourself more time to remember." His hand moved of its own volition to stroke her hair. He froze for a moment but then continued. Surely it would not be wrong to exhibit some husbandly behavior.

Elizabeth sighed, nuzzling his hand with her cheek. The simple gesture brought him a sense of warmth and contentment he had never experienced before. "Please tell me about my home," she said in a muffled voice.

Darcy tried to conjure the image to mind. Truthfully, the estate was not particularly impressive, and Mr. Bennet was not an especially careful landowner. But he tried to picture it through the eyes of a woman who had grown up in the house and loved it. "There are many trees and copious shady lanes for walks. A picturesque stream winds its way through the property and into the home of a friend of mine. You mentioned to me once that you especially enjoyed the walk to Oakham Mount where you could view all of the surrounding countryside."

"Did I never take you there?"

"No…we never had that pleasure. Perhaps when we return." *If you are still speaking to me.*

She turned her head, and he was transfixed by eyes as green as holly in winter. His hand was tangled in her hair, and his face was inches from hers. *You cannot kiss her. She is not your wife.* It was growing more difficult to remember that fact with every passing minute.

"Will you tell me how we met?" she asked.

The request threw a bucket of cold water on his ardor. How could he describe those circumstances without inadvertently revealing the truth of their relationship? However, he was saved from a response by the entry of the maid with a tray of food.

He carried Elizabeth's hand to his lips and murmured, "Another time, my dear. You should eat and then try to rest again."

There was a stubborn set to Elizabeth's shoulders, but already her energy was flagging. "Very well, I will eat. But I shall expect the full story when I awaken."

***

Elizabeth watched William bustle about, removing the last of her dishes and handing the tray to the waiting maid. He moved with such grace and such economy that she would guess he was an excellent dancer. *If only I could recall dancing with him!* She imagined facing him across a line of dancers, taking his hand for the turns, or speaking to him as they waited while others danced. But she did not glimpse even the shadow of a memory. It was as if her life had started the moment she awakened in this room two days ago.

William fussed with opening the windows and drawing the curtains, making sure she caught the early afternoon breeze without enduring too much sun. He was so attentive to her needs—the quintessential gentleman. How could she have believed he was anything else? He was accustomed to ordering the servants. His teeth and skin were quite good, his accent quite precise. She had been foolish not to notice before.

"Would you sleep?" he asked.

"I am not as fatigued as I was. May we speak a little longer?" He nodded his assent.

His words about his property suggested that he was not just a gentleman but also a man of considerable means. Now Elizabeth rather suspected she had married above her station. Perhaps far above it. William contended with not only a poor wife, but a poor wife who did not remember him. *If only I could will myself to remember!* But she had found nothing buried in her mind, save a few disjointed images of places and people she did not recognize.

Her husband certainly could tell her something to provoke a memory. "Tell me about when you made your offer of marriage."

William froze, one hand on the curtain. "Perhaps it is best if you recall that in your own time."

He did not want to describe how he had proposed? Surely that was a safe and joyful subject for a conversation. He seemed to be hiding something, but she did not know him well enough to guess what it might be. Ha! She did not even know *herself* well enough.

She had noticed yesterday that he was more at ease discussing her family or his estate than anything pertaining to their relationship. Very well. "Tell me about your family."

His shoulders loosened as he slipped into the armchair. Yes, this was the right approach. "My parents have been gone for a long time. I have a sister who is just turned seventeen. Her name is Georgiana."

"What is she like?"

Did he know how he smiled when he spoke of her? "She is a very accomplished musician—playing the pianoforte and the harp—but she is very shy around strangers."

"Does she like me?" Elizabeth could imagine forming a friendship with such a girl. *I like music, do I not?*

William started. "You have not met."

How curious. Had his sister objected to the union? Elizabeth's face must have revealed her consternation.

"Recall that we have not been married long," he said hastily. "I have no doubt that you and she will become good friends."

"Where is your sister now?" Elizabeth asked.

"She should be in London by now. She was to leave our home, Pemberley, in Derbyshire a few days ago to visit my aunt and uncle in London."

Yes, he must be very wealthy. "Is Pemberley a very grand house?" she asked.

"Many would call it grand." He did not make a great effort to conceal his pride.

"I must have liked it exceedingly."

He flinched again and did not answer at once. After a long pause, he said, "You have not yet visited Pemberley, but I am certain you will approve."

Not met his sister? Not visited his estate? Apparently they had quite an odd—and brief—courtship. Why had they married so hastily? *I am the kind of person who would marry a man without sufficient acquaintance. Am I so impetuous?*

One possibility occurred to her. "Was it an arranged marriage?" *Wait! I did not intend to blurt that out.*

His eyes widened. "No," he responded immediately.

Something in Elizabeth's chest loosened, but her fears were not completely assuaged. She stared down at her hands. "If that is the case, I will understand. Many marriages are contracted under such circumstances."

"No! Nothing like that. Why would you believe such a thing?" He leaned toward her, resting both hands on the edge of the bed.

Elizabeth shrank back against the pillows. Was he angry with her?

"Why?" he demanded.

"I have not met your sister or visited your home," she explained. "It is so odd. I do not understand unless…" Her hand flew to her mouth. "Oh! I did not entrap you into marriage?"

Elizabeth had heard of such things, although she could not recall the source: women who led men into compromising situations or who deliberately created rumors of an imminent engagement so that a man would feel honor bound. *Please God that I am not such a woman!*

Instead of exploding in anger, William exploded into laughter—for the second time that hour. The sight quite transformed his face. Before she had thought him terribly handsome, but when he laughed, the harsher lines of his face softened, a dark curl fell over his forehead, and he seemed far younger. Sober William was attractive, but laughing William was…irresistible. No wonder she had consented to be his wife.

Elizabeth wished she had the courage to throw her arms around his neck and kiss him. A wife ought to do such things when she wanted, but it felt wrong. She did not truly know this man.

"The things you think of! You did not entrap me." William chuckled. "In truth, I had quite a difficult time convincing you to marry me."

Elizabeth's mouth dropped open. *He had? Why in the world would I resist such a handsome, caring man?*

He surged to his feet, holding her hand as he stood by her bedside. "Elizabeth, I am very much in love with you...and most likely have been since the first day I met you."

Elizabeth blinked. This was not what she expected such a solemn, composed man to say. "Oh...I thought...since you did not wish to discuss our courtship..."

He shook his head ruefully. "Of course, you noticed that. You notice everything, do you not? Even when you cannot recall your own past and or leave your bed."

She shrugged, uncomfortable with such praise.

William sunk to the edge of the bed, her hand still in his, close enough that she could feel the warmth of his body through the sheets. "I owe you an apology, love." He paused for so long she was unsure if he would speak again. "I...some parts of our...courtship did not proceed smoothly. I am not eager to revisit those days or share them with you."

Oh. Elizabeth had not considered the possibility there might be something painful in their past, and she immediately speculated about its nature. But she must respect his desire to avoid the subject. How sad that their courtship should provoke unhappy memories! Had they quarreled, perhaps before she left England? Was that why she had boarded a boat without her husband?

But his hands clutched hers so tightly and he regarded her so earnestly that there could be no doubt he cared about her. Abruptly, Elizabeth felt a little queasy. How could she question a man who had traveled so far to find her? She owed him everything. A cold shiver ran down her spine. What would happen if the memories were gone forever? She could not possibly be a good wife to him if she never recalled the details of her previous life—their courtship, why she had fallen in love with him, who she really was.

He was a wealthy man, and sometimes wealthy men put their wives aside if a marriage failed. Was he such a man? Would he send her to live in a distant country house while he installed a mistress at Pemberley? Tears welled up in her eyes. Heavens, she was becoming such a watering pot!

Surely I would not have married such a man. Or would I? I do not even know my own character! Despite her husband's hand and the closeness of his body, she experienced an aching, overwhelming loneliness. He was here, but she was still alone inside her head.

"Elizabeth?" William asked gently. She looked up, only then realizing that she was squeezing his hand unmercifully. With an apologetic smile, she let it go. "What will happen if I never remember?" Oh, she had not intended to raise that subject.

"It will not matter, love," he said, brushing tears from her face with warm fingers. "You are still the woman I fell in love with." He chuckled softly. "There is no doubt about that."

Elizabeth wished she could be so sure.

She leaned into his hand until he cupped her cheek tenderly. His touch felt so natural on her face, so familiar. They must have experienced many moments like this.

His face was quite near hers. His dark blue eyes were so mesmerizing she could not possibly glance away. Then his eyes dropped to her lips. Would he kiss her? His lips drifted closer. She could imagine how they would feel against hers—firm and demanding, yet gentle. She wanted to taste him.

Abruptly, he gave a tiny shake of his head and pulled away, standing in one fluid motion. "I should allow you to rest. You have long been awake."

I do not want to sleep. I want you to kiss me. But she said nothing. *I am in no position to make demands; I can only be a burden to him.*

She slouched back against the pillows, realizing that she was indeed quite fatigued. "Perhaps I will." But her eyes followed William as he crossed to the door. She called his name before he disappeared from sight, and he glanced back over his shoulder.

"Thank you for answering my questions," she said softly.

He gave her a quick nod before escaping through the door.

***

The small rowing boat rocked violently on the waves, tossing Elizabeth recklessly from side to side. She grabbed the hull with one hand and the bench with the other, trying not to become seasick.

But her attention was not on her wayward stomach; it was fixed on the man in the middle of the boat, rowing frantically, his face twisted with exertion. He would not have been a handsome man under any circumstances, with his heavy brow and pinched eyes, but at the moment his mouth was set in an angry line that rendered him even more unattractive.

Elizabeth swallowed back her nausea. "I pray you, return me to the ship," she pleaded with him. "I will do nothing to prevent your escape."

He gave a harsh laugh. "Returning you to the ship would do you no good."

He spoke in riddles. The ship meant safety and a way to return home. Out here in the middle of the ocean, home seemed thousands of miles away. She stared longingly at the ship, which was rapidly shrinking into a smudge on the horizon.

Leaning toward the man, she reached out her hands. "I pray you—"

Startled, the man dropped the oars and pulled a pistol from his coat, pointing it unerringly at Elizabeth's chest. "Stay! Come no closer!" he warned. "Your life has no value to me now."

Her heart pounded against her ribs. She had no reason to doubt his threat. Raising trembling hands in the air, she slid back against the boat's stern, as far from the man as was possible in such a small vessel. "I will not fight you. I simply ask that you return—"

A loud boom reverberated across the water, causing Elizabeth to start. A moment passed before she could make sense of what she saw. A fire now raged on the horizon—just where the ship had been. With growing horror, she realized the ship had exploded. The Majestic was no more. She covered her mouth as tears sprang to her eyes. All those sailors... "Was this your doing?" she asked the man.

"I could not leave any witnesses." He shrugged. "The ship was carrying great stores of gunpowder; it would be a shame to let them go to waste."

A shudder of revulsion ran through her body. "You are a monster!" Her muscles tensed with the need to flee. His malicious smile, his hard eyes, his very presence...everything about him made her skin *crawl. But jumping from the boat would mean certain death; she was trapped.*

Her horror seemed to amuse him as he stowed his pistol and resumed rowing. So, this is how evil looks, *she thought.*

Elizabeth turned away from the sight of the burning wreck that had once been a ship full of sailors. Clasping her hands in her lap, she said a desperate prayer. Now there are no witnesses…nobody knows that this man has abducted me.

On the heels of the prayer came another revelation: she was the only person remaining who could identify the man. He cannot allow me to live.

Chapter Seven

Darcy stared at the ceiling from his pallet on the floor. The lace curtains did not completely conceal the moon—nearly full—a blur of silvery light outside the window. Movement caught his eye, but it was only the curtains fluttering in the breeze, for which Darcy was thankful. The room had been quite warm when they retired for the night, but now it was cooler. Perhaps he should cover Elizabeth with another blanket.

She sighed and turned in her sleep. Today, the third day since she had awakened, she had ventured from her bed for the first time. They had started small, just a few steps from the bed to the window and back, but they had met with more success than Darcy dared to hope. After she rested from her exertions, she had insisted on another journey, a slow stroll around the upstairs corridors. Her steps had been hesitant, but she had been less fatigued than either of them had expected. It gave Darcy hope that she would be recovered enough to travel within a week's time.

However, her return to health created other problems. Darcy found it more and more difficult to ignore that she was a very beautiful woman. The doctor had expected Darcy to sleep next to Elizabeth; the bed certainly had ample room. Darcy had said he did not wish to disturb her sleep, but how long would that excuse seem plausible?

Every day she grew stronger, and Darcy's resolve grew weaker.

Now that her cheeks were rosy with color and her eyes shone with animation again, Darcy's ardor did not wish to be contained. He found himself mesmerized by the musical sound of her voice or fascinated by the sight of a lock of hair blown by a breeze. An unforeseen consequence of his impulsive falsehood was that it removed any barriers to intimacy between them. Nobody—including Elizabeth—objected if he touched her hair, her shoulders, her cheek. Nobody had second thoughts if he would spend the night in her room—or even her bed.

However, those barriers must remain in place if he could continue to call himself a gentleman, if he did not wish her to hate him once her memory returned. He had come perilously close to kissing her that afternoon as he leaned over her bed. Every shred of willpower had been needed simply to walk out of the room.

He had wanted to kiss her so many times: at the ball at Netherfield, in the drawing room at Rosings Park, in the fields near Hunsford—before she had rejected his proposal. Although now that he thought on it, he probably would have kissed her afterward as well. He could not remember a time when he had not wanted to kiss Elizabeth Bennet.

The evil in this situation was that there was nothing to stop him. She would not object. The Martins would not object. Only his conscience stood in the way, and it was…weakening.

He dug his fingernails into the palm of his hand, continuing to stare at the ceiling as he resisted a ridiculous impulse to stand and savor the sight of her peaceful slumber. Even such a small step could be the precursor to taking her in his arms and kissing her until she could not breathe. Elizabeth deserved better.

That was why he must remain on a pallet on the floor.

Elizabeth's bed creaked. She moaned, and her covers rustled. Agitated limbs thrashed against the sheets. She panted as if in distress. Darcy's heart stuttered. She had not completely recovered from her illness. Could this be the beginning of a relapse?

Quietly extracting himself from his pallet, Darcy covered the two steps to her bedside. Bathed in the cool moonlight, Elizabeth's face was anything but tranquil in sleep. Her mouth was frozen in a horrified grimace while her head made small, quick jerks on the pillows.

A distressed noise emerged from her mouth, and she tossed and turned. Was she trying to escape some danger in her dreams? Darcy's hand stretched out to wake her but stopped in midair. Was it safe to waken her?

A fine sheen of sweat had broken out on her face. Her movements growing more agitated, Elizabeth moaned again—and every sound sent ripples of anxiety through Darcy's heart.

Darcy flinched as she suddenly shot into an upright position. "You are a monster!" she cried. He hoped never to hear such anguish in a human voice again. For a heart-stopping moment, he feared the accusation was aimed at him—that she had recognized his deception. But, though her eyes were open, she was not focused on him or at anything in the room. He was certain she dreamed still.

This must stop. The nightmare was tormenting her. Darcy grasped her shoulder. "Elizabeth." He kept his voice low and soothing.

"No…no…" Her voice was breathy with horror.

"Elizabeth," he said more forcefully, giving her shoulder a shake.

Her head turned toward him, the first sign she was aware of his presence. "Elizabeth, it is just a nightmare."

Abruptly, her body lost all its tension; her shoulder slid from his grip as she fell back against the pillows. When her eyes opened again, they focused on his face. "William..."

"Was it a nightmare?"

"Yes..." She rubbed her forehead with one hand. "My God!" She shuddered violently.

He rubbed her back soothingly. "You are safe here, safe with me." She nodded, grasping his nightshirt and burying her face in it, a sensation that was not unpleasing to him. "It was only a dream."

"I am not so sure of that." Her words were muffled. "It might be a memory." She pulled away from his body; he felt instantly cold. "I think it was some sort of memory." Darcy grew even colder. Had she remembered some of his ill-chosen words from the past? Her voice was hoarse. "I...I was on a boat. And there was a man with a pistol."

Darcy went completely still. Was it a memory of the events that had led to her near drowning? "What sort of ship?"

"It was not a ship. A boat...a small rowing boat."

Elizabeth might have taken such a small boat to board the cutter for Jersey. "Was the man a sailor?" Many of the navy men would be armed.

"No. He was dressed as a tradesman." Her eyes had a faraway look as she remembered. "He was so angry; he aimed the pistol at me." She shivered, wrapping her arms around herself. Without thinking, Darcy pulled her against his body, sharing his warmth.

"He was an awful man..." She was so very frail in his arms; he wanted to stand between her and the rest of the world. "A monster..."

She had uttered that word before. "Why was he a monster?"

Her brows drew together. "I...I cannot remember. He did something...monstrous. Something horrible. I could not believe..." She stiffened in his arms. "I wish I could remember."

An invisible hand clenched Darcy's heart. No doubt it was some incident from the ship's demise. Had she encountered the Black Cobra?

Perhaps by the time they returned home, Elizabeth would recall enough to give information to the War Office. Darcy had no desire to pursue the blackguard now; Elizabeth's safety was far more important.

Darcy laid her gently onto the pillows. "You should sleep." He pulled up the counterpane and tucked it around Elizabeth's shoulders. "Think no more upon it. Dreams rarely make sense."

"That is so," Elizabeth said sleepily, her eyes drifting closed. Darcy stood, pleased the dream had not disturbed her further, but before he could move, her eyes opened again. "William, what happened to the other people on the ship?"

"You should sleep," he murmured.

Instead she struggled into a seated position. "Please tell me. You said the ship had an accident. Was it an explosion? I think there was an explosion in my dream."

Not trusting himself to speak, Darcy simply nodded.

"What happened to everyone else on the ship?"

He owed her the truth. Darcy closed his eyes. "The War Office believed there were no other survivors."

She gasped. "All those people!" Her voice throbbed with grief.

"Yes." His hand stroked her hair gently. The moonlight shone in her curls.

Leaning toward him, Elizabeth relaxed against his chest. After a few minutes, he thought she had fallen asleep again, but then she stirred in his arms. "How did you know I was alive?"

Darcy's mouth opened, but he could think of no plausible response. After a moment Elizabeth's head jerked up at him. "You believed I was dead!"

Darcy closed his eyes; he would have preferred she remain ignorant of how close she came to perishing. But when he opened them again, Elizabeth was regarding him with a calm, steady gaze. "You came to France hoping to find my body." It was a statement, not a question.

"Yes," he admitted miserably.

Tears glistened in her eyes. "I am sorry to be the source of such anguish."

He grabbed both her hands in his. "Do not apologize. You live. I could ask for no greater gift."

They embraced for many minutes, but soon the weariness in her body returned. "You should sleep," he whispered.

Elizabeth allowed him to lay her down on the pillows and pull the counterpane around her again, but her eyes were wide open, anxiety evident. "I cannot help but think about those poor people. I do not know if I shall be able to sleep."

Darcy cursed himself for having no immediate remedies for the horrors she must be imagining. "I will not leave you alone, my darling." He brushed hair from her face and placed a kiss on her forehead.

When he stood, Elizabeth clutched his hand. "I pray you, do not leave me." She gestured to the bed. "There is space. Please lie here with me."

Darcy's body was instantly on fire with the possibilities. He froze, fighting to control his reaction. "I do not want to jeopardize your recovery," he said with very sincere regret.

"You will be helping me to heal," she insisted. "Tonight I cannot be alone."

It was so tempting, but... "Elizabeth, I should not—"

"Please!" Tears glittered in the moonlight, unshed in the corners of her eyes. "I will sleep more peacefully if you are with me."

Darcy was tired of fighting his need to touch her. Surely he could indulge the longing and give her comfort without surrendering to his more carnal desires. Of course, she likely would hate him when she recovered her memories, but...

"Very well." He lifted a corner of the sheets and slid between them. When Elizabeth rolled to her side, Darcy's body molded itself to the back of hers. His arm encircled her waist. Legs tangled together. It was sheer bliss.

And complete agony.

***

The next morning, Elizabeth watched Darcy pensively as he arranged her breakfast tray. "I thank you for all your care and attention," she said in a soft, low voice.

Darcy shrugged. To his mind, he had only done what was necessary in caring for the woman he loved. *I should thank her for the privilege of caring for her.*

"I have had occasion to imagine awakening in the Martins' house alone," she said gravely. "Coming to my senses among strangers, unaware of my identity, and unable to speak French well."

Fortunately, she does not know that her "husband" is something of a stranger to her as well.

"It would have been quite a trial," Elizabeth continued. "I am very grateful for your presence. You have been my anchor in this storm."

If only she knew how little he deserved the praise!

Elizabeth fell silent as she consumed her toast and eggs, but after a few minutes she announced, "I would like to walk outside. I am tired of being confined to this room."

Darcy smiled and shook his head. Even without her memory, she was still Elizabeth: chafing at being confined indoors. "Darling, you have ventured no further than the top of the stairs."

Her chin rose. "I walked nearly a half hour together yesterday and did not fall." She was not wrong, but Darcy had died a thousand deaths envisioning the disasters that could have occurred. Her expression softened. "I know you worry…"

Worry was such a paltry word to describe his nearly constant agitation. He could so easily lose her again—to illness or injury, war or treachery. The world was full of perils that could rob him of her once more.

"But," she continued with some asperity, "I must get stronger so we may return to England. France is not safe."

"I would not have you compromise your health."

Her hand slapped the mattress in frustration. "My health is compromised because I stare at the same four walls every day! A bit of sunshine will do me a world of good."

"You *are* feeling improved."

A chagrined smile crept over her lips. "Is impatience a natural part of my character?"

"You have been known to be stubborn upon one or two occasions."

She folded her arms over her chest, a playful gleam in her eyes. "Then I would imagine we often are at odds."

He shook his head in mock innocence. "Never. I always yield to your inclination."

She burst into laughter, and after a moment he joined her. His delight could not be contained; she was teasing him! As the laughter died down, they stared at each other like besotted lovers, basking in the glow of their shared mirth. Finally, Elizabeth averted her eyes and cleared her throat. "I thought perhaps a walk out of doors…"

Darcy stood, eager to encourage her happiness however he could. "The Martins' garden is enclosed by a high wall. Nobody would see us there. But I must consult the doctor about the advisability of such a plan."

Her grateful smile was like a gift.

***

William was exceedingly talented at making things happen. When he decided something would be so, everyone hurried to accomplish the task. Within half an hour, Elizabeth was seated in a wrought iron chair and viewing the Martins' small garden. Carefully manicured in the French tradition, the garden was a profusion of roses, peonies, delphiniums, and lupines—all arranged in orderly beds. A few fruit trees and larger pines edged the perimeter, and the whole was surrounded by tall, red brick walls to provide privacy.

The trip down the stairs and through the kitchen to the garden had been slow but uneventful. Her legs had threatened to buckle once, but William had braced her arm and prevented a fall. It was so pleasant to feel the sun warm her skin that Elizabeth would not for the world admit to experiencing moments of lightheadedness.

In the chair beside hers, William watched her like a mother bird who feared her fledgling would fall from the nest. "Would you like your bonnet? Or perhaps your shawl?" He leaned closer to her.

Elizabeth flicked open her fan and fanned herself briskly; they enjoyed the shade of a cherry tree, but it did not shield them from all the sun's rays. "I am not at all chilled, I assure you."

"Do you require a glass of water? Or lemonade? Perhaps we should return inside."

"I am enjoying the fresh air."

"Very well."

Elizabeth reached out to pat his hand where it rested on the arm of his chair. "I am not so fragile as all that," she assured him. "I feel quite myself today. Well, I assume this is how I must feel—at least some of the time."

His lips twisted into a rueful smile. "Have you recalled anything?"

"I sometimes remember things, but they are only disconnected images. They amount to nothing coherent."

He drew her hand into his. "I would imagine you will remember everything when we return to England. Familiar surroundings will help provoke your memories."

Unable to bear the hopefulness in his expression, Elizabeth turned her eyes to the neat rows of rose bushes. What would she do if she never remembered? Having had the good fortune to secure the affections of such a man, how could her mind have erased him from her recollections?

Elizabeth had been cheated; something precious had been stolen from her. "I have forgotten everything of importance. Your offer of marriage...our first kiss..." Tears leaked from her eyes.

William's eyes were fixed on the ground; a slight blush tinged his cheeks. Did the mere mention of kissing discompose him? "We will make new memories," he said.

Hmph. Such sentiments were very well and good, but Elizabeth was growing impatient. "When?"

"Hmm?" He gave her a sidelong glance.

His lips were pale red—the ideal shape. How would they feel pressed to hers? It was especially unfair that she did not recall kissing when it seemed like quite a pleasurable activity. "*When* shall we make new memories?"

He swallowed. "You would like to do so now?" Why did he appear so nervous? He was the one who remembered their previous kisses.

"Since"—she cleared her throat— "Since I awakened, you have not kissed me." Of their own accord, her eyes again drifted down to fix on his lips.

He made a noise that sounded like a gasp. She had not thought her request so shocking. Was she too forward? "Elizabeth, I am a stranger to you." His entire body seemed to be leaning away from hers.

A pang of disappointment took her off guard. "But *I* am not a stranger to *you*," she retorted. "This should be simple for you."

His shoulders tightened as he hunched forward in his chair. "I would not make you uncomfortable."

She blew out a frustrated breath. "A kiss might help to stimulate my memories."

Still, he hesitated.

"Is kissing me such a chore?" She smiled, trying to hide her apprehension. *Perhaps he no longer desires me.*

His eyes rose to meet hers, and there was no disguising the desire in them. *Thank God.* "No, quite the opposite."

In the next instant, his lips were upon hers, as soft and warm as she had envisioned. He kissed her with such passion it stole her breath away.

Her own reaction took her by surprise. Her entire body leaned into the kiss, wanting more—more sensation, more closeness, more tastes of William upon her lips. Her eager response encouraged him to deepen the kiss, exploring her lips with his questing tongue. She shivered at the unexpected pleasure.

His hands plunged into her hair, drawing her head closer. Her hands likewise needed purchase. One grasped his shoulder while the other slid into his silky hair.

Their lips parted for a moment. "Elizabeth," William whispered. The desperate edge in his voice was impossible to resist. She pressed her body to his, her lips to his. This time he was less gentle, thrusting his tongue between her lips and stroking the inside of her mouth with vigor.

She had not even known people did such things, but it made kissing infinitely more pleasurable. With such delights to experience, how had Elizabeth torn herself from William's side long enough to board a ship?

Without her awareness, he had drawn her into a standing position, allowing their bodies to merge even more closely together. One of his hands slid down her neck, skimming the top of her shoulder and trailing down her arm, leaving a tingling sensation behind. Her skin was so sensitized to his touch that she could feel the impression of each individual finger.

With a sudden twist, William wrenched his lips away from hers.

She made an inarticulate noise of protest, reaching for him. But he stepped away, staring at the high garden wall as his chest heaved. "Forgive me." He swallowed hard. "I…should not have lost control…"

"There is nothing to forgive, sir," she said.

He pressed a fist to his lips. "You do not know…" His eyes squeezed closed. "I am still a stranger to you."

"A bit less of a stranger than five minutes ago," she said with a smile. He did not return the grin, and hers quickly melted away.

"I cannot take advantage."

"You are my husband. There is no impropriety."

"If you only knew…" The words were uttered under his breath.

"Knew what, William?"

He did not respond. After a moment he shook his head and said, "I cannot impose myself."

"You did not. I requested—"

"I— Please forgive me." Without meeting her eyes, he turned on his heel and stumbled toward the house, leaving Elizabeth standing alone in the sunny garden.

***

Darcy knew it was cowardly to abandon Elizabeth in the garden, but he feared that he would never stop kissing her once he started—and that he would go beyond kisses. Preoccupied with his thoughts, he did not realize the doctor had a visitor until he passed the open drawing room door. By then it was too late to escape notice. Damnation! He had been so careful and now—

He continued walking, hoping the other man would ignore his presence.

"You there! Stop!" The man's voice held a note of command. Darcy froze outside the door. "Come here."

With no good reason to refuse, Darcy shuffled closer but stopped in the doorway. He had no desire to get any closer to the stranger. The man was medium height, with a beaky nose and receding hairline. But his clothes were well made, and he appeared quite prosperous.

"Guillaume," Martin said slowly. "This is Sub-Prefect Roget."

Chapter Eight

Blast! Fighting to keep his dismay from his face, Darcy gave the man a cautious bow. At least Martin was using his alias; that was a hopeful sign.

Still, Darcy's heart pounded painfully in his chest. The sub-prefect had nearly unlimited power in his assigned territory. He could order Darcy arrested on little more than a suspicion—and then what would become of Elizabeth?

The doctor evinced no anxiety over the secrets they both concealed. "You said the neighbors had seen a stranger enter the house," he said in a level tone. "Guillaume is my wife's cousin from Toulon, here for a short visit."

The official leaned back in his chair, the expression on his face assessing rather than suspicious as he scrutinized Darcy. "He looks healthy enough. Why is he not a soldier?" Darcy held his breath; conscription into the French army would be little better than being arrested. "I need thirty-three men to meet my quota this month." The sub-prefect's voice rose querulously. "You know how difficult it is nowadays to find able-bodied candidates. But they do not understand this in Paris; they only demand more recruits each month."

Darcy suppressed a shudder; a man this desperate could do a lot of harm if they did not cooperate.

Seemingly unconcerned, Martin barked a laugh. "You do not want him. His body is healthy enough, aye. But his mind…" The doctor shook his head sadly. "He is quite insane. I tell his mother to put him in an asylum, but she refuses."

Oh, Good Lord.

The sub-prefect examined Darcy carefully. At least his encounter with Elizabeth had left his hair disordered, and his clothing was suitably disreputable. Were he dressed like Fitzwilliam Darcy of Pemberley, it would be almost impossible to play the fool.

Even so, his heart quailed. Darcy had no pretentions to thespian talent. Disguise of any kind had always been his abhorrence. But Martin had declared Darcy's insanity, and now his life—and Elizabeth's—relied on convincingly acting the part.

Darcy did not have extensive experience with madmen, but there had been a young man—the son of a tenant—whose parents often were advised to place him in an asylum. They had been horrified at the thought and, knowing what such places were like, Darcy had supported their decision, ensuring that the family always had enough to make ends meet.

Now he did his best to recall Robert's outrageous behavior so it could serve as a guide for his own. Letting his mouth go slack, Darcy searched distractedly about the room. "Lucinda?" he mumbled, staring at nothing in particular. "Lucinda? Where is the hedgehog? I need it, you know. I need the hedgehog—and a bucket."

The sub-prefect's eyes went wide with alarm, but Martin's startled grin nearly provoked Darcy's laughter. Recovering quickly, the doctor twisted his lips into a scowl of disapproval. "I do not know what you mean. Go to your room."

How would Robert behave when given such a command? He was never terribly cooperative. "No. I want to see the baby Jesus."

Martin rolled his eyes. "My apologies, monsieur," he addressed the sub-prefect. "Apparently today is not one of Guillaume's good days."

The sub-prefect narrowed his eyes as he stared at Darcy. "So I see." Did he suspect? In such situations, the doctor's interest in helping young Frenchmen avoid conscription would work against them.

Darcy needed to be more convincing. What had Robert done? Darcy wished he had paid closer attention. His eye was caught by a tea tray on the table, laden with an assortment of biscuits. Darcy pounced on a biscuit as if it were a mouse. "I caught it!" He held the biscuit up triumphantly. "Did you see?" he asked Martin.

"Indeed." Martin was suppressing a smile. "No biscuit is safe from you."

Darcy laughed maniacally. "Except the ones the birds have already eaten!"

Martin shook his head with a great show of chagrin. "Guillaume, perhaps you should retire to your room for a rest."

"Will Baby Jesus be there?" Darcy asked, assuming an innocent expression.

"Perhaps," Martin said with a sigh. "You should search your room thoroughly in case Baby Jesus is visiting."

Edging toward the door, Darcy suppressed a desire to race from the drawing room; nothing could make the sub-prefect suspicious. Cradling the biscuit in his arms, Darcy began to sing a French lullaby to it.

He continued to sing—deliberately off key—as he slowly climbed the stairs and only ceased once he was inside the room he shared with

Elizabeth. There, he sank onto the bed. *Thank the Lord none of my friends in England observed that!*

***

When Elizabeth returned to the room, she fell immediately into a deep sleep, and they never discussed his precipitous departure from the garden. But Darcy had no doubt it occupied her thoughts.

That evening she was well enough to join Darcy and the Martins for dinner in their formal dining room. The doctor regaled her with a description of Darcy's mad act, and she laughed until tears leaked from her eyes. Darcy was so pleased to see her in good spirits that he could not even protest being the object of the joke.

Once the housekeeper had cleared away the dinner plates, the conversation turned to more somber subjects, particularly Elizabeth's safety. Darcy had regarded Elizabeth carefully throughout the meal. Her movements were graceful and natural. Dark circles still lurked under her eyes, but her skin no longer had the grayish pallor he had found so alarming. Despite spending several hours outside, she did not seem particularly fatigued. He caught her eye as Elizabeth placed her napkin on the table. "Do you think you are well enough to travel, dear heart?"

She answered instantly. "Yes, if you deem it necessary."

Darcy had arrived at a reluctant conclusion. "I believe Elizabeth and I should depart," he told Martin.

The other man pressed his lips together. "Mrs. Darcy is not good enough to travel. Not with enough health." His English was strongly accented but intelligible.

"I know you would prefer that we waited a full week, but I do not want to risk arrest. It would be difficult for Elizabeth to return to England alone."

"It is probable the sub-prefect will not come back here," Martin said.

Darcy sighed, trying to quiet the uneasiness in his stomach. "If he talks again with someone in the market, he might learn that my description matches that of the stranger who injured his hand. And the longer we are here, the greater the risk of discovery—and the greater danger to you."

Martin waved this away. "This is our risk."

"No. William is right. We remain in danger while we are on French soil." Darcy heard Elizabeth's words with some surprise. Although they had not discussed the danger, she understood it very well.

"But your health—" Martin objected.

"Is *mine*," Elizabeth said firmly. "Perfect health will not be of much assistance if my husband is imprisoned in France."

Martin scowled, and his wife gave him a sympathetic look, covering his hand with hers. His shoulders relaxed, and he gave her a rueful smile. "Marguerite reminds that I wish to make everyone better all the time, but sometimes this is not possible. I often forget such things."

"Where will you go?" Mrs. Martin asked in halting English.

"I was given the name of someone near Saint-Malo who should be able to find us safe passage." Indeed, the original plan had been that Mr. Dreyfus would help Darcy escape France once he completed his mission. Richard had given him the names of other English agents if Dreyfus was not available. Surely one could help.

Martin's eyebrows rose. "English agents?"

Darcy fiddled with his fork, not meeting the doctor's eyes. "I cannot say." It was best for Martin if he knew few details. "If all else fails, we will travel to Calais and hire a boat."

"Often for the sake for Mrs. Darcy's health you must rest," Martin said. "She cannot travel like she is healthy person." Darcy nodded his understanding. "If her cough becomes worse or her breathing is very bad, you must find doctor at once."

"Yes, of course," Darcy murmured, saying a silent prayer. What if it was too early to leave? How would they obtain help if Elizabeth fell ill on the journey? But remaining in Saint-Malo risked discovery. He tried to push the doubts from his mind. "We will need a conveyance. Do you know of someone who would sell us a carriage?"

The doctor exchanged a look with his wife. "Even better. I will give you mine!"

After an hour of haggling, Darcy managed to get the doctor to accept a few coins in exchange for his curricle. Martin assured him that he rarely used the vehicle and was happy to be rid of it. Darcy would have been more pleased with a larger, enclosed vehicle, but a curricle at least would be fast. The doctor also promised to find a horse for hire, and Darcy went to bed tolerably pleased with the plan.

***

The next morning, the plan went smoothly—hopefully a good omen for their future success. He paid Martin for the curricle and for Elizabeth's medical care, although the other man steadfastly refused any remuneration for food or shelter.

In the pre-dawn light, the streets were empty of all but a few men and women hurrying to work, so their departure was likely to go unnoticed. Elizabeth gave the Martins—and their housekeeper—each a hug and bade them a fond farewell in halting French.

Darcy noted Elizabeth's stiff movements with some misgivings. Was he rushing her recovery? What if she fell ill along the journey? The strain of travel might add to the confusion and stress caused by her amnesia. He bit his lip against the desire to tell Martin that they would remain another few days after all.

The process was rendered more difficult by a chastising voice at the back of his mind reminding him that he should not be traveling with Elizabeth at all—at least not without a chaperone. Unfortunately, he could not voice those misgivings with anyone; he could only push them from his mind.

He took her hand to help her alight to the high curricle seat. Thank goodness he was not compelled to wear long skirts when performing such maneuvers. Clutching Darcy's hand, Elizabeth put a foot on the curricle's wheel, preparing to climb up. But her foot slipped, causing her to stumble forward. Darcy hastily grabbed her waist, pulling her back down to safety.

For a moment they stood frozen, clutched together with their faces only inches apart. His hands did not seem to want to relax their grip on her. Under his palms, he could feel her breath quicken. Was their nearness affecting her as well?

Her head was tilted back. Cool green eyes met his, as deep and inscrutable as a forest. Her lips, plump with a dark rose color. He could not help remembering how they tasted—or prevent himself from wanting another taste.

"William." Her voice was a low, throaty murmur as she moved toward him, her head tilted back provocatively. He had no doubt about what was on her mind, and he wanted it. Badly.

Darcy closed his eyes, as if blocking the sight of Elizabeth could somehow prevent temptation. Instead his nose was filled with her faint rosewater scent. *Concentrate on the facts*, he told himself. *She is not my wife. I have no right to kiss her. If I kiss her, it would be under false pretenses.*

He repeated these phrases over and over in his mind until he had steeled himself against the onslaught of her beauty and had the strength to open his eyes. Forcing his hands to release his grip on her waist, he stepped away so they were no longer in such intimate proximity. Elizabeth regarded him with perplexity.

Only then did Darcy recall their audience; a glance at Martin showed the doctor was smirking. Elizabeth might not have recognized Darcy's desire for what it was, but Martin did.

Darcy took a deep breath and returned his attention to Elizabeth. "Shall we try that again?"

This time he handed her into the seat with no mishap. As Elizabeth settled herself, Mrs. Martin handed up a blanket. Elizabeth good-naturedly wrapped it about her shoulders, although the day was already quite warm.

Darcy settled his knapsack under the seat and then took a second bag from the doctor to stow beside it. The Martins had filled it with clothing for Elizabeth—and had refused to accept any payment. After shaking Martin's hand and again giving Mrs. Martin his thanks, Darcy swung himself up into the seat, the springs bouncing slightly under his weight.

With a flick of the reins they were off. Darcy kept his eyes fixed on the road while Elizabeth turned to wave until the Martins' house was out of sight. Carefully, Darcy navigated the rig down the narrow streets of Saint-Malo and through the old city gate. Past the gate, the roads were considerably wider, and Darcy was able to increase the pace.

As the sun rose in the sky, the heat began to affect Elizabeth, and Darcy kept a worried eye on her. She had stowed Mrs. Martin's blanket under the seat, but the sun still beat down on her shoulders and shone in her eyes if she did not hold her bonnet at the proper angle. Sweat stained the neck of her gown and dripped down the side of her face. Aware of his scrutiny, she scowled. "I will be fine." Unfortunately, her body chose that moment for a coughing fit.

Darcy watched, helpless, until it subsided. She clenched her hands together in her lap. "There is no need to be anxious on my account. A little water will set me to rights." But Darcy could not prevent the return of his misgivings.

Fortunately, at that moment he recognized the dirt path to Dreyfus's house and pulled on the reins, directing the horse. "Perhaps you should join me in the house to enjoy some of the cooler air."

"Very well." She frowned at him. "How will you make yourself known to Mr. Dreyfus? Surely you cannot simply alight from the carriage and declare, 'I understand you are an agent of the English government.'"

Darcy chuckled. "My cousin, Colonel Fitzwilliam, works for the War Office; he wrote to Dreyfus about my visit. He also gave me a token by which English agents make themselves known to one another." Leaning to one side, he pulled the small slip of paper from the pocket of his worn jacket and handed it to her.

***

Elizabeth examined the scrap of paper. There were no words, just an ink drawing of a red flower. "Hmm, it looks like a pimpernel," she mused.

"I believe it is supposed to be a rose."

She returned the paper to him. "The War Office needs better artists."

"I do not believe aesthetics are their primary concern," William said with a grin.

"But in such a business as espionage, surely the smallest mistake could lead to peril," Elizabeth said archly. "What should we do if Mr. Dreyfus believes it to be a pimpernel and that is the War Office's code for 'shoot on sight?'"

He laughed heartily; at least she had made him forget his concerns about her health. "Or perhaps the pimpernel is the flower assigned to agents of the Dutch government. Mr. Dreyfus might expect us to arrive with tulip bulbs in our pockets."

"That is a danger indeed." William's voice was warm with laughter. "I suppose espionage is fraught with all sorts of risks."

He sobered as he pulled the horse to a halt in front of a warm stone house; the front entrance opened directly onto a circular drive. Vines climbed up the front façade, and a few bedraggled roses grew in a clump under one window.

All seemed well. But why did the sight give her a sense of uneasiness? Shivers ran from the nape of her neck down her spine, and her stomach roiled with tension. After a moment she realized there was none of the activity that she would expect from the kind of busy and prosperous house this appeared to be. No servants were fetching water. No grooms were exercising the master's horses. No chickens wandered about searching for food. How odd.

Apparently happy to be at leisure, the horse, a young mare, immediately availed herself of the grass at the side of the drive. William alighted from his seat, crossed to Elizabeth's side of the carriage, and offered her a hand. She looked down uncertainly; the curricle seat was very high. But William simply put both hands on her waist—as he had in front of the Martins' house—and swung her to the drive. She again had a fluttery sensation in her stomach as her body thrilled to his touch; she longed to lean into his arms, feeling his body enclose hers.

A long moment passed while they stood in this attitude. Touching William was so pleasant that Elizabeth was loath to let go.

William released her so rapidly that he nearly tripped over his own feet. "Right, well, shall we see if Mr. Dreyfus is at home?" Turning toward the house, he offered her his arm, and they traversed the dirt drive toward the front door.

William knocked at the door, and they waited. Nobody answered. William scowled. "Even if Mr. Dreyfus is away, I would expect his ill-tempered housekeeper to answer once more." He knocked again. After a long moment the scuff of a shoe on the floor sounded inside the house, and thumps suggested someone was removing a bar on the other side of the door.

Unsurprisingly, William's chivalry compelled him to stand between her and the door as if she required a bodyguard. His body obscured most of Elizabeth's view of the person who opened the door. She had the impression of a paunchy man, not tall, in his forties, and with graying hair, but she could not glimpse his face.

"Mr. Dreyfus?"

"Yes?" The other man's tone was suspicious.

"I am Darcy. We are in need of your assistance." William extended his hand with the scrap of paper held between thumb and forefinger.

The other man grunted in recognition. "Yes, I heard about you. Come in, then." His tone was rather begrudging, and the sound of his voice was oddly familiar. She dismissed it; without her memory, everything provoked a sense of oddness these days.

William stepped back, gesturing for Elizabeth to enter the house before him. Only then did she truly glimpse the other man's face. She started, struck forcefully by a sensation of recognition. But how could she recognize this man when she recognized nothing else in her life? Surely she had never encountered him before.

However, Mr. Dreyfus's reaction to Elizabeth was far more striking. His eyes bulged, and his face paled. "But-But you are dead! I saw you fall from the boat! You could not have—after that blow to the head—"

Images from her dream came rushing back to Elizabeth in an instant. The rowing boat. The gun. The explosion. Naked hatred on a man's face. *This* man's face. She did not understand all the images, but she knew she had encountered this man before when he kidnapped her from the ship.

Chapter Nine

She had to escape.

But her body refused to cooperate. She shook with tremors, and her feet were afflicted with acute paralysis at the moment she most needed them to act. She grabbed William's arm, and his eyes shot to her face in alarm. "It is the man!" she hissed. "The man from my dream—with the pistol."

Realization dawned on Darcy's face. "From the rowing boat?"

"Yes!"

"*You* are the Black Cobra!" Darcy hurled the accusation at Dreyfus. "A double agent."

Dreyfus smiled, showing all his teeth, but his eyes darted around in a panic to see if they were overheard. "I do not know what you mean. This woman must be confusing me with another man. Please, come inside and we can discuss—"

Darcy had pulled Elizabeth behind him once more. Now he gave her a push. "Run for the carriage," he insisted urgently. Elizabeth hesitated a moment, unhappy about leaving William. "I will be right behind you!" he hissed.

Dreyfus had ducked inside his house for a moment, but now he stepped out, brandishing a pistol.

"Run!" William pushed her again.

Elizabeth ran. Grabbing bunches of skirts in her fists, she pounded her feet on the dirt of the drive. Reaching the curricle, she grabbed the seat, stepped on the rim of the wheel, and hoisted herself onto the bench, heedless of rips or dirt on her gown.

She whirled around to glimpse William grappling with Dreyfus over control of the gun. "Don't be a fool, Darcy!" Dreyfus shouted. "I have agents all over this countryside. You will never escape France!"

A loud crack split the air, startling Elizabeth. The horse even stopped munching the grass for a moment. Elizabeth feared for William's life, but as the smoke cleared, she saw the pistol still pointed upward as both men struggled to control it. The bullet must have fired into the sky.

Dreyfus released his grip on the now-useless pistol, and Darcy pulled it away, striking Dreyfus in the jaw with his other fist. The man fell backward through the doorway onto the wooden boards of his hallway floor. Turning on his heel, Elizabeth's husband sprinted toward the curricle. In a moment his weight jostled the seat, and he whipped the reins. Dreyfus's pistol dropped from his hand to the floorboard of the carriage. The horse, demonstrating a hitherto unseen energy, jumped forward and took off at a run. William leaned forward in the seat, urging her to faster speeds.

"Crouch down," Darcy ordered Elizabeth. "He may have another pistol—"

Elizabeth bent over at the waist, grabbing the seat with both hands as the carriage lurched and jumped over the bumps in the drive. As they passed behind a line of trees near the road, she breathed a sigh of relief.

Within a minute they were back on the road. William directed the horse away from Saint-Malo, keeping to a gallop.

After nearly twenty minutes of hard driving, he finally slowed the horse to a walk. The beast was sweating, its flanks heaving with exertion. Glancing behind them, Elizabeth saw no sign of pursuit. "Do you think he will follow us?"

William's mouth was a grim line. "Undoubtedly. We know he is a double agent. He will be desperate to prevent us from sharing that information with the War Office." After a moment he asked, "What do you recall from the boat?"

She stared at the road, willing herself not to shudder. "The sight of that man helped me recall additional memories from the dream." She wrapped her arms around herself. "Somehow the sailors on the cutter discovered his identity. He held me in front of him, with a pistol to my head, so he could escape."

William grunted in realization. "A young, gently-bred woman— probably the only woman aboard—would make an effective hostage. Nobody would risk your life to prevent Dreyfus from escaping."

"He made me climb into the rowing boat with him. When the ship was just a silhouette on the horizon...there was an explosion." Elizabeth squeezed her eyes closed, wishing she could forget the sight—ironically, the only memory from her previous life. "I had been pleased that I was the only soul at risk, and the rest of the crew would survive." Her voice cracked on the last word. "But he set the gunpowder afire."

William covered her hand with his. "He would have carried out the scheme even if you had not been present."

"Perhaps. But it hardly seems fair that I lived and they..." She could not finish the sentence.

William grimaced. "Dreyfus did not intend for you to survive either. Did you attend to his words? He hit you on the head and pushed you over the side of the boat, the blackguard! You simply did not oblige him by drowning. And I, for one, am very happy you thwarted his plans."

Elizabeth rubbed her forehead, chasing after foggy memories. "I believe I clung to a bit of driftwood until I came to shore." She shivered. "I could so easily have died."

Enough, Elizabeth resolved. *I cannot dwell on the past when the present is more pressing. Our escape from France is now more complicated and less certain.* "Can we reach any other English agents in Brittany?" she asked William.

"I have other names," he said slowly. "But I dare not contact them. Who knows how many others secretly work for Napoleon?"

Elizabeth's stomach churned at this unwelcome news, but of course, William was correct. "Perhaps we should make for Calais?"

William stared at the horse's ears as it ambled along the road. "Dreyfus cried out that he has agents all over the countryside."

"It may have been just an attempt to scare you."

He expelled a harsh breath. "Or it might be accurate. If he alerts a whole network of agents throughout Brittany and Normandy… They know we will travel to the coast. We are so conspicuous. His colleagues could simply monitor the roads and await our arrival." He gritted his teeth. "If this were Derbyshire, I could find a hundred little country roads they would never think to monitor. But I do not even possess a map of France!" His hands clenched convulsively on the reins.

They were both silent as they contemplated the situation. Elizabeth wiped more sweat from under the rim of her bonnet and wondered yet again if the hat was doing more harm than good. "Perhaps we are safest if we do not do what they expect."

William gave her a sharp look. "Go away from the coast, you mean?"

She shrugged. "They would not anticipate such a move."

William stared without seeing as he contemplated the idea. "There is nowhere else we could so easily disappear as in Paris," he mused. "Although it does seem rather like entering the belly of the beast."

"Do you know of any English agents in Paris?"

"No." William snapped his fingers. "But I do know someone who could help us! My old governess lives in Paris. We correspond, although rather infrequently of late. But I have not heard of her decease."

"Are you certain she would help us?"

"She loves me and Georgiana like a mother. Plus, the Darcy estate pays her pension." He nodded briskly. "Very well. We are for Paris!"

***

They embarked on the next phase of their journey in high spirits. Although Darcy did not urge the horse to run, he set a brisk pace, and they made progress as the noonday sun climbed high into the sky. They did not stop for lunch, but Elizabeth retrieved some cheese and bread from a hamper that the Martins' housekeeper had insisted on packing for them. The roads were sparsely traveled; everyone they saw appeared to be farmers or tradesmen, with nary a soldier in sight.

Elizabeth's health held for most of the day, with only three episodes of coughing. By late afternoon, however, she was visibly wilting. Although she had not uttered a word of complaint, her conversation had faded to single words, and her face was notably paler.

Increasingly, Darcy drove with one eye on Elizabeth. When her head began to droop, he feared she would fall. Transferring the reins to his left hand, he drew her close until her head rested on his shoulder. She showed no impulse to flinch away but made an approving noise and burrowed closer to his side. Darcy held his breath, fearing he would disturb her.

He ignored the voice in his head that screamed about the impropriety; her body was such a warm and welcome weight—its presence provoking tender, protective sentiments—that surely there could be no evil in it.

He allowed himself a brief fantasy that she was his wife in truth: she might lay her head on his shoulder at any minute of the day, and he would have the privilege of encircling her in his arms whenever the mood struck him. No wonder men pursued marriage.

Darcy was drawn from his reverie by the welcome sight of a village in the distance. Given the uncertain state of Elizabeth's health, they would need to rest for the night. As they entered the hamlet, Darcy was pleased to find a coaching inn almost immediately. It appeared to have been built when Henry VIII had been on the throne in England, but it would have to do.

When Darcy reined in the horse, Elizabeth started, blinked, and raised her head, leaving his shoulder cold and bereft. "Should we stop already?" She peered at the sun, low in the sky and casting long shadows but not near dusk. "It is not so very late."

"An early night will do us both a world of good," Darcy said gently. "We can set out tomorrow at the crack of dawn." Elizabeth viewed the inn anxiously. "We would have encountered any pursuers by now," he reassured her.

Elizabeth allowed her shoulders to slump. "I must admit to fond thoughts of a warm dinner and soft bed."

The inn was shabby but clean enough. It was not crowded; the innkeeper was quite happy at the sight of Darcy—and even happier at the sight of his coins. Taking the best accommodations available, he ordered dinner to be brought to the room right away. Darcy regretted that he could not avoid temptation by ordering separate rooms, but he could not protect Elizabeth effectively from another room.

Elizabeth leaned heavily on his arm as he escorted her up the stairs. An alarmed Darcy felt her forehead for fever, but it was cool.

After settling Elizabeth in the room with an admonishment to eat before sleeping, Darcy visited the stables to arrange for a fresh horse in the morning. The stablemaster was quite accommodating despite giving Darcy many puzzled glances. Only as he climbed the stairs to their room did he realize why. As his hand reached for the banister, he noticed the roughly woven fabric encasing his arm.

Darcy swore under his breath. Living with the Martins, who had guessed much of his secret, he had forgotten to play the role of a simple laborer. His clothes suited the role of a poor wanderer, but he had approached the inn as the master of Pemberley. He had commanded the finest room, ordered the best meal, and arranged a new horse. "Some spy you are," he said to himself under his breath. Britain was fortunate that her future did not rely on Darcy's thespian skills.

He paused at the top of the stairs, considering whether his blunder was sufficient to require an immediate departure. But he had promised both the innkeeper and the stablemaster additional payments in the morning. If they alerted the provincial authorities to the presence of a pair of odd travelers, neither man would receive those coins. Darcy continued toward the room with some misgivings. *I will be a better actor in the future*, he vowed.

He strode quickly to the end of the narrow hallway, worn boards squeaking with each step, and eased the door open just enough to slip inside the room. The sun was just beginning to set, but Elizabeth was already deeply asleep. A nearby tray attested to her worthy attempt to eat a dinner of hearty stew and bread. About half the food had been consumed, but sleep had plainly stolen over her before she had finished.

The innkeeper had provided a bottle of red wine, and Elizabeth had drunk half of it. Darcy chuckled to himself; no wonder she had fallen asleep so quickly. Mr. Martin had admonished her to avoid any spirits during her recovery, so the wine had a strong effect on her.

Her hair spread wantonly over the pillow in a profusion of dark curls while her hand rested next to her cheek in a gesture at once innocent and completely alluring. Darcy's gaze slipped down her body, now clad only in her shift. Of course, he had seen her before in her nightrail and had contemplated her sleeping form. But earlier it had been easy to think of her as an invalid. Now…

Now, he was all too aware that she was an attractive, healthy woman.

Darcy ran a hand over his face, reminding himself yet again why he should not touch her. Still, his eyes wandered to Elizabeth's chest as it rose and fell with each soft breath. She had not climbed under the coverlet before surrendering to slumber, so her bare legs and feet peeked out from beneath the shift's hem. He could not tear his eyes from the sight, as if he had never glimpsed bare legs and feet before. But they were so well shaped, so impossibly graceful. And they belonged to *Elizabeth*.

His hand itched with a desire to stroke her lower leg and make her sigh with pleasure. Darcy swallowed hard. Yes, separate rooms would have been a far superior choice.

Resolutely, he averted his eyes from the alluring sight and sought his own dinner, which had been set on a small table. Suddenly realizing how ravenous he felt, Darcy tore into the meal, devouring every last crumb of bread and drop of stew. The red wine also disappeared quickly, leaving Darcy in a more mellow state of mind.

His attention was again caught by Elizabeth's slumbering form. There was no harm in looking, he reasoned. Elizabeth would never know.

Her mouth had opened slightly, her delicately pink lips parted in just the right position to kiss. Darcy groaned. His fingers tingled with the need to touch her—at least caress a bare upper arm or stroke his thumb over her lips.

You do not have the right. She is not your wife. In the past few days he had acted like a husband to her, protecting her and attending to her needs, but it was merely a habit of mind, not reality.

Mustering his willpower, Darcy turned his attention to preparing for bed. Pouring some water into the basin, he used it to wash some of the road grime from his hands and face, wishing he could have a full bath. Then he slipped out of his clothing and into the long, loose nightshirt from his pack. Elizabeth might be deeply asleep, but he kept his back turned to her.

Darcy pulled the covers around Elizabeth's sleeping form, tucking her in securely. She gave a little sigh and a half smile but did not awaken. He climbed under the covers on the other side of the bed, an action that felt at once all wrong and far too right. Allowing himself one indulgence, Darcy leaned over and tenderly kissed Elizabeth's brow before retreating to his side of the bed and dropping off to sleep.

***

Darcy awoke disoriented, unsure where he was or what was happening. Someone loomed over him, launching his heart into a frantic rhythm. "It is just me, my love," a warm voice murmured.

Oh yes. Elizabeth. The coaching inn. Good Lord, he was sharing a bed with Elizabeth!

The moon had risen and cast a silvery glow through the window, turning Elizabeth into a dark silhouette. She peered down at him, her curls tumbling around her face, the long ends brushing against his cheeks. Elizabeth's shift draped loosely around her body, providing tantalizing glimpses of ivory skin. Her forearms rested on his chest and her breasts were...

Darcy hastily raised his eyes to her face. "Elizabeth?" he whispered.

"Yes." She drew out the word like one long exhalation.

Darcy's conscience warred with his body's desires. "Er...you should sleep; we must rise early in the morning."

Her lips curved into a smile he could only describe as seductive. "I slept for a long time, and I am no longer tired."

That much was plain to Darcy.

Her eyes held his gaze—the green so much darker in the dim light. Her lips were so close. The sight and the scent of Elizabeth made his heart pound and his breathing quicken.

No, this was wrong. He locked the muscles in his arms, keeping them stiff at his sides so they would not enclose her—no matter how much he longed for the embrace.

"You need more rest." He tried to sound firm, but he was too breathless.

"Why have you not kissed me again?" Her mouth made a little moue of disappointment. "We only kissed the once, but it was very pleasant." She lowered her head until their mouths were only inches apart, and he could smell the wine on her breath.

"How much wine did you drink, love?"

Her brows drew together. Good Lord, even her frowns were beautiful! "I am not foxed."

"Of course not, but—"

"Although, I must admit the wine did go to my head earlier. I feel quite...warm and...delightfully...distracted." Darcy found her attention far too focused for his peace of mind. She settled onto his chest, giggling as if the situation were a minor inconvenience rather than the potential disaster Darcy knew it to be.

Gently, he tried to slide her back to her side of the bed, but she resisted. "Elizabeth—"

She pouted. "Just one kiss?"

What could be the harm in a single kiss? Especially if she then surrendered to some much-needed rest. Her lips were so very pink and...close...and difficult to ignore. "Very well," he breathed.

Before he had a chance to act, Elizabeth's lips descended onto his, pressing and demanding a response. Oh, it was heavenly. How often had he dreamt of kissing Elizabeth? Yet the reality far exceeded any dream. Her lips tasted of wine, appropriately enough since he felt intoxicated by every touch. Her lips avidly sought his as if she, too, could not get enough of his taste, and her eagerness further stoked his desire.

Darcy opened his mouth, and their tongues swept together in a loving duel. The need for air meant their lips must reluctantly part, which prompted a throaty moan from Elizabeth. "I have nothing with which to compare, but surely you bestow the best kisses of any man in England—or France." She moaned again, and the sound traveled down Darcy's spine to radiate excitement throughout his body.

Darcy flushed with pleasure. "I can only say I am happy you have been kissing nobody else."

She smiled and lowered her head for another kiss. As their lips parted, both Elizabeth and Darcy were panting for breath. He had expected her energy to flag by now, but she still lingered, seemingly prepared for another kiss.

He patted her arm reluctantly. "Elizabeth, love, you must sleep."

"I am not tired."

"Still…" Darcy had been avoiding touching her more than necessary, but he feared his will would soon break. Placing both of his hands on her waist, he attempted to roll her back to the other side of the bed. But Elizabeth used his momentary distraction to slide one of her legs over both of his. Now her entire body rested atop of his, straddling his pelvis. Darcy's body reacted in an unmistakable way.

He groaned, mind and body at war. "Elizabeth, we cannot—"

"Shh." She laid a finger on his lips. "I am recovered from my injury and illness. There is no reason we could not resume…marital relations." She blushed at the words, not meeting his eyes.

Damnation! Darcy's body was in complete agreement with that plan. His desire had been restrained by concern that she did not return his feelings, but these actions seemed to answer that question. Yearning surged through his blood, lashing his entire body into a frenzy.

As she bent down to kiss him again, her entire body pressed against his, their night clothes providing only a flimsy barrier as body parts rubbed against each other. Darcy swallowed hard, on the verge of losing control of the situation.

With an effort of will, he grabbed her arms and flipped her onto her back. Now he loomed over her, his body covering hers.

Elizabeth's eyes widened and she gasped, but she made no complaints. She recovered quickly, entwining her arms around his neck, and brought his head toward hers for a passionate, impossibly long kiss.

The bodice of her shift had moved, almost to the point of revealing a mound of creamy flesh…If Darcy just…

His hand reached out and…

Chapter Ten

What the hell am I about? This woman is not my wife!

Darcy yanked his hand back as if she had suddenly burst into flames. Fool! he berated himself. I cannot indulge in "marital relations" with Elizabeth. I would be taking advantage of her in the worst way.

But his body protested. She was lying beneath him, flushed and wanton, entirely too willing for someone he would take advantage of.

Ignoring his body's pleas, Darcy rolled off Elizabeth's warmth with a muffled oath and landed with his feet on the cool floor.

"William?" Elizabeth was stricken. "Have I become less desirable to you?" Moisture gathered in the corners of her eyes.

Oh, Good Lord! Let her believe anything but that! Darcy felt like the worst sort of blackguard. "Nothing could be further from the truth, my love. But I—" He cast about for a plausible explanation. Unfortunately, his brain was still befuddled by lust. "I—You—You are not completely well," he finished lamely.

Her brows drew together. "If I am well enough to travel, surely I am well enough for...the marriage bed." The plea was followed by a wiggle of her hips that did nothing to dispel his desire.

What could he possibly say? Then inspiration struck. "Darling, we are currently trapped in France."

"Yes." She nodded warily.

"I do not want to take the risk that you could become with child. We do not know how soon we can return to England."

"Oh." Her lips formed a perfect circle. "I had not thought of that."

He leaned over her and stroked her silken hair. "It is not a lack of desire, darling. That is impossible."

Her shoulders slumped in resignation. Darcy hated the defeated expression on her face. How could he experience guilt over not taking her virginity? He had wandered into a mirror world where right was wrong, up was down, and left was right.

She slid down into the covers. "Very well. Will you at least hold me as I fall asleep?" Her voice was plaintive and small.

"Of course." He climbed back into bed and pressed his body against hers, savoring the warmth against his skin. The sensations of her moving beside him were almost enough to undo the vow he had made so recently.

He could not completely deprive himself; one more kiss would be his reward for restraint. Cradling her head in both his hands, Darcy captured her lips with his. This kiss was slow and tender, unlike the earlier frenzied collision of lips. When he reluctantly pulled his lips from hers, she sighed with deep contentment, her body relaxed and supple.

"I love your kisses, William," she murmured, her eyes heavy.

"And I love yours."

He watched as her eyes fell closed; soon her breathing became deep and slow and regular. Still, he could not shake a feeling of unease. What would he do if she became amorous again? When would he tell her the truth? What would happen if her memory returned?

Darcy was more than willing to marry her to compensate for the ways he had compromised her reputation. But once she learned how he had lied to her, she might never wish to see him again.

Still… Darcy rubbed his finger along his swollen lips in wonder. He could not bring himself to wish those kisses away.

***

People streamed along the street, hurrying to work, buying bread, or chatting with friends. Paris seemed even more crowded than London, not that she could remember a specific trip to London. Elizabeth fought the desire to shrink down on the bench as they entered the city. Perched on the high seat of the curricle, she felt as if she wore a sign proclaiming her to be an Englishwoman. It was nonsense, of course. She was wearing French clothing, and her face alone could not betray her national origin. As long as she was not called upon to speak, she was safe. Fortunately, she understood French far better than she spoke it; they had managed throughout the past two days with William speaking French while Elizabeth listened and nodded in appropriate places.

However, the sheer number of people in Paris made her apprehensive. Surely some of them would want to speak with Elizabeth. How could she avoid revealing her secret? If their identities were revealed, the consequences would be bad enough for her, but far worse for William. The gendarmes were unlikely to be very harsh toward a woman, but they were imprisoning all Englishmen. William had been so good to Elizabeth, so patient; she could not be the cause of his downfall.

If anyone suspected, they would claim to be a Frenchman with an English wife, but Elizabeth foresaw many potential problems with the plan, not the least of which was that an Englishwoman living in France should speak better French.

To make matters worse, she had awakened that morning feeling far more weary and stiffer than the day before. She had experienced fewer coughing fits, but her breathing was more constricted, wheezing roughly in and out of her chest. Elizabeth strove to minimize the sounds and conceal her fatigue, but William's solemn expression suggested that he was not fooled. A stiffness in his posture betrayed his anxiety.

She tried not to stare at him, but he was very handsome. At times she experienced such desire for him, as she had the previous night. But other times he seemed far too magnificent for her—like a fine silk gown one might admire in a shop window but knew would be far too dear. How had he ever fixed on her as the future companion of his life? It seemed impossible that such a creature would desire her.

Although she had only seen him in rough laborer's clothing, she knew they did not suit him. His bearing was too commanding, his posture too erect for him to be anything other than a gentleman. William would be resplendent when dressed the part: in a waistcoat and jacket with a starched cravat neatly tied around his neck. Was such an image fixed in her mind as a memory?

His hands were strong as they handled the reins. She could not help recalling the night before as his fingers pressed into her skin—firm but caressing. Even his profile suggested the strength of his character: his determined mouth and sharp eyes. And then there was the unruly dark hair she longed to run her fingers through.

How had she managed to capture the attention of such a handsome man? Elizabeth had viewed herself in a mirror; she had her share of beauty but nothing out of the common way. Nor was there any reason to suspect William had married her for her dowry.

Recognizing her scrutiny, William gave her a quick, reassuring smile before returning his attention to negotiating the teeming Paris streets. At such moments she had no difficulty believing in his deepest love. Indeed, it was the only explanation for his behavior. Yet at other times she wondered. Would she discover one day that it was all some bizarre mistake or waking fantasy? Without her memories, everything seemed slightly unreal. Perhaps she was still lying unconscious in the Martins' guest chamber, only dreaming of Paris.

On the outskirts of the city, William had stopped to ask a shopkeeper for directions to Rue DuVal. The neighborhood in which they now found themselves was neither for the most prosperous citizens nor the city's poorest residents. Women on the street wore sensible, sturdy cotton dresses, and the men in drab brown jackets were most likely shopkeepers or clerks. Houses were small, even by London standards, but well maintained and neat, with boxes of summer flowers blooming at their windows.

William guided the horse down a narrow side street, little more than an alley; a sign tacked to one building proclaimed it to be Rue DuVal. Elizabeth allowed herself a sigh of relief; she was quite prepared to quit the curricle. He reined in the horse in front of number twenty-three, an unprepossessing townhouse little different from its neighbors. Lacy curtains adorned the windows facing the street, and the door had been painted a cheerful red.

"This is her house?" Elizabeth asked as William helped her down.

"Yes." Darcy took a deep breath as he gave her his arm. "We can only pray she is at home."

As at the Dreyfus farm, William positioned himself between the door and Elizabeth while he knocked. She did not know whether to be annoyed or touched by the unnecessary chivalry; surely his former governess was unlikely to be a source of danger.

The door was opened by a young man—probably in his late teens—tall and thin with dark hair. He was not dressed as a servant. A family member perhaps? William had said the governess had returned to France to nurse a widowed sister through her final illness; then she had remained in Paris to raise her niece and nephew.

"Good afternoon," Darcy said politely in French. "Is Miss Laurent at home?"

The man's eyes narrowed. "Who are you?"

"My name is for Miss Laurent. I am an old friend."

The frown deepened. "Is she expecting your visit?"

William huffed out a laugh. "No, but I have no doubt she will be pleased to see me."

The man hesitated, not opening the door to admit them, torn between protecting his aunt and his duty to visitors.

An older woman's voice floated out from the depths of the house. "Who is it, Bernard?"

"He will not grant me his name, but he wishes to speak with you."

"Nan!" William called out in English. "'Tis I."

At these words a stout woman in her early sixties came bustling down the hallway. Her eyes went round with shock when she saw William. "It is you!" Instantly, her eyes darted around the street behind them to see if their presence had been noticed. "Bernard, let them in. Let them in at once!" She gestured urgently.

With a dubious expression, Bernard admitted William and Elizabeth. Only once the door was safely closed behind them did the woman fling her arms around William and embrace him as one might a child. Had the woman been younger, Elizabeth might have been seized by jealousy.

"Will!" she cried. "What an unexpected treat! Mon Dieu! You are in good looks, although a bit informally dressed." The woman chuckled, but her torrent of words continued. "Why are you in Paris? And who is this lovely creature? And how is Georgiana? Is she with you? And—"

William laughed. "I will answer your questions, Nanny Laurent, if you will stop talking long enough to listen."

Miss Laurent laughed, too. "I simply cannot believe it! Let me look at you." She stepped back to scrutinize William from head to toe. "Ah, you are a fine figure of a man! The very image of your dear papa." She leaned toward Elizabeth, confiding, "In his youth he was prone to stoutness, but it seems he has outgrown that tendency."

William rolled his eyes as Elizabeth put a hand over her mouth to disguise her smile. "I do not believe it!" she said.

The older woman waggled her finger at Elizabeth. "You must believe it. I have known Will since he was a babe in arms."

"I may regret introducing the two of you." William gave the older woman a tolerant smile.

Miss Laurent raised an eyebrow meaningfully at Elizabeth. "I do not believe we have been introduced."

"Ah, forgive me. Miss Adele Laurent, this is my w-wife, Elizabeth Ben—" William caught himself and began again. "Elizabeth Darcy."

"Your wife? Upon my word, I heard nothing of a wife in your last letter." At these words, William stared at his feet and fidgeted. "It must have happened very quickly. How wonderful!" The woman could not help but draw Elizabeth into an embrace, kissing her on both cheeks. "Nothing could make me happier than to meet Will's wife." She turned to William. "You have given me a great gift."

Elizabeth blushed. It would be difficult to accept such effusions under any circumstances, but it was particularly hard when she could not recall their courtship.

William's face sobered. "This is not a holiday, I am afraid. We have found ourselves in France by mischance and now seek to return home."

The older woman clapped her hands together. "Of course. We will help in any way we can." Behind her, Bernard stood with his arms crossed over his chest, not appearing at all inclined to help.

"We need shelter for two or three nights, if possible," William explained. "Elizabeth requires rest, and we must find a way to cross the Channel."

"Why does Mrs. Darcy need to rest so badly, eh?" Miss Laurent nudged William in the ribs. "Is she, perhaps, in an interesting condition?"

Elizabeth could not imagine many people treated William with such familiarity, nor had she known his face could turn that particular shade of red. William coughed. "Not at all. Elizabeth was recently ill with a lung fever."

"Oh, my dear!" Elizabeth found herself embraced for the second time by a woman she had known for fewer than five minutes. "What do you require? Hot compresses? Leeches? An apothecary?"

"Just a place to rest, I thank you," Elizabeth murmured.

Miss Laurent kept an arm around Elizabeth's waist as if she needed to be propped up. "I pray you, remain as long as you need. We will do whatever we can to be of assistance."

Bernard's eyes darted to his aunt. "Aunt, it could be dangerous if we were found sheltering an Englishman," he objected.

Miss Laurent gave her nephew a level look. "We will not turn away friends in need, and do not forget that Mr. Darcy's generosity helped me buy this house and feed you and your sister. We owe him everything. What has Napoleon ever done for us? We owe him nothing."

"If there is a danger—" William started.

"No." Miss Laurent waved her hand dismissively. "There is no danger. The gendarmes do not even know who I am. There is no reason they should pay us a visit."

"We will depart as soon as we are able," William promised.

"But not too soon, I pray you. I must hear how everyone fares at Pemberley. And you must tell me the story of how you arrived in Paris." She gestured William to a small but stylish drawing room. Elizabeth followed them, attempting to ignore the scowling Bernard trailing in their wake.

***

Adele poured Darcy another cup of tea, adding the amount of milk and sugar she knew he preferred. He and Elizabeth had explained their situation to his old governess. At the conclusion of the story, she had patted his cheek and exclaimed over him. "My poor dear!"

Darcy had smiled and endured. Despite his age, Adele still tended to view him as her young charge. But the tilt of Elizabeth's eyebrows suggested she found Adele's informality a bit shocking.

Less sympathetic, Bernard had excused himself after only a few minutes of conversation. Soon the conversation had turned to stories about the inhabitants of Pemberley. Although Elizabeth tried valiantly to participate, she could not conceal her fatigue. Adele took her upstairs and settled her in the guest bedchamber.

Upon Adele's return, the old friends had an opportunity to conduct a private discussion. "Have you decided when Georgiana will be coming out?" Adele asked. Every question demonstrated how she had attended to the details in each letter Darcy and Georgiana had written to her.

Darcy hesitated before answering. London. Georgiana. His life as the master of Pemberley seemed so remote. What would happen if he and Elizabeth never returned from France? Would Georgiana even have a season? No, he must not think in such a way. Their situation was not so desperate. Yet. "Probably next year. She could have come out for this season, but she did not desire it." In fact, she had begged him to delay it another year.

"She never did enjoy having her share of attention. But she will be beautiful." The older woman wore a fond smile. "Perhaps Mrs. Darcy can help her overcome her shyness."

Darcy blinked in surprise. The thought had never occurred to him since Elizabeth was not actually his wife, but now that he thought about it…she could be good for Georgiana. Yes, he could see Elizabeth being of great help to his sister. If she agreed to marry him. Or speak to him. Once they returned to England.

"Ah, I wish I could see her coming out." Adele lowered her eyes and smoothed her skirts. "But of course, I am needed here."

"Your home is quite lovely," Darcy said. He wished he could say something kind about her nephew, but Adele would detect any insincerity. Hopefully when the niece returned from school, she would provide an opportunity to praise Adele's parenting skills.

"Thank you." She smiled gently. "Mrs. Darcy seems like a delightful woman."

"Oh, she is," Darcy breathed. "Clever, kind-hearted, and beautiful, of course." Only when he glanced down at his lap did he realize he had inadvertently pulverized the biscuit he was holding. With a chagrined look at Adele, he brushed the crumbs onto the tea tray.

"What is the problem, Will?" Adele's gaze was sharp.

He raised an eyebrow. "Is it not obvious? Elizabeth and I are trapped in France."

Adele gave an unladylike snort. "Do not try to fool me. I did not believe you when you denied feeding your horse a lemon biscuit, and I do not believe you now. What makes you so uneasy about Mrs. Darcy?"

Darcy opened his mouth to deny the assertion, but then he sighed. Adele would pry it out of him eventually; she knew him too well. And there was no one he would trust more with his secret. "We are not actually married," he blurted.

Adele slowly lowered her teacup to the table. "Fitzwilliam Darcy! You have been living in sin with that lovely young woman?"

Darcy ran his hands through unruly curls. "No. Well, not precisely." Adele sat quite straight in her seat, one eyebrow raised. "Elizabeth believes we are married."

"Not a matter which is usually the subject of confusion," Adele said dryly.

"I told you she sustained a blow to the head and suffered memory loss—amnesia the doctor called it."

Adele nodded. "In all my years I never heard of such a thing."

"She does not recall me or anything about her previous life." Darcy tugged at the cuffs of his shirt. When had the room grown so warm? "I had believed her to be dead. When I first saw her at the doctor's house, I was so surprised that I claimed her as my wife. Perhaps because I wished it to be true, or perhaps I knew the doctor would not allow me to take her back to England unless I had such a claim to her." He swallowed convulsively. "The lie has proved to be something of a necessity. It is unlikely she would have trusted me so easily or traveled with me so readily if she knew the truth."

"Trust built on a lie." Adele covered her face with both hands. "This was not well done of you, Fitzwilliam."

Darcy's shoulders hunched; she only called him Fitzwilliam when he had done something wrong. He wanted to deny her words, but he could not. There may have been conveniences attending to his falsehood, but it was still a falsehood.

"Have you considered what will happen when she discovers the truth?"

Darcy shrugged. "After traveling so long as husband and wife, we must needs marry. We have shared many rooms, although—of course— we have not conducted…marital relations." This was a rather uncomfortable subject to be discussing with one's former governess. "Long before I arrived in France, I realized that marrying Elizabeth was the best way to secure my happiness."

Adele eyed him shrewdly. "But is it what Elizabeth wants?"

Darcy grabbed his teacup and took a hasty swallow. "The mistress of Pemberley will have many compensations."

"Enough to compensate for all the falsehoods?"

Darcy felt as if he had been punched in the stomach. "Sh-She is fond of me," he said, aware how weak it sounded.

Adele scoffed. "I am sure she is fond of her sisters and puppies and boiled potatoes. That does not signify."

Darcy leaned forward as if closer proximity would help Adele understand. "But she must marry me. Her reputation is too compromised to marry anyone else."

"That will make a very fine marriage proposal," Adele said tartly.

Darcy could not help remembering the disastrous proposal at Hunsford. Why would Elizabeth accept his advances now when she had so decisively spurned them before? He squirmed in his chair, trying to get comfortable. The room definitely had grown warmer. What a mess he had created. "What can I do?"

"You should tell her the truth at once."

His whole body protested the idea. "I cannot do so now!" he exclaimed. "She still remembers nothing about her past. I cannot risk losing her trust."

Adele's face was impassive. "You would prefer that she discovers a basic fact about her life another way? Perhaps when she recovers her memories?"

The thought made Darcy faintly nauseous. "I cannot tell her while we remain in France. Who knows what her reaction will be? Once we are safely on English soil, I will tell her immediately."

Darcy had trouble identifying the emotion he read on Adele's face. Was it...pity? "I just hope you have the time," she said sadly.

***

The bed at *chez Laurent* was very comfortable—wide and soft. Elizabeth sank into the pillows gratefully. Miss Laurent had provided a simple dinner and, noticing Elizabeth's continued fatigue despite her afternoon nap, had encouraged both of her visitors to retire early. William had not objected; no doubt he was more fatigued than he appeared.

As Elizabeth relaxed, her mind drifted, supplying her with the sorts of nonsensical ideas and images that populated the state between wakefulness and deep sleep. Eventually her drifting thoughts coalesced into an image of a scene...a ballroom, no, an assembly room.

The assembly room at Meryton. Somehow she knew the name.

Other people were dancing, but Elizabeth was not. With insufficient men to partner all the women, she was sitting out, watching the dancers and trying not to observe the two men standing before her. As their shapes sharpened in her view, Elizabeth recognized one as William. The other man, blond and smiling, seemed familiar, but she could not recall his name.

"Come, Darcy," the man said. "I must have you dance. I hate to see you standing about by yourself in this stupid manner."

William drew himself to his full height. "I certainly shall not. You know how I detest it, unless I am particularly acquainted with my partner." He sniffed disdainfully. "At such an assembly as this it would be insupportable. Your sisters are engaged, Bingley, and there is not another woman in the room whom it would not be a punishment to me to stand up with."

This declaration might have provoked Elizabeth's ire, but it was all so amusing. Mr. Darcy obviously thought very highly of himself if he could only bring himself to dance with two women in the entire assembly.

"I would not be so fastidious as you are," cried Mr. Bingley, "for a kingdom! Upon my honor, I never met with so many pleasant girls in my life as I have this evening; and there are several of them you see uncommonly pretty."

"You are dancing with the only handsome girl in the room," said Mr. Darcy, *regarding a very pretty blonde woman across the room. Elizabeth immediately recognized the woman as her sister Jane.*

"She is the most beautiful creature I ever beheld!" Mr. Bingley *exclaimed. "But there is one of her sisters sitting down just behind you, who is very pretty, and I dare say very agreeable. Do let me ask my partner to introduce you."*

He means me! Elizabeth realized, *frozen in her chair. She had no desire to stand up with a man as proud and disagreeable as Mr. Darcy, but it was already too late to escape his notice.*

"Which do you mean?" Glancing around, Mr. Darcy *caught Elizabeth's eye. She hastily glanced away, but he had noticed her and knew she was without a partner. How awkward!*

Mr. Darcy replied to his friend with cool civility. "She is tolerable, but not handsome enough to tempt me; I am in no humor at present to give consequence to young ladies who are slighted by other men. You had better return to your partner and enjoy her smiles, for you are wasting your time with me."

Mr. Bingley shook his head at his friend but made no further comment before hurrying away to find Jane. Mr. Darcy's head turned in Elizabeth's direction, but she kept her face impassive and hoped she was not blushing. Once he had disappeared into the crowd, her breath came more easily.

There was no reason to be ashamed. Nobody had overheard. And really, the conversation had revealed nothing more than Mr. Darcy's lack of character. A fine gentleman indeed! He might be rich in wealth but certainly not in manners.

She allowed her eyes to range about the room, but the sights blurred in her eyes. Upon most days she might have ignored such a slight or laughed at it, but today it was more difficult to forget. She had not yet managed to secure a single partner while she watched her friend Anna Preston dance with her newly betrothed. She was happy for her friend, but the news was another reminder that Elizabeth's own chances of marrying well were vanishingly small.

And then Mr. Darcy found her tolerable, but not handsome. Her hands clenched into fists. I will not cry. I will not cry. *Nonetheless, one tear escaped from her eye; she dashed it away impatiently. No doubt her skin was decorated with ugly pink blotches as well. If only she could depart the assembly that very minute! But all her sisters were agreeably engaged, and her father had disappeared into the card room. She was quite trapped.*

She stood, making her way blindly through the crowd to the ladies' retiring room, where she could dab her eyes and blow her nose—and claim she suffered from a trifling cold. Tears pricked her eyes, and Elizabeth quickened her steps so she would reach the retiring room before she disgraced herself further.

Elizabeth forced her eyes open to stare at the brown linen canopy, willing herself awake as she might do after a nightmare. Well, it was a sort of nightmare. Mr. Darcy—William—had been vile to her, insulting her without any provocation. Her heart pounded against her ribs, and her lungs labored to obtain sufficient air. She slowed her breathing lest she trigger another bout of coughing.

It was only a dream. I am not that person. I am not attending an assembly in Meryton; I am lying in bed in France. The repetition did little to calm her racing heart, and Elizabeth knew why: the source of her unease was lying beside her in the bed.

It was only a dream. It had no connection to reality. But the words failed to soothe her. In truth, the images had not felt much like a dream. Events had unfolded logically and sensibly in the way that dreams never did. It felt as if she had uncovered a buried memory—a memory of her first meeting with William.

Rubbing her eyes, she felt moisture and silently berated herself. It was fruitless to cry over something that happened months ago—or perhaps was an invention of her befuddled mind. But the melancholy from the dream persisted.

Resigning herself to wakefulness, Elizabeth sat up and rested her head against the headboard. The man in the dream had been haughty, arrogant, and uncaring of others' feelings. Had her William ever behaved in such a way? It seemed impossible to reconcile that William with the man she knew. Perhaps it was only a dream.

As she dried her eyes on the sleeve of her nightrail, she tried to take a rational view of the situation. Perhaps her dreaming mind had combined different memories. Perhaps the incident had unfolded as she remembered, but with a different man. Her memory was nothing if not faulty. The dream might be part memory and part fantasy.

As she prepared to slip under the covers again, William stirred and looked up at her. "My love, are you all right?" Even in the dim light cast by the moon her tears must have been quite visible.

No. Such a tender man could never have said such awful things. Her dream must have been a very flawed representation of reality.

"Darling." William's arms encircled her shoulders, drawing her down to his chest. "Did you have a bad dream?"

Elizabeth seized on the explanation. "Y-Yes. Just a b-bad dream."

He pressed a tender kiss to the top of her head. "Will you tell me about it?" he asked.

A recounting of the dream would not reflect well on Elizabeth and might hurt William. She shook her head. "I would rather forget it." How ironic: she struggled and strained to remember everything else.

William murmured his agreement and pulled her down next to him, nestling her body against his. "Very well. Go to sleep, my darling." Her muscles were tied in knots, her body as pliable as a wooden board.

But he made a contented noise and pulled her closer. His warm breath tickled the back of her neck, and the warmth of his body seeped into hers, helping her to relax. As she dropped off to sleep, Elizabeth was still contemplating the dream. She had wished for her memories to return, but perhaps her life was better without them.

Chapter Eleven

Recovering from the rigors of their journey, Darcy and Elizabeth slept quite late that morning. He noticed happily that the dark circles under Elizabeth's eyes had lightened, and her eyes regained some of their sparkle. His fear that her exhaustion heralded a relapse of her lung fever abated.

After they arose, Adele served them a leisurely luncheon in her garden. It was simple fare—a bit of ham, cheese, grapes, and bread—but the food was fresh and delicious. To Darcy's delight, Elizabeth ate with relish.

The garden itself was small but well-maintained, surrounded by high walls that preserved its privacy from the surrounding houses. The roses were in bloom, and their subtle fragrance added to the meal's pleasures. Elizabeth and Darcy were introduced to Marie, Adele's niece, a girl of fifteen who was as bright and cheerful as her brother was dark and brooding.

Conversation soon focused on how Darcy and Elizabeth would reach the coast. After clearing away the food, Adele spread a map on the table so she and Darcy could debate which roads to travel and which ports would be safest. Finally, they settled on a rather circuitous route that would eventually lead to Calais while avoiding the roads most likely to be frequented by soldiers.

The conversation then turned to other subjects. Bright-eyed and fascinated, Marie asked Elizabeth many questions, particularly about the amnesia. "You do not remember anything at all of your life before awakening in Saint-Malo?"

Elizabeth hesitated briefly before replying in stilted French. "Recently I have had a few memories."

Darcy leaned forward in his chair at this news; his skin prickled with apprehension.

"Only a few remembrances from my childhood," she reassured him with a smile. "I recalled when my sister and I thought we must rescue a baby rabbit from beside a pond, but the rabbit ran away and we both got wet." Everyone joined Elizabeth's laughter. As it died down, Elizabeth said wistfully, "I do not remember my sister's name."

Darcy's heart ached anew. How lost Elizabeth must feel!

Elizabeth mustered a smile. "I do not believe such was an unusual occurrence. I think my mother complained about my 'wild ways.'" She looked ruefully at Adele. "I am sure William did not provoke similar complaints as a child. He must have been always polite and well-behaved."

Oh no. Darcy was not pleased with this turn in the conversation, but Adele had a knowing smile on her face. It was already too late to prevent disaster. "Oh, he was *very well* behaved."—she rolled her eyes— "except, of course, for the time he slid down the front stairs on the best silver tray from the butler's pantry."

Darcy could feel the heat rise in his cheeks. Naturally that would be the story Adele chose first.

"William!" Elizabeth exclaimed in mock horror. "*Now* I learn the truth of your misspent youth? Did you disclose this to me before I married you?"

"Another time," Adele continued, "he climbed into Pemberley's attic and dropped apples and potatoes into the courtyard."

Elizabeth gave him a dubious look.

"I had been studying about Sir Isaac Newton and thought to conduct my own experiments with gravity," Darcy said with as much dignity as he could muster.

The hand over Elizabeth's mouth surely concealed a smile. "And what did you discover?"

He could not completely suppress an answering smile. "I discovered that when you drop apples and potatoes into the courtyard, it creates a mess on the stones that your governess will require you to clean up."

Adele nodded. "Precisely. And you never did that again." Everybody laughed.

"Of course, it was your cousin Richard who caused the most trouble," Adele remarked. "I certainly hope the army has tamed his wild ways."

Darcy drank from his teacup. "That might be beyond their power."

Adele turned to Elizabeth. "Richard would organize all the local children into battalions and send them into battles with sticks and wooden shields. I was forever treating bruised shins and scraped arms."

Darcy smiled reminiscently. "I rather enjoyed Richard's visits to Pemberley." As the second son, his cousin had never experienced the sense of responsibility that weighed on Darcy's shoulders.

Elizabeth gave him a teasing look. "And what do you do for amusement now?"

Darcy absently rubbed his chin. Amusement? He could recall few things he did purely for amusement. Everything advanced some purpose or another. Even when he went into the country, it was with the aim of benefiting from the clean air and the exercise of riding and hunting. *Good Lord, when did I grow into such a dullard?* However, one thing sprang to mind immediately. "I have had far more amusement since you came into my life."

Elizabeth blushed, but Adele clapped her hands together. "Well said! Well said indeed!"

After a short pause, Darcy asked Elizabeth, "Have you recollected anything from your time as an adult?" *Anything about me, for instance?*

Elizabeth hesitated and then shook her head, her eyes fixed on her lap. "No, nothing."

Darcy did not know whether to be relieved or disappointed. Had she forgotten him because he was not important to her life? Or should he count his blessings that she could not recall some of their less agreeable encounters? The somberness of Elizabeth's expression troubled him.

Adele drained her teacup and set it on the table with an air of finality. "Your memories will return in time, I have no doubt." She leaned over to pat Elizabeth's hand reassuringly. "In the meantime, I am very pleased fate has brought you here."

***

Over the next two days, Elizabeth rested and recovered her strength while Darcy worked with Adele to perfect their escape plan. They developed alternative routes in case of unforeseen obstacles and packed away cheese, apples, and other food that would not spoil quickly. With Darcy's money, Adele discreetly purchased additional clothing for the journey. Elizabeth passed many pleasant hours in conversation with Marie and Adele, who seemed to find her good company. Despite the circumstances, Darcy was pleased he had the opportunity to introduce his former governess to Elizabeth.

By necessity, Elizabeth and Darcy did not leave Adele's house except for occasional forays into her walled garden. But on the third day, Darcy was forced to venture out to sell the curricle and horse. The carriage was simply too noticeable and too ostentatious for a laborer and his wife;

they were fortunate indeed that it had not aroused suspicion on the road to Paris.

The very act of slipping out of Adele's back door made Darcy's palms sweat. His mind instantly conjured up a variety of horrific consequences, from the French army descending on the house to Elizabeth suffering a terrible relapse.

Darcy traded the curricle for a dogcart and a sturdy mare. Such a conveyance would slow their pace, but it was a necessary inconvenience. To avoid drawing attention to Adele's house, Darcy arranged for the man to deliver the cart and horse the following morning, when they planned to depart.

His head full of last-minute preparations, he returned to Adele's house from the back alley, muddy and strewn with refuse as it was. However, as he unlatched the garden gate, the hairs on the back of his neck lifted, causing him to freeze in his tracks. Something was not right.

The windows on the first floor were wide open. Despite the heat and the pleas of her niece and nephew, Adele had steadfastly refused to open any windows because of her distaste for flies. Now, however, the lacy curtains in the rear windows fluttered in the lazy summer breeze. Also, the cat was sitting on the back step. A rather elderly yellow tom, Adele's cat always stayed indoors. Fearing it had grown too old to fend for itself, the older woman allowed it a quiet retirement at her fireplace hearth. Yet here it was on the doorstep, extremely disgruntled and meowing piteously to be readmitted.

Something was not right at Adele's house.

Darcy slipped through the gate and closed it softly behind him. Rather than stroll up the back pathway, he skulked along the wall where he was partially concealed by vegetation. Drawing closer to the house, he could hear voices; clever of Adele to open the windows. The rumble of a deep masculine voice did not belong to anyone in the household. Darcy inched closer until he crouched under the windowsill where he could discern the words.

"When will your husband return?" the man demanded.

The voice that replied was Elizabeth's; her French was halting and heavily accented. "As I said before, monsieur, he traveled to Toulon. He is looking for the work. He will be far away for plenty of days." Whoever their unexpected visitors were, Elizabeth did not want Darcy to encounter them.

"If you do not wish to tell me, madame, we will wait." The man's tone was mocking.

"I assures you my husband is a French citizen." Darcy winced at her conjugation of "assure."

The man, who must have been a gendarme, chuckled. "And no doubt his French is as good as yours."

Elizabeth huffed indignantly. "Yes, I am from the England, but Georges is French—born in Normandy. It is not a crime for marrying to an Englishwoman." *She tries to protect me*, Darcy thought sadly.

"No, but being an English spy is a crime," said a different male voice. There were at least two gendarmes. How had Darcy been discovered? They had been so careful.

"Georges is not an English spy," Adele scoffed. "Why would you think this?"

One of the men cleared his throat. "Your neighbor heard English being spoken in your garden."

"Which neighbor?" Adele asked shrilly. "Was it Mr. Renard? Was he eavesdropping from his side of the wall? He is a senile old man. You should not listen to anything he says!"

Elizabeth's voice was calmer. "Me and my husband do talk in the English. It means nothing."

"We will make that determination for ourselves," the gendarme said coolly.

A long silence followed. Darcy pictured Adele and Elizabeth sitting on one side of the drawing room, glaring at the gendarmes in the tense stillness.

Finally, Elizabeth cleared her throat. "Many Frenchmen married to Englishwomen. Why do you bother my husband?"

The pause was so long that Darcy believed they would not answer. Eventually, one of the men cleared his throat. "We seek a spy who was last seen in Brittany."

Darcy's heart raced. How had that news traveled so fast?

"We believe he has some connection with Miss Laurent," the man continued.

Icy chills crept down Darcy's spine. If they suspected his true identity, they would not give up easily. How had they discovered that connection?

Elizabeth barked a laugh. "You believe my husband might be this man, Lieutenant? We are living in Marseilles for months." *She is good.*

Her outrage seems quite genuine. But her accent does not suggest a woman who has lived long in France.

"You will forgive me, madame, if I do not take your word for it." The Frenchman's tone was oily. "When I speak with your husband, I will judge his story for myself."

Under the window, Darcy stiffened; his accent was good, but he could not vouch for its perfection. A careful listener might notice mistakes.

Blast and damnation! The safest course would be for Darcy to depart, and swiftly, but that would leave Elizabeth and Adele—and possibly Bernard and Marie—alone and undefended. The gendarmes seemed focused on him, but they might imprison Adele or Elizabeth on a whim.

He felt for the handle of Dreyfus's pistol in the pocket of his coat. It slid in a palm slick with sweat. Darcy had purchased ammunition and powder; however, a single pistol would not be sufficient against two or more armed men. Cold perspiration trickled down his neck and between his shoulder blades.

"My husband is not returning for weeks. Will you to sit in Madame's drawing room for such a whole time?" Darcy wondered if Elizabeth's words contained hidden meaning. Was she warning him that he should leave the city? She should know him better.

The man chuckled. "Madame, if your husband tries to leave the city, we will soon be informed. Our men guard all the streets leaving Paris. At the moment we seek several spies; he is but one." Darcy shivered. So much for their plan of sneaking quietly from Paris.

Elizabeth made a slight sound; a noise of distress? Darcy longed to put his arms around her and assure her that all would be well.

"Is this your plan?" asked Adele with some aspersion. "Sit here and await his return?" She snorted. "As he is on his way to Toulon, it will be a long wait. And I have no intention of feeding your men."

"We shall see," the man said smugly. The hairs rose on the nape of Darcy's neck; did the gendarme know something about his whereabouts?

"Well, Adele," Elizabeth said in English, "I suppose we can only wait for them to weary of this exercise."

"Indeed."

As the sun began to lower in the sky, Darcy crouched immobile under the window—not daring to leave for fear the gendarmes might harm the women. His muscles cramped and protested the uncomfortable position, but he could not risk the slightest movement.

There was little conversation in the drawing room. The two women talked a bit about the weather, fashion, and similar topics, pointedly ignoring the gendarmes. Adele provided a small dinner for herself and Elizabeth; apparently she had sent her niece and nephew to stay with friends. As promised, she did not offer any food or tea to the men occupying her house.

Although the gendarmes spoke little, the sounds of coughs, pacing, and muffled curses suggested that the men were tiring of the activity. Based on the noise, Darcy guessed there were at least three men. Finally, at around eight o'clock, the lieutenant stood with a scrape of his chair legs on the floor and announced their departure. Darcy breathed a sigh of relief.

"Madame," the gendarme said in a clipped voice, "your lack of cooperation with the gendarmerie will be noted."

"I cannot help it if my guest has left for Toulon," Adele replied serenely.

"He *will* cooperate." The gendarme's voice had dropped an octave. "We will be taking his wife to the Temple."

Chapter Twelve

All breath left Darcy's lungs in a rush. The Temple was the most notorious prison in Paris.

Adele's voice was panicked. "The Temple? She has done nothing wrong!"

The gendarme chuckled. "Then her husband will have no difficulty retrieving her."

"It will be several days before he can return!" Adele protested.

"I assure you that she will be fed in the meantime," the man said dryly.

Darcy's heart pounded so loudly he thought the gendarmes might hear. Rescuing Elizabeth from the Temple would be nigh impossible; he had to act now. Briefly he considered turning himself in, but Elizabeth might not be able to escape France without him—she might refuse to even make the attempt.

Still, he needed to find some way to prevent them from taking Elizabeth away.

In the growing twilight, Darcy darted up the front path to the street, a plan taking form in his mind. Fortunately, the street urchin he had passed earlier still lingered at the corner. Darcy jingled some coins in his pocket. "Would you like to earn some money?"

A few minutes later Darcy was back in position under the window, listening as Elizabeth and Adele tried their best to delay the process. "Elizabeth," Adele asked, "do you have the handkerchiefs I purchased for you?"

"Oh! I failed to pack them."

"I believe they may be in Marie's room. I will fetch them for you."

A gendarme growled, "She does not require a fresh supply of handkerchiefs. She is going to prison, not a tea party!"

"Do not be a brute!" Adele admonished.

"I hardly think—" The man broke off with an exasperated noise. "No more delay! You will accompany us now."

"What will you do?" Adele challenged. "You will shoot an innocent woman because you cannot wait for her to gather a few handkerchiefs? Has France lost all semblance of civilization?"

There were several uneasy coughs from the other gendarmes. No doubt some were uncomfortable arresting a woman.

"Very well." The lieutenant sighed.

Adele's retreating footsteps sounded on the stairs. Darcy held his breath. Now would be an excellent time for a distraction.

"Lieutenant! Lieutenant Jardin!" Right on cue, the urchin's voice sounded on the street.

"What do you want? What is it?" One of the gendarmes shouted at the boy through an open front window.

"Were you looking for that woman's husband? He was approaching the house, but when he got close, he ducked down the Rue Marvel."

"We can get him!" the lieutenant cried. "Go! Go!" Feet pounded across Adele's floors, and the front door burst open. "Luc, you remain here with Madame Laurent," the lieutenant said before the door slammed behind him.

Darcy had hoped they would abandon the house altogether. Using a convenient tree root as a footstool, Darcy peered through the open window. The sole remaining gendarme had his back to the window, looming over Elizabeth where she sat on the sofa. Anger sped Darcy's heartbeat. Was such intimidation necessary?

Grasping the edge of the windowsill, Darcy managed to pull himself up without making any noise. As he sat in the window, he pulled out the pistol, tempted to shoot the man. But the gendarme was only following orders, and murdering an officer would compound their problems.

As silently as possible, Darcy crept toward the man's back. Standing by the fireplace, Adele watched him with wide eyes but made no sound. Just as Darcy closed in on the man, a floorboard under his foot creaked. The man whirled around, but too late. The butt of the gun met the base of the man's neck with a dull thud, and the gendarme crumpled in a heap on the floor.

"William!" Elizabeth stood in one motion and fell into Darcy's arms, a warm and gratifying weight.

Adele hurried toward him. "Will! Thank God!"

Darcy embraced her quickly. "We must leave immediately. The gendarmes will not be distracted for long. By now the street urchin will have disappeared."

Elizabeth nodded, handing him his knapsack. "I knew you would come." She shrugged in reply to his surprised look.

Pistol at the ready, Darcy led the way through Adele's back door, moving swiftly but warily past the garden and into the alley, now swathed in evening shadows. It appeared empty, but the darkness could hide anyone.

"They watch all the roads, Will!" Adele huffed as she rushed to follow him. "You cannot leave Paris now. We must conceal you in another location…"

Darcy's stomach knotted with tension. The longer they remained in France, the greater the risk of discovery, but he saw no alternative.

"I had a thought," Elizabeth said, her eyes bright as she looked up at him. "They are watching all the *roads*, but there must be another way to leave Paris. Perhaps the river?"

Adele's mouth dropped open. "Of course!"

Darcy shook his head in wonder. "That is a magnificent idea, Elizabeth." She blushed at his praise. He turned to Adele. "How often do boats go north?"

Her answer came in short gasps as they hurried along the alley. "Many depart every day. Barges bring coal and firewood daily to the city from Belgium and Normandy."

"They return up the river empty?" he asked.

"Yes, or laden with goods manufactured near the city. The gendarmes could not possibly watch all the boats on the Seine even if it occurred to them. Wharfs line the river in many different locations, and boats leave at various times of the day." She looked thoughtful for a moment. "My friend Therese is married to a dockmaster. Perhaps he could find a boat that would take you upriver."

Darcy nodded. "Lead the way. There is no time to lose."

***

Adele's friends, Mr. and Mrs. Girard, were surprised to receive visitors so late at night but were eager to help. Naturally she did not relate the entire story, merely explaining that her friends needed to reach the coast quickly. The couple might have guessed William and Elizabeth were fleeing from the authorities, but they did not ask questions. Many people in France, it seemed, were eager to defy the government.

Mr. Girard indeed knew of a barge that was departing for Rouen in the morning. No doubt the captain would be amenable to taking passengers—for an exorbitant fee. Elizabeth was relieved to have a plan, although she would not rest easy until they were safely on the barge—and probably would not sleep soundly again until they were back in England.

Darcy gratefully accepted the Girards' offer to occupy their guest chamber for the night. All that remained was to bid farewell to Adele.

The older woman had tears in her eyes as she said goodbye to Elizabeth and William. She embraced Elizabeth first. "How fortunate we had an opportunity to meet! You are exactly the sort of woman I would have chosen for Will."

"A woman with amnesia?" Elizabeth joked.

Adele shook her head, her eyes serious. "Even with amnesia, it is clear you are a woman of character who will not always allow him to have his own way. This is what he needs, whether he knows it or not." Over her shoulder, she gave William a fond look; he merely shook his head, as if he had expected her to say something of the kind.

When the former governess released Elizabeth, she pulled William into an all-consuming embrace. "I knew you would mature into a fine man. Your father would be proud." She pulled a letter out of her reticule. "Here, I have written a note to Georgiana. I pray you, deliver it for me."

William carefully put the note in his pocket. "Will you be safe after we depart?"

She waved away the anxious expression on his face. "I will stay with friends for a few days. Once the gendarmes realize you are gone, they will chase after some other 'spy.'"

William took both of her hands in his. "If they give you any trouble, please write to me. I will ensure that you and your family may leave the country. We would be most pleased to have you at Pemberley." Elizabeth realized he meant they could host Adele and her family at his country estate…forever. The idea of such wealth was quite overwhelming.

"Yes, and you must write to me when you arrive home," she insisted. With another swift hug, she was gone.

***

Elizabeth dreamed. *She played the pianoforte in a drawing room she did not recognize. The house was very grand, with chairs upholstered in silk and gilt décor verging on gaudiness. Some instinct told Elizabeth that it was too ostentatious to be Longbourn. A sandy-haired man sat on a chair near the pianoforte, listening to Elizabeth play. His appearance tickled her memory, but Elizabeth could not recall his name. Mr. Darcy's sudden appearance at her right shoulder startled her, causing her to strike the wrong key. As she recovered from the faux pas, the master of Pemberley positioned himself so he could view her face while she played.*

By the end of the piece, Elizabeth was fighting a rising irritation. "You mean to frighten me, Mr. Darcy, by coming in all this state to hear me?" She gave him a poisonous smile. "But there is a stubbornness about me. My courage always rises with every attempt to intimidate me."

A small smile played about Mr. Darcy's lips. "You could not really believe me to entertain any design of alarming you; I have had the pleasure of your acquaintance long enough to know that you find great enjoyment in occasionally professing opinions which in fact are not your own."

Elizabeth suppressed a desire to roll her eyes. She had told him he intimidated her; her request for him to desist could not have been any plainer. And his response? He assured her that she was joking, as if she did not know her own mind! Did the man understand no subtlety at all?

Covering her irritation with a polite laugh, she directed her next comment to the man who sat beside the piano. "Your cousin will teach you not to believe a word I say. Indeed, Mr. Darcy, it is very ungenerous of you to mention all that you knew to my disadvantage in Hertfordshire for it is provoking me to retaliate and such things may come out as will shock your relations to hear."

"I am not afraid of you," Mr. Darcy said. Of course, he was not. His position insulated him from whatever criticism his unpleasant demeanor so richly deserved.

"Pray let me hear what you have to accuse him of," said the cousin. Colonel Fitzwilliam: *the name rushed into Elizabeth's mind. "I should like to know how he behaves among strangers."*

For a moment Elizabeth was tempted to tell the truth: that the man was rude, condescending, and aloof. Oh, it would be so lovely to voice such sentiments. But her triumph would be brief. She would be sent away from Rosings Park, and Mr. and Mrs. Collins would suffer the consequences of having invited such an ill-mannered guest.

Instead Elizabeth fixed an insincere smile on her face. "Prepare yourself for something very dreadful. The first time of my ever seeing him was at a ball and what do you think he did? He danced only four dances, though gentlemen were scarce and more than one young lady was sitting down in want of a partner."

The colonel's knowing smile suggested that Mr. Darcy had behaved this way upon other occasions. Mr. Darcy himself grinned as if Elizabeth had paid him an immense compliment. Infuriating man. Yes, she had said it in a teasing manner, but he should be ashamed of his rudeness; instead he appeared to be proud of it.

Elizabeth pulled herself up through layers of sleep until she lay gasping and staring at the low ceiling of the Girards' cottage. There was barely space for a bed and washstand in the room, and the bed was so small she was pressed quite close to William's body. Slow, regular breaths demonstrated that *his* sleep was undisturbed by memories of past conflicts.

Elizabeth increasingly was certain that this dream—like the last— was the record of a memory and not random images from her life jumbled together in a nonsensical narrative in the usual way of dreams. These visions were too linear, logical, and sensible to be anything other than memories—although she would have preferred otherwise.

When musing about the first dream (assuming it was a memory), Elizabeth had supposed that she and William quickly overcame the negative feelings about their first encounter. She had imagined that William apologized, and they laughed over the misunderstanding before embarking on their courtship.

But this memory—from some months later and in a completely different place—suggested that they were still very much at odds, even if William did not recognize it. Sitting at the pianoforte, Elizabeth's thoughts about William had been extremely unfavorable. Her words had been bitter, even if she concealed her anger with a teasing tone.

In Saint-Malo, William had suggested their acquaintance was short before their marriage. How had she gone from disliking the man to accepting his hand? It was a puzzle. She shivered despite the heat in the room. *I am missing something, an important piece of information; without it I am groping for answers in the dark.*

She cursed the holes in her memory. William's concern for her wellbeing was indisputable; he had risked his life on her behalf many times. But she had the persistent sense that he was concealing something from her. A fundamental rift? A mutual disdain? Some kind of forced marriage?

Staring into the dark, she listened to the thumping of her racing heart. What would she do if the one person she relied upon completely was the one person she could not trust?

William rolled over in his sleep and threw his arm around her, pulling her close against his body. The sensation of his hands on her arms made her skin crawl, but Elizabeth did not struggle lest she awaken him. She expected to remain awake for the rest of the night, but she soon fell into an uneasy sleep.

Chapter Thirteen

In the morning, Mr. Girard introduced Darcy to Mr. Moreau, the captain of a barge bound for Rouen. A gruff fifty-year-old with a fringe of white hair, Moreau eyed Darcy with a raised eyebrow. "Do you support Napoleon?" he asked in a harsh voice nearly as weather-beaten as his face.

Unsure of the "correct" answer, Darcy simply gave the honest one. "No."

Moreau grunted. "Good." He spat on the floor. "I spit on Napoleon!"

Darcy said nothing.

"Do you support Joseph Fouche?"

Fouche was the director of the Paris gendarmes—someone Darcy had no desire to encounter. "No."

"Good." Moreau spat on the floor again. "I spit on Fouche!"

Again, Darcy said nothing.

"And what of the gendarmes of Paris?" Moreau's eyes narrowed at Darcy.

By now Darcy felt comfortable revealing some of the truth, so he shrugged. "Well, they tried to arrest me."

Moreau spat on the ground again. "I spit on the gendarmes!"

Girard rolled his eyes. "We get the idea, Moreau."

Moreau grinned at Darcy. "If taking you to Rouen would make Napoleon's gendarmes unhappy, I am pleased to help." Then he named his price.

Darcy grimaced; the captain was not solely motivated by altruism, but they had little choice. "We have a deal."

***

The barge did not move swiftly, which gave Darcy plenty of time to enjoy the passing scenery from the deck. One bank boasted fields of golden wheat as far as the eye could see; they gleamed in the noonday sun and rippled whenever a breeze brushed over the sheaves. A picturesque village occupied the other bank.

Hearing footsteps, he turned to find Elizabeth climbing the stairs to the deck. The voyage so far had been uneventful, and he had enjoyed the opportunity to relax his vigilance.

Genuinely pleased to see her, he gave her a warm smile, but her answering smile was brief and tight. It was not his imagination; although the trip on the barge should have helped Elizabeth relax, she seemed more distant with every passing hour.

He had been poised to inquire about her change in mood numerous times, but he feared the answer. What if she had remembered something he would prefer she forget? What if she had decided she could not love him?

Despite his unease, he longed to take her hand, as much to reassure himself as to express affection for her. However, he could not forget—even for a minute—that he did not have the right to touch her as a husband would. He held his breath, hoping she would extend her hand to take his, but she joined him at the railing with only a cursory glance in his direction.

Restraint was the proper course, but Darcy's arms ached with emptiness—particularly now that he knew exactly how they would feel wrapped around Elizabeth. It was pure torture sharing a bed with her every night while trying not to touch her.

"The view is very beautiful," Elizabeth said.

"Yes," he agreed.

She leaned against the railing, savoring the scenery while Darcy savored her beauty.

They had been fortunate in the weather; since departing Paris, the skies had been blue and sunny. The crew was pleasant but kept the two passengers at a wary distance. When Darcy and Elizabeth dined with Captain Moreau, he generously shared his opinion of Napoleon, the emperor's generals, the march on Russia, the Peninsular War, taxation, the state of the roads, men's hats, or any other subject. Indeed, he appeared to have a decided opinion about everything. Thus, conversation with the captain consisted primarily of listening.

Otherwise, Elizabeth and Darcy were left to their own devices for entertainment—a situation that would suit Darcy admirably were it not for the shadows in Elizabeth's eyes. Even now when she had sought his company, she stared persistently at the vista and showed no inclination toward further conversation. Perhaps he should give her an opening to discuss the source of her unease. He took a deep breath and said, "Have you remembered anything else of your past?"

She hesitated and then shook her head as her hands squeezed the railing. "Nothing substantial. Just wisps of memories, images that are unconnected to specific events. Words and sounds that make no sense to me."

How bewildering such an experience would be. Lost in a forest without any sign of a path to lead you back home. No wonder her eyes were shadowed.

"Perhaps if you describe the images, I might be able to help you recall what they are. I could put them into context."

She pressed her lips together. "I doubt it. After all, you and I have not known each other very long."

"True." Why was she insisting on that point? She presented a calm façade, but underneath there seemed to lurk a great disturbance of spirit. Did she doubt his feelings for her?

Or was she questioning her feelings for him?

I am still a virtual stranger to Elizabeth, he reminded himself. *Everything is disorienting. Of course, she is uncertain about the stability of our relationship. No doubt she is uncertain about the stability of her entire life.*

The need to reassure her urged him to speak, but he faltered over finding the right words. He had been deliberately vague in describing their relationship, but there was nothing vague or false about his feelings for her. Recalling that emptiness following her "death" was like pressing on a bruise, yet it gave him strength. Nothing that happened now could be as painful as those days.

"As I said before, I had great difficulty convincing you to marry me."

She bit her lower lip. "Yes, I recall. But I thought…" Her voice trailed off.

"Yes?"

Her gaze touched him briefly and then returned to the water. "I thought possibly that my father wished the match and I did not."

Tension twisted his stomach. The supposition came a little too close to the truth for his comfort, and yet he must not let her suspect.

His hand covered hers where she gripped the railing. "Elizabeth, I…" *How may I reassure her without weaving additional lies into our story?* "I assure you that my proposal was borne of nothing other than the deepest and most ardent affection and admiration."

That much was the complete truth. She need not know that she had *rejected* the aforementioned proposal. He gave her hand an affectionate squeeze.

Elizabeth finally lifted her eyes to his. "It was?"

He had said this before; why did she find that hard to believe? Did she have a contrary memory? "Yes." His voice was louder and more forceful than he had intended. "I was slow to recognize and comprehend my feelings." He stared at their intertwined hands. "But it was irrevocable."

"Oh." She breathed out the word, a look of wonder on her face. After a long silence she asked the question he had been dreading. "And what of my feelings for you?"

He swallowed convulsively. "I cannot speak to your sentiments."

"Did I not tell you I loved you?"

Darcy's entire body stiffened as he fought to keep the panic from his face. What could he tell her that was not a lie?

"I…we did not speak much of our feelings." *That much was certainly true.* "I have actually spoken more of what I feel here in France than before." *Also true.* He drew her hand to his chest. "And I will always do everything in my power to make you happy."

A few of the anxious lines on her face smoothed out at this declaration. He wanted to make all her worries disappear, but he had already told so many falsehoods… Was there another way to reassure her?

He studied her forest green eyes, absorbed by his concerns about her turmoil. *I should not touch her, and I certainly should not kiss her.* But Darcy would have defied any man to resist those soft eyes and slightly parted lips. Every passing day brought them closer to the restoration of her memories—when she might turn away from him forever. Every day could be his last opportunity to kiss her. Even if they managed to cross the Channel with the deception intact, the truth must be revealed the moment they set foot on English soil.

He stepped closer to her and, when she did not move away, bent his head toward hers. Still, she voiced no objections. When he enfolded her in his arms, she melted softly against him, a gesture so trusting that it took his breath away.

Darcy intended the kiss to be a taste, a quick reassuring pressure on her lips, but he was unprepared for her reaction. She pressed herself against the full length of his body, urging him to explore her mouth more deeply.

Every kiss with Elizabeth was intoxicating, like the finest wine he had ever tasted—rich and sweet and smooth. He could not get enough. Soon he was giddy with passion and lack of air; he might as well be foxed.

Many minutes passed before he could bring himself to pull away from her.

She stared at him, two parallel lines etched between her brows. "I do not understand..." Her voice trailed off.

"Understand what?" he asked.

She shook her head. "A vague memory of a dream. It probably means nothing." He would have asked her more, but she looked away, her expression shuttered.

"I do love you, Elizabeth. Most ardently." *Please believe that much, even if you doubt everything else.*

Her eyes fixed on a willow hanging over the river bank. "I wish I could say the same, but I cannot remember..." A tear slid down one cheek.

Darcy brushed it away with gentle fingers, cursing himself for even raising the subject. "I do not expect it. You are not sufficiently acquainted with me."

Her gaze dropped to her hands. "I am sure when I do remember, I will..."

Darcy wished he could be so certain. "I have no doubt all your memories will return in time."

She nodded stiffly. Darcy felt so impotent in this situation. With all his fortune and station in life, he could do nothing to mend the operations of Elizabeth's mind.

They stood at the railing, still as statues, for long minutes. Finally, Elizabeth withdrew her hand from his. "I am tired. I think perhaps I will lie down."

Darcy watched her retreating form, unable to repress the feeling that he was losing her.

***

Elizabeth dreamed again. *She walked in the park of some great house accompanied by the man she had encountered in the previous dream: Colonel Fitzwilliam. They were speaking of Mr. Darcy's sister, whom Elizabeth had never met. "She is a very great favorite with some of the ladies of my acquaintance, Mrs. Hurst and Miss Bingley," Elizabeth said.*

"I know them a little," the colonel replied. "Their brother is a great friend of Darcy's."

For some reason these rather innocent words frustrated Elizabeth. "Oh yes," she said drily, "Mr. Darcy takes prodigious care of Mr. Bingley."

"I really believe Darcy does take care of him. I have reason to think Bingley very much indebted to him."

"What do you mean?"

"He congratulated himself on having lately saved his friend from the inconveniences of a most imprudent marriage, but without mentioning names or particulars." The colonel cleared his throat diffidently. "I only suspected it to be Bingley."

A terrible thrill shot through Elizabeth's body, and she quivered with the effort to conceal her reaction from her companion. He must be speaking of Jane; surely Mr. Bingley did not form "inappropriate" attachments so very frequently. "Did Mr. Darcy give you his reasons for this interference?"

"I understood that there were some very strong objections against the lady."

Elizabeth's heart swelled with indignation. How could Mr. Darcy have presumed to do such a thing? Only that day she had been reading Jane's letters and musing how out of spirits her sister seemed. Who was Mr. Darcy to judge that Jane was unworthy?

He had ruined her sister's chance for happiness.

That high-handed... The gall of... Such an officious... Elizabeth could not think of epithets vile enough to express how she felt about Mr. Darcy at that minute.

The force of words unspoken pressed on the inside of her skull until she felt as if it would explode; her head throbbed and the muscles in her neck tightened as if preparing for a battle with Mr. Darcy. She desperately wanted to be alone but forced herself to continue walking and bantering with the colonel. He must not suspect anything...

Elizabeth awoke panting and sweating, twisted in the sheets. The dark walls of the barge's cabin loomed over and around her, enclosing her in a room no larger than a jail cell. Pounding in her head alerted her that the headache had followed her from the dream into waking.

But was the dream a memory or a fantastical construct of her sleeping mind? A sister by the name of Jane? Yes. Such a sister had danced at the Meryton Assembly. But she could remember nothing about her sister save a vague memory from the earlier dream. Did she resemble Elizabeth? How old was she? What was her favorite color?

Other parts of the dream also coincided with things she knew to be real. Colonel Fitzwilliam was indeed a cousin of William's. Mr. Bingley was the man who had liked Jane at the assembly ball. She was certain that the park from this dream belonged to the house from the previous dream. Its name was— The name remained elusively out of reach.

Likewise, the William described in this most recent dream greatly resembled the one she had seen in her previous dreams, although he did not seem at all like the William she knew in France.

Therefore, she could conclude that this dream was most likely a real memory and not a fantasy. The thought was more disturbing than reassuring.

Why had Mr. Darcy—William—objected to Jane's behavior? It was possible Jane was a terrible flirt or seemed too immature, or perhaps she simply did not like Mr. Bingley. But Elizabeth's reaction to the colonel's news suggested otherwise. She had felt that Jane deserved a chance for happiness with William's friend and that it had been unjustly denied to her. Elizabeth had been furious at his interference.

William stirred, turning his head toward her as his voice emerged from the darkness of the cabin. "Elizabeth? Are you unwell?" Without awaiting a response, he sat up in bed, the covers falling around his waist.

She scrubbed her face with the heel of her hand. "Nothing but a dream." She did not feel equal to describing its particulars to him, but perhaps he could help her ascertain their accuracy. "What is my sister Jane like?"

William hesitated before responding. "She is very pleasant and sensible. Quite pretty. I believe you are very close to her." *He finds nothing objectionable about her now?* Elizabeth was beginning to feel as if she were traveling with a completely different man than the one depicted in her dreams.

"Have I met your cousin, Colonel Fitzwilliam?"

William startled slightly. "You met him when visiting Rosings Park."

Rosings Park! Yes, that was the name she could not quite recall.

He leaned closer to her, his face deeply creased with worry. "What did you remember?"

She refused to tell him the whole of her disturbing dreams until she understood them better. "Bits and pieces only. I remember he listened to me play the pianoforte."

William's shoulders relaxed. "Yes, upon more than one occasion. Your playing is quite good."

"Where is Jane now?"

She must have appeared anxious for William took her hand. "She was at Longbourn with your family before I left England."

Was she still heartbroken over Mr. Bingley? "How did she seem to you?"

If William found these questions odd, he did not show it. "She was quite worried about your disappearance. All of your family was, but perhaps Miss Bennet and your father took it the hardest." He rubbed a hand over his mouth. "I arrived at Longbourn with my friend Charles Bingley. He stayed in Hertfordshire, and I hope his presence is a comfort to her."

Another piece of the puzzle! Elizabeth fought to contain her excitement. "Mr. Bingley," Elizabeth said slowly as if just recalling the name. "Did he court Jane?"

"Indeed." William's smile seemed a bit strained. "Your memory *is* improving."

"Only a little." Elizabeth shrugged. "I have a vague recollection of his face, but do not remember even the smallest detail about him." She hesitated before saying anything else, but William was her sole source of information. "Do you believe he will make Jane an offer?"

He gave her a startled look. "He may very well. I have reason to believe he was not happy while they were apart." So far, William had corroborated every particular in the dream. Her stomach churned; while it was exciting to regain memories, their content raised more questions than they answered.

Elizabeth scrutinized his face as much as the dim light would allow. He evinced no dissatisfaction with the idea that her sister might wed his friend. Had he changed his mind about Jane? Or had the colonel been wrong about the identity of William's friend? Perhaps she had drawn the wrong conclusion at Rosings Park.

Elizabeth rubbed her forehead. Partial memories were nearly worse than no memories at all. She would prefer to believe the dreams were lies, fantasies spun by a mind not completely recovered from its recent ordeal. Yet she could not dismiss them completely when so many of the details were accurate.

While her mind was confused, her body had no reservations about William…kissing him or craving more of his touches. Surely that was a sign of past intimacies. Their kiss had been…

The memory alone gave her goosebumps.

"You should try to get more sleep. Lie down under the covers again, my darling. Your hands are like ice."

She could have no doubt he cared about her as she allowed him to pull her down beside him, enjoying the feel of his warm body cradling hers. But she could not shake her misgivings. Despite his concern for her, she could not prevent her opinion of her husband from being influenced by something as insubstantial as dreams.

Chapter Fourteen

Darcy was once again admiring the view from the deck of the barge—there were few other ways to pass the time—when the captain joined him. "We will arrive in Rouen tomorrow morning. What will you do then? You are hoping to cross the Channel, are you not?"

Darcy was not surprised the man had guessed they were destined for England; no doubt he had noticed Elizabeth's accent. He took a minute to scrutinize the captain. There was no reason to distrust the man; his hatred of Napoleon seemed genuine. "We will need to hire a carriage for Calais."

The captain frowned. "Hmm."

"You disagree?"

"The army is thick on the ground at Calais. It is the place, above all, where they are most wary of spies."

"We must take a boat from somewhere to cross the Channel."

"I would suggest Gravelines. Boats leave for Kent and Sussex every day."

The name sounded familiar, but Darcy could not recall where he had heard it. "What is in Gravelines?"

"Napoleon has created a smugglers' village there." The captain gestured expansively. "French merchants visit Gravelines to sell silk clothing, brandy, and lace to English smugglers in exchange for guineas. Napoleon is always short of cash. His wife needs tiaras and golden furniture." The man spat on the deck. "I spit on him!" He spat on the deck again. "I spit on his wife!"

Darcy moved his boots out of range. "Yes, so you said before."

"Because so many boats go back and forth, Gravelines should be safer. You should find a smuggler who will take you to England for a price."

Darcy had his doubts about trusting the honor of smugglers, but Gravelines still seemed safer than Calais, where Elizabeth's accent would be noticeable to agents of the French government. "Very well. I like this plan of yours, but we cannot embark on it immediately." They would arrive at Rouen too late in the day to begin a journey. "I will need to rent a carriage, and Elizabeth will need to rest."

"I would be quite pleased to offer you and your lovely wife a room in my house for the night. For a very small fee, of course." Moreau grinned widely enough for Darcy to see all his crooked teeth.

"Of course."

Oddly, Darcy found the captain's greed reassuring; if money was Moreau's primary motivation, he was unlikely to betray them. "Thank you, we would be honored."

***

They arrived at Rouen around noon and disembarked from the barge without attracting any attention. The captain's home was located near the port, but it proved to be a good-sized townhouse decorated in the modern style.

As they stood in the nicely appointed home, Darcy realized that the captain could not possibly be fooled by their disguise. Not only had he guessed their true nationality, but he also must have an idea of Darcy's station. A man of Moreau's means would not have invited a common laborer to this house. Darcy wondered what had given them away. The abundance of funds? His commanding presence? Perhaps the truth was that Darcy did a spectacularly poor job of pretending to be a laborer.

The back of his neck prickled as they ventured further into the house; he was wary of everything these days. But Darcy saw nothing out of the ordinary. The captain introduced his wife, a short, plump woman, and his children, who had to be coaxed downstairs to greet the strangers. A fine luncheon had been spread out for them in the dining room, Darcy saw gratefully. The fare aboard the barge had been meager.

Once they had seated themselves and started eating, conversation quickly turned to the next stage of their journey. "Is it difficult to enter Gravelines?" Darcy asked the captain.

The other man nodded slowly. "It is strictly controlled by the military and the customs services. Everyone who enters or leaves the encampment must have the appropriate papers."

Darcy's stomach churned. Perhaps Calais was a better bet.

The other man grinned, leaning back in his chair as he shoved his hands in his jacket pockets. "Fortunately for you, I know an export forger. He has created papers for many other 'merchants' who need entry to Gravelines. His services are not cheap, but he is fast. I would be happy to take you to him—for a small fee."

Of course. Darcy agreed and thanked the captain. Perhaps this plan would work.

After luncheon, the captain led them into a large, well-appointed drawing room. Through a doorway, a smaller room was visible with a—

"A pianoforte!" exclaimed Elizabeth. Her eyes shone with an excitement that had been too often absent of late.

Mrs. Moreau dimpled. "Yes. Do you play?"

"I believe so," Elizabeth responded, not noticing the puzzled looks this earned. She drew closer to the instrument as if pulled by a magnet.

"Would you play for us?" Darcy asked. He had not had the pleasure of hearing her play for months. Perhaps she was not the best musician technically, but the expression with which she played brought the music alive for him.

As if enchanted, Elizabeth seated herself and brushed her fingers over the keys. Darcy searched among the pile of musical manuscripts on a nearby table for a piece he recognized. But music immediately emanated from the piano, so he seated himself to enjoy her performance. Captain and Mrs. Moreau positioned themselves on a loveseat near the door.

It was a simple melody, the kind a child might practice when learning the instrument. But Elizabeth played it with a sense of discovery and childlike wonder that eased Darcy's heart. At the end of the piece, Elizabeth lifted her hands from the keys and met his eyes. "I remember."

"Yes, you played the piece perfectly."

"No. I *remember*." She tapped her temple.

Darcy's hands trembled as he rose and went to her. What would she do when she recalled that he was not her husband? "What do you remember?"

Her expression was dazed. No doubt the sudden onslaught of memories must be like standing under a powerful waterfall.

She blinked, her eyes focusing on him. "My childhood. Longbourn. My parents. Jane, Mary, Kitty, Lydia. Aunt and Uncle Gardiner. How could I have forgotten them?" She raised a hand to her mouth.

Captain and Mrs. Moreau watched curiously from the loveseat but did not interfere.

"Nothing of your later years?" Darcy asked.

She shook her head. "I recall my twelfth birthday, but I do not believe any memories date from after…"

His knees weak, Darcy sank onto the bench beside her, feeling like a prisoner who had been granted a stay of execution. Perhaps they need not discuss such unpleasant matters until they were on their way to England. "It is a good sign," he said. "Other memories might follow shortly." *But hopefully not all.*

"Perhaps." Her face glowed. "It is so wonderful to remember! I feel more like myself than I have since I awakened in Saint-Malo. For what are we, after all, but the sum of our memories?"

Darcy was happy for her. He was. But his hands still shook. *How much time do I have before everything crashes down upon me?*

***

Elizabeth's good mood persisted for the rest of the day. Whirling in a sea of reminiscences, she would occasionally laugh aloud as a particularly amusing memory struck her or hold back tears at the recollection of some more solemn incidents from her childhood. Buoyed by her rediscovered memories, she was especially charming with Mrs. Moreau and the children as they begged for songs on the pianoforte. How good it felt to play again!

William and the captain returned before dinner with the necessary papers for a departure the following morning. Memories flooded Elizabeth throughout dinner. The taste of potato recalled a funny story about Lydia. A sip of wine reminded her of Jane's preferences for the drink. She had opened a previously locked door to find an endless series of rooms just waiting to be explored.

At the same time, she was extremely impatient for dinner to end so she could inundate William with questions. Possessing memories that ended at age twelve was endlessly frustrating. Were all her sisters yet at home? Had any married? Had Mary ever outgrown her tendency to moralize? Had Lydia developed better sense? Had Kitty lost the annoying lisp in her speech? Were they all in good health? Every new worry sent a thrill of anticipation racing through Elizabeth's body.

Her sisters must have grown and changed, but Elizabeth did not know how. Unfortunately, William would likely lack answers to many of her questions since he did not seem particularly well acquainted with her family. *How did I come to marry a man who showed so little interest in my family?* She recalled Colonel Fitzwilliam's story about Darcy's attitude toward Jane. *Does he dislike my family? Would she have married such a man?*

However, by the end of the meal, Elizabeth was faltering again. Perhaps the excitement over the new recollections had drained more energy than she recognized.

After dinner, William departed to hire a horse and wagon for the morrow, suggesting that Elizabeth rest before their long journey. She did lie down on the bed in the guest chamber. Her body was weary, but her mind was too alert for sleep. Although she knew the memories of her adult life were inaccessible, she could not help but strive to uncover them. In particular, she wished she could remember her association with Mr. Darcy. Her dreams had given her vexingly incomplete glimpses.

The memories provided other information she found to be useful. She now understood how unprepossessing the Longbourn estate was and that her dowry would be very small. Why had William chosen a wife who was virtually penniless? As a girl, she had occasionally fantasized about falling in love with and marrying a handsome rich man. But the adult Elizabeth recognized that such men usually married beautiful rich women—which she decidedly was not.

Was there some other reason for their marriage? Had he accidentally compromised her? Or perhaps it was a case of "marry in haste, repent in leisure." No, he had vowed his love for her on more than one occasion.

But why he had made no effort to claim his marital rights? Whenever she had tried to move their lovemaking beyond kissing, he had rebuffed her. Yes, he treated her tenderly, but perhaps his affection was more akin to the fondness one might feel for a friend or a sister.

Earlier he had claimed that he did not wish to get her with child, though surely that could not be the only reason. She had assumed he was being a gentleman, but perhaps his ardor toward her had cooled. Perhaps she was no longer so attractive after her illness. Perhaps he did not want a damaged wife. Despite the warm air, the room suddenly felt very cold.

If she approached him again with amorous intentions, how would he react? The thought set butterflies flitting about her stomach, a not completely unpleasant feeling. The truth was that William was quite a handsome man, with intelligent eyes and dark curls that she longed to thrust her fingers into.

The idea that such a handsome man loved her…was intoxicating. The excitement fizzed in her veins like champagne bubbles. She could imagine a wonderful future being married to such a man. The few kisses they had shared had been…exquisite.

Was William a magnificent kisser because he really loved her, or simply because he was practiced at the art? She did not wish to pursue that line of thought.

Of course, she wanted the answer to be true love, and yet it was difficult to fully believe in his love given the contradictory information in her dreams. It was a puzzle, and a number of the pieces were still missing.

***

She awoke when William opened the door, blinking sleep from her eyes. "What time is it?"

"Nearly nine," he said softly. "I visited earlier, but you were sleeping so soundly I thought it best to let you get the rest you need."

She stretched her arms over her head, noting that William's eyes followed her every movement. "Thank you. You are kinder to me than I deserve."

He gave her an odd look. "Not at all. I regret that I cannot give you anything close to what you deserve in the present circumstances."

She sat up, tugging her shift into place. "You have taken excellent care of me."

"But you deserve to be back at Pemberley with a doctor to monitor your return to health and servants to care for you. Not being dragged across France during a war—and without any memory to boot."

"None of the circumstances are your fault."

William strolled to the window without a word. Why did the subject disturb him so? Did he feel some guilt about her presence in France? Perhaps something he had done or said precipitated her trip to Jersey. Perhaps they had a row before she departed. But she had been visiting an old friend… The endless mysteries were beginning to wear on her.

With his eyes focused on the street below, he told her of his successful efforts to hire a horse. "Captain Moreau's friend has given us papers naming me as Maurice Thibeaux, silk merchant, which would give me reason to enter Gravelines. You will be my wife, of course."

"But will they not expect us to have silk to sell?"

William gave her a brief smile. "Indeed, which is why I also purchased a dozen bolts of silk to transport in the back of the wagon. They are quite fine quality. It is a shame we cannot take one with us."

He seemed confident about their plan, yet he kept his eyes averted from her. And why did he remain on the far side of the room?

"It sounds like a good plan," she complimented him.

He did not respond, and the room fell silent.

When she was not focusing on the future, Elizabeth's thoughts turned inevitably to the past—and everything she did not know about it. "When you left England, was everyone in my family in good health?"

"Yes, they all enjoyed excellent health."

"Are all of my sisters living at home? Are any married?"

"None are yet wed, and they all remain at Longbourn with your parents." Although his answers were reassuring, he spoke with a terseness that suggested he would rather avoid the subject. Perhaps he did dislike her family.

Other questions about her family crowded her mind, but few were on subjects he would be familiar with. Once again the conversation faltered. William continued to peer out of the window. *Perhaps he cannot bear to look upon me.*

Finally, Elizabeth could contain herself no longer. "Why are you avoiding me?" she asked plaintively.

His head whipped around, and he regarded her with horrified eyes. "I-I-I—I am not—Well, look at yourself!" He gestured toward her shift.

Glancing down, Elizabeth saw that the semi-transparent fabric hid little of her body and clung to her curves. But he was her husband! Did the sight of her body horrify him so? Tears pricked her eyes, and she swallowed hard, trying to keep them at bay.

"You no longer find me attractive?" Her voice was little more than a whisper.

William gaped at her, and his face paled. "Why would you think—? No! You are so lovely it makes my heart ache just to regard you. I cannot believe my good fortune that I have found a woman who is not only beautiful but also clever, well-informed, and kind-hearted." He took several steps toward the bed. "At times I think I must have imagined you."

Oh...That was... His words took away her breath and obliterated her thoughts. Was it possible that anyone really felt that way about her? Was it possible that *this man* felt that way?

"It is all I can do not to touch you when I see you like this." The wave of his hand encompassed all of Elizabeth. "But I fear if I begin to touch you, I will never cease." His voice was rough with emotion.

Despite her misgivings about what he was concealing, despite the unease engendered by her dreams, William heated her blood. Of all the memories she had lost, the one she regretted the most was the recollection of their wedding night. Being intimate with the man...feeling his body against hers...his skin rubbing against hers. Just imagining it made her flush with heat. "I would not prevent you from touching me," Elizabeth whispered. The thought of his hands upon her was not unpleasant.

Although several feet still separated them, William stretched out his hands as if preparing for just such a touch. For a moment she believed he would close the distance between them, and she would feel his hands on her skin.

But he let his arms drop with a sigh and turned back to the window. "No, you are recovering, and we are fleeing for our lives. This is neither the time nor the place." He held himself very stiffly, grasping the edge of the windowsill as if it would buttress his self-control.

Yet when he raised his eyes to hers, they told a different story as they blazed with desire. At times such as these, she had no difficulty believing in his love or understanding why she had accepted his offer. Such passion would be irresistible.

Surely they could be intimate again. It would be like a second wedding night.

She leaned forward, aware that it provided him with a tantalizing view. "Perhaps increased intimacy would help to restore my memories."

William swallowed, the muscles of his throat working. He was breathing more rapidly, his eyes fixed on her lips as he took two stumbling steps toward the bed. She trailed her fingers up his arm. "Music helped to restore some memories. Perhaps you could do even more..."

He was on the bed beside her now, gathering her into his arms. His lips parted slowly and then he bent his neck, pressing his lips against hers. The kiss was long and languorous. Elizabeth lost herself in the sensations. Nothing existed except for lips touching lips, tongue sliding over tongue. Someone moaned, and Elizabeth realized the sound had emanated from her own throat.

One of William's hands explored her back while the other cradled her head as he imbued his kiss with greater passion. Everywhere he touched, her skin tingled. She pressed herself against him, hoping he would proceed to the next stage of intimacy.

Instead he tore his lips from hers, sliding off the bed and whirling away with a groan of protest. She remained in the bed, bereft and untouched. "No…Elizabeth, it is not right. I am a virtual stranger to you."

"But if I do not object…"

"Your trust in me is humbling. But I cannot. It would not be right until you recover your memories of our relationship." He took great gulps of air, his chest heaving. "And I cannot get you with child," he added as an afterthought.

She looked at him from under her lashes. "You still desire me?"

He gave a harsh bark of laughter. "If I were not a gentleman, I would show you how much I desire you."

"At the moment I wish you were not such a gentleman," she murmured irritably.

William breathed out a laugh. "As do I."

Elizabeth allowed her shoulders to slump.

"When we are safe in England," William promised. "If you still wish it…"

"I will," she whispered, a little shocked at the depth of her own desire. Proper young ladies were not supposed to have such feelings, although her brazenness did not appear to disgust her husband.

"I hope so," he said just as softly.

Before she could question this peculiar response, he took a deep breath and spoke in a more normal tone. "You should get more rest."

"Will you hold me?" she asked shyly.

He gave her a tender smile. "Of course."

With his back to her, William quickly changed into his nightshirt. Raising up the coverlet, he extended his body beside hers. He turned her onto her side, his front to her back, engulfing her as he wrapped his limbs around her.

***

The following morning Darcy and Elizabeth bade the Moreaus adieu and took the road leading from Rouen. A far cry from the high-flying curricle, the wagon Darcy had purchased was worn and shabby, moving at a slow pace. The very sight of the vehicle made Darcy clench his teeth in vexation. *This is a necessary part of the disguise,* he reminded himself. Soldiers searching for Dreyfus's English spy would not give the wagon a second glance.

The streets of Rouen were crowded; departing from the city was an exercise in patience as their wagon joined a crowd of produce-laden vehicles, grand carriages, and gigs out for a morning ride. Frustrated at their speed, Darcy pulled his watch from his pocket to check the time.

"Oh!" Elizabeth exclaimed, her face turning quite white.

Darcy followed her gaze to the watch. He had taken pains to keep it concealed since Mr. Martin had reminded Darcy that laborers did not own watches. However, Elizabeth was not staring at the watch itself, but something on the fob.

The amber cross.

Darcy had completely forgotten that he had hung her cross as a pendant from his watch fob. Now her eyes were mesmerized by the sight. He slid the cross off the chain. "I did not think to return this to you before now. It was around your neck when you washed up on shore."

He dropped it into her waiting hand, and her fingers closed around it. Elizabeth swayed on the bench, causing Darcy to reach out a hand to steady her. "Dearest?" Her pallor was a little alarming, and he had an irrational fear that the cross was somehow causing her pain.

"Memories," she murmured through gritted teeth.

"Oh." Darcy swallowed, hairs rising on the nape of his neck. Was this it? Would she now remember the true state of their relationship? His palms grew damp; he was ill-prepared for such a conversation.

She swayed alarmingly, and Darcy wrapped an arm around her shoulders, pulling her against his body for safety. Even if she did remember, even if she hated him, she was still his responsibility. His beloved. She might choose her own path once they arrived in England, but until then he would not leave her side.

"What do you remember?" he asked in a hushed tone.

She stared at the pendant in the palm of her hand. "Everything."

Chapter Fifteen

Darcy's heart clenched.

"The cross was a present from my aunt and uncle Gardiner for my nineteenth birthday. Uncle Gardiner bought it on one of his trips. Jane has one with garnets...." She fell silent, her eyes open but not seeing anything around them.

"Everything...except..." Her brows drew together. "Except I do not remember meeting your friend Mr. Bingley...or you...or visiting—what was the name of the place? Rosings Park." Under the brim of her hat, her free hand massaged her forehead. "What is the year?"

"1812." He was squeezing the reins with unnecessary force and fought to relax his hands.

She shook her head in bewilderment. "I recall the summer of 1811, but nothing after. How strange! Everything...except for the last year."

Darcy had been granted a reprieve, but she had recalled so much in such a short time. The memories of the previous year could not be too far out of reach.

And why should she recall everything except the past year? Would she prefer to forget any part of her life that concerned Fitzwilliam Darcy? The breakfast he had consumed less than an hour ago sat like a lump of lead in his stomach. "Those memories will return soon, no doubt." He strove to keep his tone hopeful, but he feared it sounded discouraged.

"Yes," she said faintly.

As the traffic lightened, Darcy urged the horse to greater speed. But the wagon was an unwieldy vehicle and simply would not allow a decent pace.

After a long pause he ventured a new subject of conversation. "I had hoped to reach Gravelines today, but I fear this pace will have us on the road another day."

"Yes," Elizabeth said absently, tucking the cross into her pocket.

Just let us reach England before she remembers all, he prayed fervently. If she discovered his lies before they departed France, he could not predict the results. Darcy winced as he recalled her words at Hunsford parsonage. When she learned the truth—however she learned the truth—no doubt she would have some cutting words for him. He could only hope she confined herself to words and did not decide to separate herself from him before they reached home.

They traveled in silence past fields of wheat and isolated farmhouses. Elizabeth stayed absorbed in her own thoughts, unaware of the scenery. Finally, she remarked, "Yesterday I felt as if my life were a book that was only half-finished. This morning I have been granted access to several more chapters—but not the ending."

"There is no ending," Darcy observed. "You are still writing the book."

Elizabeth squinted in the bright sunlight. "Ha! I suppose you have the way of it. Still, I would give much to recall the past year. I worry that something dreadful has occurred, and my mind is suppressing the memory."

Darcy clenched the reins more tightly. *Could I be something dreadful? Could I have caused her to suppress her memories?* "I know of no tragedy that befell your family in the past year," he said.

Elizabeth bit her lip. "But what of my friends? Charlotte Lucas has been my good friend for my entire life."

"She lives in Kent now," Darcy said absently as he steered the horse around a hole in the road.

"Kent?"

Darcy cursed himself silently. He could not relate to Elizabeth most of the events of the past year; it would inevitably lead to a revelation of the true state of affairs between them. "Yes, she is now wed to a Mr. Collins who is a parson in Hunsford parish."

What may I tell her of her friend's life that would not reveal too much? Certainly I can say nothing about Aunt Catherine. "They live in a cozy parsonage near the grand estate of his patroness." Too late, Darcy remembered that Collins was her cousin; would that provoke additional recollections?

"Mr. Collins?" she said. "I do not believe I know him."

Darcy breathed a sigh of relief. Apparently her acquaintance with her cousin was recent.

"But everyone in my family is well?" she asked, looking for reassurance.

"Everyone in your family enjoys the best of health."

"And the Gardiners?"

"The Gardiners?"

"My aunt and uncle Gardiner who live in London—and their children?"

"I am not acquainted with them."

"Did they not attend the wedding?"

Damnation! He had forgotten the "wedding." This is why he abhorred deceit; one lie begat a whole series of falsehoods. "They did not attend the wedding," he said truthfully enough.

"I hope nobody in the family was ill!"

"I heard nothing of any illness," Darcy reassured her. "You were their only source of anxiety."

"They believe I am lost at sea." Elizabeth's hands twisted in her lap. "Oh, we must hurry home so I may lighten their hearts!"

"Indeed."

She pressed fingertips to her forehead. "If only I could recover the rest of my memories!"

Darcy could only pray that she did not recover them too soon.

***

Elizabeth dreamed.

She did not recognize the place: a modest drawing room with well-worn furnishings and a blazing fire in the hearth. Several unremarkable paintings on religious themes adorned the walls.

His face quite pale and drawn, Mr. Darcy leaned against the mantelpiece on the other side of the room. This was not the proud, distant man she recalled from previous encounters. Obviously in the grip of some strong emotion, his chest heaved with each breath. Was he angry?

Finally, he spoke in a strained voice. "And this is all the reply which I am to have the honor of expecting! I might perhaps wish to be informed why with so little endeavor at civility I am thus rejected."

Elizabeth's entire body trembled with an unaccustomed fury. "I might as well enquire why with so evident a design of offending and insulting me, you chose to tell me that you liked me against your will, against your reason, and even against your character! Was not this some excuse for incivility if I was uncivil? But I have other provocations. Do you think that any consideration would tempt me to accept the man who has been the means of ruining, perhaps forever, the happiness of a most beloved sister?"

He did not deny it. In fact, he looked even more tranquil—and far haughtier. Such superciliousness further stoked her anger. "Can you deny that you have done it?"

"I have no wish of denying that I did everything in my power to separate my friend from your sister, or that I rejoice in my success. Towards him I have been kinder than towards myself."

Such effrontery! Calmly agreeing that he had ruined Jane's life! Elizabeth wanted nothing more than to hurt him the way he had hurt her sister. *"But it is not merely this affair on which my dislike is founded. Your character was unfolded in the recital which I received many months ago from Mr. Wickham."*

His face grew red. *"You take an eager interest in that gentleman's concerns."*

"Who that knows what his misfortunes have been, can help feeling an interest in him?"

Mr. Darcy scoffed, *"His misfortunes! His misfortunes have been great indeed!"*

Anger surged through her veins, giving her energy. *"And of your infliction. You have reduced him to his present state of poverty. And yet you can treat the mention of his misfortune with contempt and ridicule."*

Abandoning the mantelpiece, Mr. Darcy took a few steps in her direction; a muscle twitched in his jaw. *"And this is your opinion of me! But perhaps these offences might have been overlooked had not your pride been hurt by my honest confession of the scruples that had long prevented my forming any serious design. I am not ashamed of the feelings I related. They were natural and just. Could you expect me to rejoice in the inferiority of your connections? To congratulate myself on the hope of relations whose condition in life is so decidedly beneath my own?"*

Elizabeth marveled for a moment, staring open-mouthed at the man. He actually believed she would have accepted him if he had made her the offer in a more acceptable way! Did he not understand how contemptible he had rendered himself? Well, she would correct that misapprehension. She drew herself to her full height. *"You are mistaken if you supposed that the mode of your declaration affected me in any way than as it spared me the concern which I might have felt in refusing you—had you behaved in a more gentleman-like manner."*

He started at her words, his face a frozen mask. Had she gone too far in accusing him of being ungentlemanly? It was, to be sure, quite an insult. But he still offered no apologies or excuses. Apparently he still found his behavior acceptable.

Well, she certainly had more to say. *"You could not have made me the offer of your hand in any possible way that would have tempted me to accept it." His eyes widened with astonishment. "From the first moment of my acquaintance with you, your manners impressed me with the fullest belief of your arrogance, your conceit and your selfish disdain for the feelings of others. I had not known you a month before I felt that you were the last man in the world whom I could ever be prevailed upon to marry."*

Mr. Darcy finally moved, taking a jerky step away from her. "You have said quite enough, madam. I perfectly comprehend your feelings and have now only to be ashamed of what my own have been. Forgive me for having taken up so much of your time and accept my best wishes for your health and happiness."

His face a stony mask, he strode swiftly through the door and then was gone. Elizabeth sank into the nearest chair, barely perceiving the room around her.

Gradually, awareness crept over Elizabeth. She was no longer in that drawing room. She was in a bed. In the inn where William had bespoken a room.

Where William was in the bed beside her!

Her shift—and even the sheets—were plastered to her body with sweat. Her breath was coming in quick, audible pants, and she tried to slow it lest she wake William. Lying immobile in bed, she considered the dream. These were memories, she was quite certain of that now, but she knew not what to make of this latest one.

Mr. Dar—William had apparently proposed to her in that little drawing room. And she had rejected him in a decisive manner, blaming him for Jane's heartbreak and for reducing a man named Wickham to poverty. Try as she might, Elizabeth could not recall anyone of her acquaintance named Wickham; the last year of her life still proved elusive. William had not denied the accusations about Wickham or about Jane. And then Elizabeth had accused him of pride, selfishness, and ungentlemanlike behavior. She nearly gasped at that last one: such an insult for a man like William!

Very well, the circumstances of the proposal and the reasons for her rejection were quite clear, but how had she later ended up married to the man?

Her hands clutched at the sheets. Was this all part of some elaborate plot? Had William abducted her for the purpose of—what? She could think of no reason why kidnapping her would be to his advantage. Her family had no fortune, and he certainly could secure a wife by conventional means.

Goosebumps rose on her arms. Her experience with Dreyfus had shown how untrustworthy some men could be. Was she making a mistake by trusting William now?

Was it possible that William was plotting with Dreyfus—and the French? Perhaps his concern for her was only a mask that concealed his true purposes. Perhaps the true William was the cold, proud man, and the one she knew now was only a construct, an act perpetrated to fulfill some unknown scheme.

No, their race across France had been too complicated to be a ruse, and then there was the question of motivation.

Obviously I have been reading too many novels from the circulating library.

But still she was left with the fact that William had proposed in that unnamed house, and she had violently rejected his offer. How had they wound up here?

No matter how she considered it, nothing made sense.

If only she could remember the past year! But she had strained and searched for any wisps of memories, and her mind was still a blank.

Why had William proposed in the first place when Elizabeth had disliked him so decidedly? He seemed shocked by the vehemence of her rejection—or that she rejected him at all. Of course, few women in England would decline Mr. Darcy's fortune; he would not have expected it. But he must have been quite violently in love with her to have made the offer in the first place.

"I perfectly comprehend your feelings and have now only to be ashamed of what my own have been." William had been in love with her when he made the offer; there was no other possible explanation. The memories occasioned her considerable anxiety, but she also experienced a pang of pity at the disappointment she had inflicted upon him. He had been quite shattered when he departed the drawing room.

He had loved her then. And—she thought of his declarations on the barge—he loved her now. There could be no doubt. Every word, every action had demonstrated his love for her. He had risked his own life again and again for her sake. Her safety was his utmost concern. Despite her rejection, his love had been unwavering.

Elizabeth's muscles unlocked, and she relaxed into the bedding. *I may trust William. He will not do anything to harm me and will do everything to protect me.* She repeated these words silently to herself over and over until most of the tension had drained from her body.

Still, he was concealing something from her. Perhaps it related to the question of why Elizabeth had changed her mind about marrying him. What had he done or said since her rejection to make her accept him? Like unread chapters in a book, there clearly was more to the story that she did not know.

She stared at William's blanket-clad form as if it could somehow answer her questions. Here, he was quite different from the cold, condescending man who haunted her dreams. She did not blame her past self for wanting to avoid such a proud, difficult man. Unease prickled over her skin. Which William was the true one? Would he revert at some moment to his previous demeanor? That thought left her feeling very alone.

Or perhaps he had an identical twin. Elizabeth suppressed a snort of laughter. *Definitely too many novels.*

Perhaps she was losing her grip on reality. Her dreams told one story while she lived a far different story when awake. Elizabeth clasped her trembling hands together. *I must endure until we reach England. It will all be sorted out,* she assured herself. *Once there, I will determine the truth about his feelings—and mine.*

Goosebumps returned. She was almost afraid to discover that truth. Whatever it was, Elizabeth was now William's wife irrevocably. She was bound to him forever—even if the cold, indifferent William of the past returned. How could she bear to live with such a man? Her hands shook as she wiped tears from her eyes.

After a long while, her thoughts were turning back on themselves since she had no new information to add. *This is fruitless; I should rest instead.* Perhaps in the morning Elizabeth might find a way to ask him about the events in her dream. More tears leaked from her eyes as she lowered herself back on the mattress, beside William but not touching him.

***

The next morning at breakfast, Elizabeth was very quiet, keeping her eyes fixed on her plate. Darcy had expected her spirits to improve as they grew closer to home. Gravelines was less than an hour away. Once there, they need only hire a boat across the Channel. Anticipating the end of their travels, Darcy was alive with energy. However, dark smudges marred Elizabeth's eyes, and she moved with the sluggishness of someone who had not slept well. "Did you have a difficult night?" he asked her.

She took a moment before responding. "Yes...no. That is to say my rest was rather disturbed."

"I am sorry to hear that," Darcy replied. He scrutinized her for signs of returning illness, but it appeared that she simply suffered from fatigue. "Hopefully we will quickly locate a boat so we may return home." Elizabeth nodded wearily.

Darcy believed she was concealing something. Unusually wary in his presence, she flinched from his touch as he handed her up to the wagon seat. Had she remembered something to his detriment? Unfortunately, there was no discreet way to inquire.

Although the sun was not at its height, the day was already quite warm when the high fence surrounding Gravelines came into view. It was merely a smudge on the horizon, but the back of Darcy's neck prickled with apprehension. This could be the most dangerous part of their journey.

"I do not understand why the French government wants a smugglers' encampment on their land," Elizabeth remarked as they drew closer. "Smuggling is illegal here as it is in England."

These were the first words she had uttered since they left the inn, and Darcy was happy to pursue the subject. "Napoleon sees it as a means to acquire English gold to finance his war effort. The smugglers arrive with gold guineas to purchase goods, which they transport to England for sale. The encampment is controlled by French soldiers and customs officials to ensure that the emperor receives a portion of the illicit activity."

Elizabeth stared at the distant line of fences. "Guineas leave England and go to France? Does that hurt our war effort?"

Darcy shrugged. "It is not good, but I do not believe it is crippling Britain. No doubt the Royal Navy would prefer to put a halt to all smuggling, but there are simply too many of them—and many smugglers also are legitimate fishermen. I would imagine the War Office finds Gravelines useful as well. No doubt it is a good source of information."

She was silent for a moment. "Do you have confidence in the forgeries you obtained?"

"I think so. I do not believe I was the first buyer for that particular sort of forgeries."

"What will they do if they suspect it is a forgery?"

Darcy took a deep breath. "I do not know. In that case, failing to reach English shores may be the least of our concerns."

Elizabeth's stiff nod betrayed her anxiety. Her fists clenched the skirt of her gown while she comtemplated the distant fences.

As they drew closer to the encampment, it was revealed to be roughly triangular. It was shaped by tall fences on all sides to prevent English smugglers from wandering—and spying—in the rest of the country. A gate opened to admit travelers, providing glimpses of a multitude of tents as well as a roughly built, one-story wooden building—no doubt to house the French officials. The French merchants and English smugglers would be consigned to the tents. The entire structure was only a few yards from the beach, which was covered by a number of small smugglers' galleys awaiting the return trip to England.

The road led directly to the encampment's only gateway, guarded by uniformed soldiers. Darcy said a prayer that the forger had been both competent and honest. He was entrusting both their lives to the papers the man had created. He slowed the wagon as they drew closer and stopped it right before the gate.

"What is your business here?" one of the soldiers—a man with a dark bushy mustache—demanded.

"I am a silk merchant," Darcy responded, enunciating carefully to avoid any trace of an English accent. "This is my wife."

Dark Mustache stared at them suspiciously. "I do not remember you from before."

"We are new visitors to Gravelines," Darcy said. "I have the appropriate papers."

He handed them down to the man. Mustache consulted with a man in the guard's shack, most likely his supervisor. Another man climbed into the back of the wagon, throwing back the cover over the bolts of silk so he could count them. There were sufficient guards watching the wagon so that escape would have been impossible.

A skinny blond man stared openly at Elizabeth. The lasciviousness in his expression had Darcy wishing he could punch him. "Eh, pretty lady!" he called out to Elizabeth. "You don't want a merchant for a husband. Come and live with me if you want a real man!" His fellow soldiers laughed at what seemed like a harmless jest to them. Elizabeth sat frozen on the bench of the gig, not having comprehended all his words. "What do you say?" the soldier continued. "Will you at least give me a kiss?"

Silence hung in the air as the soldier awaited a reply. The soldier searching the wagon had jumped back and watched them along with the others to see what her response would be. A pulse beat rapidly in her neck, her entire body quivering with tension; she could not reply without betraying her accent.

The blond man frowned. "What, are you too good to speak with me?" The other soldiers exchanged disgruntled looks.

Elizabeth's eyes darted in panic to Darcy. "That is not the case at all, Lieutenant," Darcy said hastily, trying to think up a good reason why his wife would not speak. "My wife is, unfortunately, deaf."

The blond soldier's face turned from suspicious to sympathetic. "What a pity! She is quite lovely. But who would want a wife who cannot hear? You should give her up and get another woman," he advised Darcy with a shake of his head.

Darcy clamped down hard on his anger and considered his role as a merchant. "Not at all!" He tried to match the man's leer. "A mute wife is the best kind. She is grateful for my attention and never complains."

The soldiers laughed uproariously at this rejoinder. Soon the mustached man returned with Darcy's papers, assuring him that they were in order and gesturing for them to proceed through the gate. Darcy surreptitiously wiped his sweaty hands on his trousers and snapped the reins to get the horse moving.

As the wagon creaked noisily into the camp, Darcy spoke from the side of his mouth. "I apologize for my coarseness."

Elizabeth said nothing—after all, she was supposed to be deaf—but she shook her head with a smile, suggesting she was not offended. As the gates closed behind them with a clang, Darcy tried not to think about how they were now essentially trapped within the encampment.

The camp was bustling with activity. Well-dressed merchants, scruffy soldiers, and even scruffier smugglers strolled around, some at their leisure while others were intensely involved in heated negotiations. Most were men, although a few merchants were accompanied by wives.

Many merchants had set up stalls while others were showing their wares to the visiting Englishmen inside their tents. The variety of wares for sale was impressive. Tables displayed lace, fine silk bonnets, gloves, stockings, and shawls. Other booths sold bolts of cloth in many different hues. In another part of the camp, signs advertised merchants who sold brandy and Dutch or French gin. It was a bit like market day in a village square, if the market were surrounded by tall, impenetrable fences.

Darcy clambered down from the gig and tied up the horse to a hitching post outside the customs office, using the time to think about his next step. Unfortunately, the helpful Captain Moreau had not known anyone within the Gravelines encampment, so they had to rely on their own wits to find an English smuggler who would take them across the Channel.

If the French authorities learned of that smuggler's part in their escape, he could be banned from Gravelines and its lucrative trading opportunities. Darcy hoped to offer a sufficient quantity of gold to encourage one of the galley captains to take the risk.

After helping Elizabeth down from the wagon seat, he tucked her arm into his and set a brisk pace away from the gate. The blond soldier's frankly carnal stare at Elizabeth had made Darcy's skin crawl. This was not a place where he could leave her alone for any amount of time.

"I shall attempt to make the acquaintance of some of the smugglers," he murmured in her ear, "in the hopes that we can identify one who will help us." *And will not turn us over to the French authorities,* he added silently.

Elizabeth nodded, her grave face suggesting that she understood the risk he had not articulated.

They forged ahead, plunging into the bustling marketplace. Darcy scanned the crowd, seeking likely captains. They had not gone far when Darcy's attention was caught by a figure at one of the lace merchants' stalls. A familiar figure.

No, it was not possible. The man's head turned toward the light, providing a clearer view of his features. The man did bear a close resemblance to Richard Fitzwilliam, but surely his cousin had never worn such ill-fitting rough clothing in his life.

It could not be. Still, as he had mentioned to Elizabeth, Gravelines undoubtedly served as a convenient location for English spies. Could he possibly be so fortunate?

Grasping Elizabeth's elbow, he maneuvered her toward the man. If Darcy had mistaken his identity, they would simply walk away.

But he was not wrong.

Chapter Sixteen

The man turned just as they reached him, and his eyes alighted on Darcy. They widened, and a relieved smile spread over his cousin's face. Then Richard noticed who accompanied Darcy, and he started violently; for a moment he seemed on the verge of apoplexy.

Of course; he thought Elizabeth was dead.

Darcy extended his hand to Richard. "I am Mr. Thibeaux, silk merchant," he said in French-accented English. "Would you, perhaps, be interested in purchasing some silk?"

His eyes fixed on Elizabeth, Richard rubbed the back of his neck. "You know, I believe I am. Shall we go somewhere private to discuss the particulars?"

Elizabeth gave Darcy a questioning look, but he gave a minute shake of his head as they followed Richard to a far corner of the camp, sufficiently deserted that nobody was near enough to overhear them.

Once there, Richard gave Darcy a warm embrace. "Darce! Good Lord, it is good to see you! When we received no word from you, we feared the worst."

Darcy laughed. "Why are you here, Richard? Are you meeting with an agent?"

Richard snorted. "Why am I here? The War Office lost track of the master of Pemberley, who failed to contact any of our agents on this side of the Channel. My superiors were very concerned that some evil had befallen you. I was sent with one of the smugglers' boats in the hopes I could slip into the countryside and search for you."

No doubt his cousin had volunteered for the mission; Darcy was touched. "I ran into various unforeseen circumstances," he said, thinking what a grave understatement that was.

"Indeed." Richard's eyes darted to Elizabeth. "This is *most* unforeseen. Miss Bennet, you look very well for a woman who has been dead for weeks."

Elizabeth stared at Richard with a dazed expression on her face. Darcy winced. Of course, she would not recall his cousin; Darcy should have thought of that earlier. "Elizabeth," he said quietly, "this is my cousin Richard."

Richard gave Darcy a puzzled look, no doubt wondering why he was being introduced to a woman he knew quite well. When she did not immediately reply, Darcy prompted, "Elizabeth?"

"You are Colonel Fitzwilliam," she said slowly.

"Yes," Richard said warily. His brows drew together as he looked to Darcy for guidance.

"She suffered a blow to the head and experienced some memory loss," Darcy explained without taking his eyes from her face. But apparently she recognized Richard; had she recovered the missing year of her life?

Richard's eyes were wide, and his mouth hung open. "Memory loss? What the devil, Darcy?"

They both ignored him. Elizabeth fixed Darcy with an accusing stare. "I remember everything now. *Everything*."

"Excellent!" Richard said cheerfully while Darcy's heart sank into his boots.

"I trusted you," Elizabeth said in a choked voice.

Darcy felt like the worst blackguard. Worse than Napoleon or any of his generals. Worse than a scoundrel who cheated a widow out of her last shilling. Worse even than Wickham.

"Darce, I pray you, explain," Richard said.

Darcy ignored his cousin. "I did not set out to lie to you—" He reached out to touch Elizabeth's arm, but she yanked it out of reach, and he let his hand fall again. "It simply happened…"

"During a week of traveling together, you could never spare a minute to tell me the *truth*?" Her eyes filled with tears. Darcy had thought Elizabeth's angry accusations at Hunsford Parsonage had destroyed all his hopes, but the naked pain on her face tore at his soul.

"I needed your trust so I could keep you safe," Darcy said, realizing how paltry his words sounded even as he said them. "I only had your best interests at heart."

She pressed her lips together until they turned white. "You have a strange idea of what my 'best interests' are." Her fists clenched at her sides as if she could hold herself together by sheer force of will.

"Elizabeth—"

She averted her eyes from Darcy's face and turned toward Richard. "Colonel, could you possibly assist me in returning to England?"

Me. Not us. It left a bitter taste in Darcy's mouth.

Richard looked uncertainly from her to Darcy. "I believe so. When the tide turns, the smugglers' boats will depart. The captain of the galley I crewed most likely could be convinced to take two additional passengers for a fee."

"Good." Elizabeth did not so much as glance in Darcy's direction. "Might you know of a place I could rest until then?"

Darcy reached out to take her arm. "Elizabeth, may we at least talk –?" She jerked her arm from his reach.

Richard watched them warily before nodding to Elizabeth. "I rented a tent for the night. You are certainly welcome to use it now."

Elizabeth took Richard's arm, and he led her back to a tent at the end of a long row of similar tents, with Darcy trailing disconsolately behind them.

The small shelter contained a serviceable cot, a stool, and a table with a washbasin. "I apologize for the meager accommodations," Richard said to Elizabeth, "but I hope it will allow you to sleep for a couple hours."

"I thank you." The bleak expression on her face made Darcy's heart ache. He had protected her for a week from the many dangers in France, but he could do nothing to ameliorate the pain from a wound he himself had inflicted. *If I could at least explain to her why…*

"Elizabeth—" His voice was weak and pleading even to his own ears.

"No." She did not glance in his direction as she lowered herself to the cot.

Richard pulled Darcy's arm, gesturing toward the entrance. He was loath to leave her, but Elizabeth rolled without hesitation, turning her back to both men.

He allowed his cousin to pull him from the tent, blinking in the sudden brightness. "Let us go over to that tree." Richard pointed to an oak with wide-spreading branches. "We will be able to watch over the tent and speak in peace."

Feeling as though he were leaving his heart behind in the tent, Darcy followed his cousin. Once they were a sufficient distance away, Richard rounded on Darcy. "You brought that woman back from the dead! What could you possibly have done to make her so angry with you?"

Darcy suppressed the retort on the tip of his tongue. "I told her we were married," he said with a sigh, dropping to a patch of soft grass beneath the tree.

Richard's jaw fell open. "What—?"

"She was rescued by a doctor and his wife, but they did not know her identity. She was unconscious. They were suspicious of leaving me with her, so I said she was my wife. The word came from my mouth without any forethought. I suppose it might have been wishful thinking; I was so shocked to find her alive. Then when she awakened and could not remember anything about her life…the falsehood persisted."

Richard sank into a cross-legged position on the ground. "And she did not realize the truth until now?"

Darcy removed his hat and ran one hand through his damp curls. "Her memory has been returning bit by bit. The last missing piece was this past year. Apparently seeing you triggered the remaining memories. Or perhaps it was when you called her Miss Bennet."

"I am sorry."

Darcy shrugged. "My falsehoods are not your responsibility."

One of Richard's eyebrows lifted. "You resurrect the woman you love from the dead and keep her safe in a hostile country only to alienate her a few days later. That takes some talent."

Darcy snorted at his cousin's sarcasm. "I will be fortunate if she ever deigns to speak another word to me."

"You will be the man who rescued her from France. Surely you have earned some gratitude."

"Gratitude! No doubt I will have that, but what I want is her *love*." Darcy plucked a blade of grass and proceeded to shred it.

"I think it likely that she does love you."

Darcy narrowed his eyes at his cousin. "In our last conversation before leaving for France, Elizabeth proclaimed I was the last man in the world she could ever be induced to marry. Then I lied to her for a week about a basic matter of her identity."

Richard blew out a breath. "When you put it that way, I suppose it is not promising…."

Darcy could not stifle a harsh laugh as he pulled up more grass to shred.

"But you have been traveling together—alone," Richard said. "Surely her reputation is so compromised that—"

Darcy grabbed his cousin's arm before he could finish the sentence. "No. Do not so much as whisper a word on that account. I do not want her forced to marry me. That would be a fate far worse than never marrying."

Richard's eyebrows shot up. "Very well, I will not mention anything about your traveling arrangements, but it will provoke many questions when you return to England."

Darcy's shoulders slumped. "I know. I had hoped to persuade her to an engagement by then." He pictured the angry rigidity in her body as she had turned her face to the canvas wall of the tent. Any type of persuasion seemed unlikely.

Richard gave a low whistle. "I thought love was supposed to make you happy."

I did, too. Darcy glared at his cousin. "Did you not need to speak to the boat captain about taking on two passengers?"

Richard gave him a rueful smile. "Very well." He stood. "I will be back soon."

After his cousin's departure, Darcy stood and circled the tent—inspecting it carefully to ensure Elizabeth was safe—but saw no signs of trouble. Returning to the tree, he shifted position until his back rested against the trunk and settled in for a long watch.

Half an hour passed before Richard returned with the welcome news that he had secured passage with the galley captain. Using the tree's canopy to shield them from the hot midday sun, they conversed in low tones as Darcy related the story of their journey. Fortunately, this part of the camp was outside the market area, and few people passed by.

When Darcy described Dreyfus's betrayal, his cousin swore under his breath. "Damn double agents! My superiors in the War Office will find a way to deal with him."

"Dreyfus and his men may still be on the lookout for us," Darcy warned.

"You will not be on French soil for much longer."

Darcy nodded in fervent agreement. They could not leave the country quickly enough to suit him.

***

Elizabeth stared at the side of the tent. With the sun bright and high in the sky, the space was filled with a dusty yellow glow. Even if she had designs on slumber, the light would have made it impossible. However, she had a far greater need for privacy and quiet in which to order her thoughts. Already she perceived the beginning of a headache in the knotted muscles in her neck.

She had suspected William—Mr. Darcy—had not been truthful, but it had never occurred to her that he was lying about their marriage. In hindsight she should have guessed; he had been so vague about the details of the proposal and wedding. But marriage was a sacrament, a sacred bond between two people. How could he have been so cavalier about the truth of it? She had been a fool to trust him. Obviously he was completely untrustworthy and devoid of higher feelings.

What else had he lied to her about?

The moment when her memories rushed back to her had been so disorienting. The sight of Colonel Fitzwilliam had provoked a flood of memories from Rosings Park: eating dinner, playing the pianoforte, walking in the park. Other recollections followed on the heels of the first, including the entirety of her history with Mr. Darcy. Now she was horrified at her behavior with him: her casual intimacy, the confidences she had shared, the kisses. He had seen parts of her body—although she had not been wholly naked in his presence. They had shared a bed!

Before today, the cold and distant Mr. Darcy in her dreams had been a puzzlement. Now she wondered the opposite: who was the attentive and caring Mr. Darcy she had encountered in France? Elizabeth would not have believed he possessed such qualities. Yet he had treated her with tender regard and protected her with everything in his power. She could scarcely believe this was the same man who had so casually insulted her family and separated Mr. Bingley from Jane.

He had every reason to be furious with her after her refusal of his proposal—and the egregious way she had credited Mr. Wickham's story over his. After the incident at Hunsford, she imagined he cursed her name and would never wish to see her again. He had believed she was deceased. Why had he even come to France?

It was such a shock, as if she had been doused with cold water. *Mr. Darcy is not my husband.* Even now, an hour later, her mind struggled to grapple with all the ramifications. Despite the restoration of her memories, it was difficult to change her habits of mind. She had grown accustomed to seeing him as her spouse, and now she needed to adapt to viewing him as an odd and unpleasant acquaintance who had once revealed his affection for her in a shocking and insulting manner. It was most disconcerting.

She could not even articulate exactly how she felt about Mr. Darcy at this moment. When she had believed him to be her husband, she had not questioned her feelings for him. Of course, she loved him; he was her husband. Without memories, it had been impossible to form a complete understanding of the various emotions he provoked. But now she was left in limbo.

How do I feel about Mr. Darcy?

It was true that in the days following the proposal, Elizabeth had regretted the manner in which she had refused his offer, particularly after reading his letter. But that did not mean her essential feelings toward him had changed.

It was also true that before her departure for Jersey she had found Mr. Darcy often in her thoughts. To be honest, he had occupied her thoughts more than any other young man of her acquaintance. However, she attributed that to their awkward encounter at Hunsford Parsonage; it had been so unexpected and unpleasant that she could not push it from her mind.

After the proposal she had often mused about their lively conversations; they enjoyed many books and pieces of music in common. He was an excellent dancer and a handsome man. She had been mortifyingly incorrect in her worst accusations against his character. And yet he had still been rude and arrogant and proud. Lively, well-informed conversation was not sufficient to induce her admiration. And yet…

The headache had crept up the base of her skull, and new pressure was building across her forehead. Why had he lied to her? Why would any man lie about such a thing? The obvious answer with most men would be to take advantage of her virtue. However, she had been in his bed, and he had steadfastly refused to avail himself of the opportunity.

She had suggested—nay, begged him—for greater intimacies. Her cheeks flamed at the memory, and she was forced to cover her face with her hands even though there was nobody to see her. How could she face him again when she had been so brazen? It was a shame amnesia could not be employed selectively; she would choose to forget a great many incidents from the past week.

What a fool I have been.

He had not avoided kissing her, and his kisses had been quite…passionate. She blushed again at the memories. How wanton she had been with a man not her husband! Still, she would admit it to herself: she would miss those kisses.

The fact was not lost on her that he had compromised her reputation most egregiously. If it were known that they had been traveling as husband and wife, he would be forced to marry her. Had that been part of his plan: to force her to marry him after she had refused his offer? Just the thought of such deliberate scheming sent shivers of horror through her body. Would Mr. Darcy stoop to such designs?

The thought of actually marrying him produced a much weaker sense of horror.

But he lied to me.

That fact was inescapable. He claimed to love her, but why would he lie so egregiously and repeatedly to somebody he cared about? Even if he did love her in his way, surely he could not possibly respect her. Or trust her.

Nor was it possible for her to trust him. Yes, she could trust him with her life and her safety, but not with her heart.

Her body broke out in a cold sweat. That was it; the decision was made. Or perhaps there had been no decision in the first place. She could not trust him with her heart. There could be no future for them.

The headache now engulfed her entire head; she tried to shift into a more comfortable position, to no avail. Even if she did occasionally have...warm feelings for him, they meant nothing without trust.

He had lied to her, and she could never trust him again.

***

The sun was sinking low in the sky when Richard decided the time was right to rendezvous with the smugglers' boat. Supposing discretion to be the better part of valor, Darcy sent Richard into the tent to awaken Elizabeth. She soon emerged, a bit rumpled and bleary-eyed but alert enough to avoid meeting Darcy's eyes. He sighed. It had been a vain hope that things would improve in such a short time.

They joined a line of smugglers trudging toward the gate. Many boats would depart at the same time as they took advantage of the high tide. Darcy took Elizabeth's arm and pulled ahead of Richard. She stiffened at his touch.

"Elizabeth," he murmured in her ear, "I understand that you are angry with me—with good reason. But we must not give the authorities any reason for suspicion. You and I must leave together and cannot be seen in Richard's company. Remember, you are deaf."

She gave the barest nod, but her body did not relax beneath his arm.

The soldier who took their papers gave Darcy an odd look since they were leaving without their wagon. Darcy scowled at the man. "One of the bastards out there"—he gestured to the galleys on the beach— "cheated me! I need to stop him before he gets away."

The man took a cursory glance at their papers. "I regret we cannot provide assistance, monsieur. We do not interfere in private trade matters."

"I understand," Darcy growled as he grabbed the papers back. With the soldier's eyes upon them, Darcy set a quick pace toward the beach, stalking his imaginary customer. They soon reached the wet stones of the beach where dozens of small galleys had been dragged to await the high tide. A few bigger fishing vessels were moored further out in the deeper water. Everywhere, men were climbing into boats, grabbing oars, settling onto seats, and securing cargo. A few vessels were already pushing into deeper water where the rowers—ten or twelve to a boat— jumped in and started their rhythmic strokes.

Darcy fought the urge to break into a run, keeping to the swift but steady pace of an angry man. With her skirts gathered in one hand, Elizabeth did an admirable job of keeping pace with him. Ahead of them, Richard ambled up to one of the bigger galleys where men were tying down cargo. The boat was low and long—built for utility and speed— without any kind of roof or shelter to protect the occupants from the elements. An older man, likely the captain, regarded Richard with some impatience, his arms folded over his chest. Darcy picked up their pace as Richard stopped to speak with the captain and gestured toward them. He was just as impatient to reach the open water as the smuggler was.

"There they are!" Someone shouted in French behind them. Darcy looked over his shoulder to see Dreyfus, leading a group of three soldiers running toward them—all with pistols drawn. "We must stop them from reaching England!"

Chapter Seventeen

Damnation! They were so close to safety.

"Run," Darcy urged Elizabeth. Picking up her skirts, she took off like a shot toward the smuggler's boat, with Darcy not far behind her. At least two shots sounded behind them; Darcy could only pray that the soldiers' aim was poor.

"Devil take you!" the captain shouted at Richard as they raced toward him. "You promised me no trouble!"

Ignoring the man, Richard pulled a pistol from his rumpled coat and took aim at Dreyfus. When that shot went wide, Richard took out another pistol. "Time to push off!" he shouted at the captain over his shoulder.

Cursing and calling Richard a string of vile names, the captain helped his men push their boat into deeper water. There was no chance the captain would wait for them to reach the boat; they had to board it before it shoved off. Elizabeth had waded into the surf with no care for her boots, but as her skirts fell into the water, they created a drag that slowed her progress.

Darcy calculated that they would not make it to the deeper water before Dreyfus and his men reached them. His imagination supplied him with images of what that failure would mean—capture, imprisonment, torture for himself and Richard, and possibly even Elizabeth. He had failed her miserably.

He pulled out his pistol but could not fire while running.

As he neared the boat, Richard fired his other pistol, hitting one of the soldiers, who fell with a cry onto the beach. Another soldier stopped to help his compatriot.

Darcy splashed through the surf, frantic to reach Elizabeth. Dreyfus crashed through the water behind him. A bullet whistled by Darcy's shoulder but did not find a target.

Darcy hauled Elizabeth, wet skirts and all, into his arms and carried her toward the galley. She was a sodden mess, wet fabric clinging to her skin and hair dripping into her eyes. Richard had clambered aboard the boat, preventing it from gliding out to sea by the simple expedient of putting a gun to the captain's head.

Staying barely ahead of Dreyfus, Darcy propelled them both through the water toward the boat. He half pushed, half dragged Elizabeth over the gunwale, where Richard steadied her with his free hand. Darcy shoved his pistol into her hand, hoping the powder was still dry. If he did not make it onto the boat, she would need it to defend herself.

The moment he released her, Elizabeth reached for Darcy, but he knew they could not escape unless he did something to stop Dreyfus. "Go! Go!" he urged Richard before turning to face the double agent.

"No! William!" Elizabeth reached with her free hand. "I am not leaving you!"

Darcy had no opportunity to argue before he was tackled by Dreyfus, the man's hands immediately clamping around his neck. Darcy tried to pry them off, but the other man had a firm grip and Darcy's hands were slick from seawater. The back of Darcy's legs hit the now-stationary boat, but he could not get purchase to pull Dreyfus's hands away.

The pressure of the other man's hands slowly constricted the flow of air, and Darcy's vision darkened around the edges. His movements grew weaker and uncoordinated. He could only hope that the galley would escape while Dreyfus took the time to kill him.

A loud bang nearly deafened him, and suddenly Dreyfus's grip went slack. The Frenchman fell on top of Darcy at the same moment hands grabbed the back of his shirt and hauled him onto the boat. Darcy instinctively clung to Dreyfus, pulling the man into the galley with him.

"Go! Go!" Richard exhorted the captain, and the boat lurched into action under their soaked bodies. Shouts and curses in French floated over the water, but nobody fired at them. Perhaps they feared hitting Dreyfus.

Gasping for breath, Darcy pushed off Dreyfus's limp body and sat up. Crouched by his side, Elizabeth gasped when she saw blood on his shirt. He shook his head, panting, "Not…mine. Dreyfus's."

Some of the tension left her body; Darcy was pathetically grateful she cared about him that much.

The men were rowing for their lives and the galley was skimming over the waves while the captain shouted. "Row! Row! Devil take it! Row!"

Darcy gave the rowers credit; they were strong and fast. The boat slid over the water like a dolphin. The coast of France rapidly grew smaller behind them.

Richard pulled Dreyfus to his feet. "Mr. Dreyfus, we have not met, but we have corresponded. I am Colonel Fitzwilliam." Dreyfus sagged in his arms at this revelation. "I never expected to encounter you under these circumstances, but I suppose the War Office will be pleased to have you in their custody. No doubt you have plenty of useful information about Napoleon's spies."

"I will tell you nothing," the man ground out. "You may shoot me again. I will tell you nothing."

Richard grinned. "'Twas not I that shot the first bullet. It was she." He gestured to Elizabeth with a dramatic flourish.

Darcy and Dreyfus both gaped at her, and she shrugged, the pistol still held loosely in one hand. "My father gave me shooting lessons as a girl."

"Bah!" Dreyfus spat on the deck. "I will not cooperate with you."

Richard shrugged. "It is your choice, but we need not bind your wound in that case." His eyes looked pointedly at the freely bleeding bullet hole in the man's shoulder.

"If you do not treat it, I could bleed to death!" Dreyfus protested.

Richard folded his arms across his chest and gave the man a relaxed grin. "The unfortunate consequence of becoming a double agent and shooting at my cousin. Perhaps you should re-think some of your choices." Dreyfus's response was unprintable, but Richard merely waggled a finger at him. "Ah, ah. Watch the language. There is a lady present."

The Frenchman sneered derisively at Elizabeth's sodden homespun clothing. "Lady!" he scoffed.

Darcy was happy he had regained his breath. His fist hit Dreyfus's chin with a very satisfying thump. The man fell back into the bottom of the boat. "Lady indeed," Darcy growled. "That is Mrs. Fitzwilliam Darcy, mistress of Pemberley!"

Dreyfus did not try to stand, but his eyes darted from Darcy to Elizabeth, his mouth gaping open. Richard's eyes were alive with merriment. "Did you believe you were chasing after a fishmonger and his wife?"

Only then did Darcy remember that the marriage was a sham—and that Elizabeth knew it to be a lie. He had grown so accustomed to the falsehood. However, her stony expression suggested that *she* had not forgotten. On the whole, Darcy much preferred the pretense.

"Will you cooperate?" Richard asked Dreyfus, his eyes hard.

"Yes," the Frenchman muttered, staring at the floor of the boat.

"Good." Richard pulled the man's hands behind him and tied them with a bit of rope. "Let us see what we can do about that wound." He pulled the double agent to the boat's stern, where he proceeded to make bandages out of silk shawls from one of the smuggled packages.

The coast of France was nothing more than a shadow on the horizon. The captain made his way to the back of the boat. His face was so red that he was in imminent danger of an attack of apoplexy. "You told me there would be no trouble!" he shouted at Richard, waving an arm in his face. "You said the French would not bother us!"

Calmly, Richard continued to bandage Dreyfus's wound. "I believed they would not, but I am afraid I was mistaken."

This admission did nothing for the captain's temper; he drew back an arm as if to strike Richard. "Now I won't be able to ever return to Gravelines," he bellowed, a Kentish accent strong in his voice. "You have ruined me!"

Darcy hastily reloaded his pistol from the kit in his pocket. If they had to fight off the captain, would the crew join his side?

Richard did not seem worried. "Actually, I have saved your business," he said calmly.

"The hell you have!" the man scoffed.

"After all, by returning us safely to Ramsgate, you are ensuring my goodwill. A clever move, sir. Otherwise I might be tempted to report your illegal activities to my superiors at the War Office. They take a dim view of smuggling, and they know whose boat I shipped out on."

"Your superiors at the—" The captain spluttered. "Well, devil take you!" he shouted, and turning on his heel, he stomped to the front of the boat.

Richard put the final knot in the bandage and grinned at Darcy. "It should be smooth sailing after this, Cuz."

Darcy's gaze traveled to the figure of Elizabeth, huddled miserably on a bench near the front of the boat, ignoring everything happening around her. "Maybe for you, but not for me."

***

Now that the captain had stopped shouting at Colonel Fitzwilliam, silence had descended over the galley. There was only the squeak of the oars and the grunts of the rowers, the slap of water on the side of the boat. Nobody spoke. Dreyfus appeared to be sleeping. Beside him, the colonel kept a watchful eye, pistol at the ready.

Before retreating to the stern once more, Will—Mr. Darcy had provided Elizabeth with a blanket that once might have been white but was now a dingy gray. Despite its uncertain cleanliness, Elizabeth welcomed it. As the wind dried her clothing, she felt truly chilled for the first time in days. Thank goodness they were not making this trip during the wintertime. The blanket kept out the worst of the cold, but she still shivered as the wind whipped the ties on her bonnet and lashed stray strands of hair into her eyes.

A fine mist had started to fall; in minutes everything she wore would no doubt be soaked through. Wonderful. But there was nowhere to go on this boat. Built for speed and maximum cargo space, the galley had no shelter.

Huddling deeper under the blanket, Elizabeth reminded herself that she would soon be home. *I will soon see Longbourn again...and Papa and Jane...* It was far better to dwell on those images than to think about her current circumstances. She would even prefer to focus on her current misery than to contemplate the state of her relationship with Mr. Darcy.

She had been so gullible. He deceived her for days, telling her she was his wife. She had grown accustomed to the idea, to anticipating a future with him once they returned to England. Now her future seemed like an empty hole. Elizabeth dug her fingernails into the palm of her hand. How he must have been laughing at her ignorance!

Of course, she could have allowed Dreyfus to strangle Mr. Darcy, but in the heat of battle she had not even considered it. Her only thought had been to save Mr. Darcy at any cost; the prospect he might be hurt had horrified her. *I cannot fathom how I managed to hit the man!* Her shot had been lucky indeed, but she was very happy he would live.

Now that she reflected on it, her need to save Mr. Darcy only made sense. For a week, she had relied on him to get her safely home. It was only sensible to worry what would become of her if he perished. Her reaction was quite rational and had nothing to do with her personal feelings for the man. Nothing.

Mr. Darcy had been very solicitous of her wellbeing; she could hardly repay him by ignoring him in his hour of need. She had done what any good Christian would do.

She pulled the blanket more tightly around her shoulders. *He said he loves me*, she reminded herself yet again. But what did those words mean to him? Men could mean so many different things by the word "love." She could not trust that it meant the same to him that it did to her. She would never lie to someone she loved.

She deliberately bit down on the inside of her cheek, focusing on the pain. *I will not cry. I will not give him the satisfaction of seeing me cry.*

Instead she conjured up an image of Longbourn's drawing room: her father sitting by the fire, Jane embroidering, Lydia and Kitty squabbling. The muscles in her back began to loosen. How lovely it would be to sit in her father's study and discuss books. Her sisters would be amazed to hear about her adventures in France, although there would be much she would need to conceal. And Jane…her embrace would be a balm. To Jane, at least, Elizabeth could confess everything without fear of judgment or consequences.

If only Jane were here now…

Darcy interrupted her as she was recreating Longbourn's dining room in her mind. "Eliz—Miss Bennet, allow me to thank you for saving my life." He took another place on the hard, narrow bench but as far from her as the plank would allow.

Drat the man! Of course, he must utter the exact words she could not reject with an angry retort!

She took a quick, involuntary glance in his direction. His clothing was as damp as hers, and he had no blanket to shield him from the wind. An occasional shiver betrayed his chill. *I will not feel sorry for him*, she vowed silently.

But civility demanded that she at least acknowledge his words. "It was the least I could do. After all, you saved my life, *Mr. Darcy*."

He winced when she emphasized the last two words. Was she being too harsh with him? After all, she would not have escaped France without his assistance. "I truly appreciate all that you have done for me, Mr. Darcy. My family will be eternally in your debt."

"If you would thank me, let it be for yourself alone," he said huskily. "I thought of nothing save keeping you safe and well."

Oh, Good Lord, why did he have to make it so difficult to stay furious with him?

"I pray you, listen to my explanation of"—he cleared his throat—"of the past week."

Elizabeth wanted to push him off the bench and watch him sprawl on the dirty boat's deck. But, she grudgingly admitted, she probably owed

Mr. Darcy her life. The least she could do was listen to his explanation. Once she was off this boat, she need not ever see him again.

"Very well," she said stiffly.

Mr. Darcy held his shapeless worker's hat, turning the rim around and around in his hands. He cleared his throat again. "When I arrived at Saint-Malo, I believed you were dead."

Elizabeth nodded. She knew this but still did not know what to make of it.

"I wanted to find the man who caused the cutter to explode and bring him to England for justice." Darcy glanced over his shoulder at Dreyfus huddled on the floor of the boat. "I just this minute realized that we actually accomplished that goal even though I abandoned it."

"Why did you want to avenge me? Did you somehow believe you were responsible for my trip to Jersey?"

"It did occur to me that you would not have been on that cutter if I had made you an offer of my hand in a way that could have tempted you." The desolation on his face took Elizabeth's breath away. "But I had journeyed to Longbourn in the hopes of changing your opinion of me. When I learned of your...demise, I thought I had lost that opportunity. There was no further service I could render you or your family, save to avenge your death."

Despite herself, Elizabeth felt moisture gathering in her eyes. Every time she doubted his love for her, he made such doubt impossible.

"But then I walked into a bedchamber at the Martins' house, and you were lying in the bed—ill but quite alive. I never even dared to hope..." He swallowed, staring down at his hands. "I was so overcome by the sight that I took you into my arms....You were warm and breathing and..."

Elizabeth could not help glancing at his profile. He was staring out over the ocean, his jaw clenched and tense. Reliving these memories was clearly a kind of agony for him.

When she said nothing, Mr. Darcy continued. "The Martins were scandalized at my behavior—grabbing an unconscious woman—so I said the first thing that came into my mind: that you were my wife." He rubbed his jaw with one hand. "Oddly enough, at the time it almost did not feel like a lie. I had been so ready to make you mine—to make you another offer at Longbourn—that it almost felt like you were...mine."

I should say something....But no words could emerge past the lump in her throat.

"I thought that when you awakened, I would induce you to play along, at least so that Mr. Martin would not be scandalized that I was in your sick room. I had no idea that you would have…"

"Forgotten everything," she supplied.

"Yes. The Martins told you I was your husband, and how was I to correct your misapprehension without destroying your trust? You did not remember who I was; I could not confess to deception. It seemed easiest to allow you to continue to believe it."

"Easiest?" Her voice was so loud that several of the rowers looked in their direction. "Easiest for whom?" she asked in a lower voice.

"For both of us." He squared his shoulders and then turned to look directly at her. "Elizabeth, if I had told you that we were neither married nor engaged, and that upon our previous meeting, you told me that I was the last person on earth you would marry"—Elizabeth flinched at her harsh words—"would you have accompanied me out of Saint-Malo?"

The first days in Saint-Malo had been so disorienting, not knowing who she was or why she was in France. She could see now that her "husband" had been a source of comfort and security. "Possibly not," she conceded. "But we have been traveling together for a week. You could have told me at any point."

His head dropped, and his eyes fixed on his hands again. "I considered telling you upon many occasions, but I feared distracting you from the all-important tasks of recovering from your illness and reaching England. Nothing was more important than getting you home safely. I vowed I would do anything to make that happen. Even make you hate me."

Elizabeth could not help recalling how he had charged into Adele's house to rescue her when he easily could have escaped on his own. He *had* put her safety above everything else, including his own life.

"I had planned to tell you the truth once we reached England. I swear to you!" His voice now held an edge of desperation.

"The truth would have been necessary." Elizabeth's voice sounded cold even to her own ears. "The population of Longbourn and Meryton would hardly have cooperated with your deception."

"I pray you, understand that I abhor falsehoods of every kind. Living such a lie felt wrong every moment of every day."

She could sense his desperation, but she was not convinced that he had no choice. "Did it truly feel wrong, Mr. Darcy, or did you get a secret thrill from pretending I was your wife? It was what you wanted after all."

Elizabeth's rage was an ice-cold core deep in her body. Mr. Darcy's words had melted it a little bit, but she clung to it like a piece of driftwood in the ocean. Otherwise the onslaught of fresh memories threatened to overwhelm her.

He opened his mouth quickly as if for an angry retort but then closed it again. "I will admit I enjoyed the fantasy of you as my wife," he said with a sigh. "Nothing would make me happier."

"Even now?" she asked. He had certainly seen her at her worst.

"Even now," he said firmly. "But I swear to God I did not embark on the deception for the purpose of coercing you into matrimony."

"No?"

A corner of his mouth quirked upward. "No. I am somewhat familiar with your temperament, Elizabeth."

She could not help responding with a small grin of her own.

"I will admit that playing the role of your husband gave me pleasure." The absentminded smile on his face was all the more charming because he seemed unaware of it. "But not as much pleasure as being your husband in truth would give me." He leaned forward. "I am very sorry," he said simply. "I cannot apologize sufficiently for the pain my falsehoods have caused."

She took a deep breath. "I accept your apology, Mr. Darcy."

"I thank you." He was watching her with something akin to hope on his face.

"But," she continued, "I do not know if I can trust you. You deceived me so thoroughly—even if it was with the best of intentions."

Chapter Eighteen

"I do not make a habit of deception," he said stiffly. "Quite the contrary."

"I know," she murmured. "Please believe that I do forgive you and hold you blameless. And you have my deepest gratitude for saving my life. I wish I could somehow repay you."

He scowled. "I want neither gratitude nor recompense."

She swallowed. This was more difficult than she expected. She had come to regard him as a friend and disliked causing him any pain. "I hope that when we part in Kent we may part as friends."

He gasped. "Part? Elizabeth, we cannot part."

"Why not?" she asked coolly. "I will go to Hertfordshire, and you will return to Pemberley—or London, perhaps."

His hands balled into fists in his lap. "You know we cannot do so. We have been traveling together for a week. Your reputation has been thoroughly compromised."

She had expected this argument, but it was still a bitter pill to swallow. "So now we must marry?"

He looked bemused. "Well…yes. Of course."

She drew herself up straight, making her back ache. If only there were somewhere else she could sit on the benighted boat. "I do not accept that premise, sir."

Now he was bewildered. Had he not considered the possibility that she would reject him? Again? "But… you must marry me," he sputtered. "We-We have been…in the same b-bed!"

She took a deep breath, reminding herself that she was on an open boat and not trapped in a prison cell, even if it did feel as if walls were closing in around her. "And do you intend to take out an advertisement in the papers to that effect?"

"Of course not!"

"I shall not tell anyone, and neither will you. Everyone who witnessed our inappropriate relationship remains in France. I think it unlikely that the gossips of Meryton have agents in Saint-Malo."

Darcy shook his head. "I knew this would go ill for me." He rubbed his forehead with one hand. "And if rumors do start—?"

The wind had grown cooler; Elizabeth shivered violently. "I will not make decisions about my future happiness based on a hypothetical."

"But—"

She interrupted. "There are worse fates than remaining unmarried: marrying the wrong man, for instance."

Mr. Darcy winced. "Is there another man you would—?"

She interrupted. "No, not at all. But the decision about who to marry is the most important decision a woman can make in her life. It determines the whole course of her future, including where she will live. A man might enter into it lightly; a woman cannot."

"I am not entering into this lightly." He scowled.

She sighed, aware that she was badly mangling the conversation. "I did not mean to imply that you are. I simply am not prepared to make such a momentous decision."

"Do you still find me so thoroughly objectionable?" he asked softly after a pause.

Elizabeth tried futilely to brush hair from her face. Why was he persisting in asking such difficult questions when she was having trouble enough just marshaling her thoughts? "No. Not at all....I may assure you that you have thoroughly destroyed my previous objections. But, I always promised myself that I would marry for love."

His expression was bleak. "And you do not love me." It was not a question.

She could not stand the intensity in his gaze and lowered her eyes to where her hands played with the edge of the blanket. "I...cannot say....I do not know how I feel about you. You were the last man in the world I would marry. Then you were my husband. Then you became the man who had lied to me and made a fool of me." Tears welled up in her eyes, and she bit her lip to prevent them from falling. "I am damp and exhausted and hungry. My family believes I am deceased, and I shot a man today." His expression softened. "I cannot truthfully say how I feel about you."

He was silent for a long moment. "It is not what I hoped to hear."

Elizabeth slouched forward on the bench, desperately wishing for a bed or even a pile of hay upon which she could sleep.

Mr. Darcy touched her cheek with one finger, and she had to fight the impulse to lean into his hand. "You are not telling me no?"

She sighed. "At this moment I am not capable of saying yes or no. You must wait, Mr. Darcy."

He snorted. "Patience is not one of my virtues, but I have received many lessons lately." His hand squeezed her shoulder briefly. "I will leave you to rest, but we must discuss this again before we part ways."

She nodded wearily.

"I will take a room at an inn for you when we reach Kent."

She could only nod again. "That would be most welcome."

"Very well." He hesitated for a moment but then stood and made his way to the back of the boat to join his cousin.

***

Thanks to the choppy waters of the Channel, they did not arrive at Ramsgate until minutes before the dawn. The sun was peeking over the horizon as the sailors finally pulled the boat onto the beach. Colonel Fitzwilliam enlisted two of the sailors to help him take Dreyfus to the nearest magistrate while Mr. Darcy accompanied Elizabeth to an inn. Eager to return to Hertfordshire, she suggested searching for the first mail coach, but he insisted that she required breakfast at the very least.

He was very careful not to touch so much as the fringe on her shawl but remained close enough to demonstrate she was under his protection. He led her to The White Hart, surely the biggest and most expensive establishment in the town.

"I have stayed here before," he said softly as they entered the building. Only then did Elizabeth recall that Ramsgate was the town where his sister had run afoul of Mr. Wickham. It would not hold pleasant memories for him.

The innkeeper looked askance at the two travel-stained peasants who dared to darken his doorway, but his expression quickly shifted to incredulity. "Mr. Darcy!" the man cried, hurrying toward them as if fearing they would collapse from exhaustion at any minute. "What has befallen you? Highwaymen? Footpads?"

Mr. Darcy grimaced. "Merely a few of Napoleon's soldiers."

The man's eyes widened comically. "Here?"

"No, we are just arrived from France."

The man nodded sagely as if he understood—when he obviously did not. "Ah. Do you need a room?"

"Two rooms. And we are sorely in need of one of your fine breakfasts." Elizabeth's sluggish brain puzzled over the need for two rooms until she realized one must be for Colonel Fitzwilliam.

Elizabeth was immediately whisked away to a back room while Mr. Darcy discussed the particulars with the proprietor. The innkeeper's wife was just bringing in breakfast when Mr. Darcy entered the room. Elizabeth's hunger had abated during the night, but the aroma of eggs and sausage awakened her appetite and she ate heartily. Once her stomach was full, she became quite drowsy, giving her second thoughts about her plan for an immediate departure for Hertfordshire.

"Elizabeth." Mr. Darcy gently laid his hand on hers, affecting not to notice when she pulled it away. "You are not fit to travel today, particularly since you are not recovered completely from your illness. Please take a room here; you need a bed and a warm bath." Her eyes were so heavy she was not sure if she could make it to a bed before falling asleep.

"My own room?" she asked.

He scowled. "Of course." He lowered his voice. "If I did not take advantage of you in France, I would hardly do so here."

Elizabeth's mind absorbed these words slowly. "I apologize. I did not mean to imply…" Her voice trailed off when she forgot the subject under discussion.

Mr. Darcy chuckled. "You should not travel in your current state. You might accidentally take the coach to Penzance."

"Very well, I suppose there is no harm in departing tomorrow." Her words were interrupted by a huge yawn.

Mr. Darcy disappeared and returned with a maid in tow. "Mary can show you to your room," he said.

Elizabeth trudged up the stairs behind the maid, trying to decide if she wanted a bath or a nap first. The choice was decided for her when she saw a huge bath of steaming water in the room. "When did Mr. Darcy order this?" Elizabeth asked Mary. "I only decided to stay a few minutes ago."

The maid giggled. "I don't rightly know, ma'am, but we've been bringing water up here for the better part of an hour."

He knew I would stay. Or at least he hoped I would. Elizabeth supposed she should be vexed by his presumption, but she could only be grateful.

"Would you like me to help you undress?" Mary asked, glancing dubiously at Elizabeth's clothing, no doubt wondering why so fine a gentleman as Mr. Darcy was escorting a woman whose clothes might be cast aside by a charwoman.

"No, I can manage." It wold be a joy to take off the rumpled and stained garments.

"Mr. Darcy asked me to hunt up some proper clothing for you." She gestured to a gown lying on the bed. "This is the best I could do on such short notice." The gown was simple muslin with little in the way of decoration, yet it was no doubt finer than anything the maid owned. Elizabeth wondered how many coins had fallen into the innkeeper's hand so the staff would produce a suitable gown in an hour's time. Beside the gown were all the appropriate undergarments and a fine linen nightrail. He had considered all her needs. Tears sprang to her eyes at his thoughtfulness.

"It is wonderful," she told Mary, who dimpled with pleasure.

After the maid departed, Elizabeth gladly removed her salt- and mud-caked clothing and took a long, leisurely bath. Emerging from the bath, she felt as though she had never been so clean in her life, but her limbs grew heavier with every passing minute. After drying herself, she pulled the soft nightrail over her head. The last thing she remembered was climbing under the coverlet and sinking into the soft mattress. She did not stir even when the footmen entered to remove the bath.

***

To Darcy's immense relief, Elizabeth's skin had lost its grayish pallor by the time she descended the stairs for dinner in the inn's private dining room. Eight hours of rest had clearly done her a world of good. Although the gown was snug in the bodice and a little long, it was a vast improvement over her previous garb. *How satisfying to see her finally dressed properly!* Although he would have preferred she wore a finer fabric, he was pleased she no longer resembled a fishwife.

Darcy, too, had appropriate clothing cobbled together by the innkeeper's wife. The jacket was too large and the waistcoat quite out of style—and he still wore the laborer's boots. But it was worlds better than his previous garb. *When I finally find some decent boots, I will see these burned.*

Having turned Dreyfus over to the local magistrate, Richard was able to join them for dinner. He had left a suit of clothing in town, so he was not only dressed appropriately but it all fitted quite well. Darcy eyed his cousin enviously.

Richard smiled and stood when Elizabeth joined them at the table. Darcy stood as well, but he could not bring himself to smile. Every time he saw Elizabeth, he feared she would tell him that she never wished to see him again.

As they ate, they spoke of neutral subjects—the weather, the war on the peninsula—and Richard relayed all the latest news they had missed. He voiced the opinion that Dreyfus would likely be imprisoned for the remainder of the war, but the man seemed willing to provide information in exchange for more lenient treatment.

Elizabeth spoke civilly to Darcy, neither avoiding nor seeking out his gaze, but there was little warmth in her tone. Her continued coldness made Darcy's heart sink; she obviously had no plans to accept his offer. When, over pudding, Elizabeth asked for Richard's assistance in arranging for her transport to Longbourn, it was like a knife in his heart.

Darcy spoke before his cousin could respond. "That will not be necessary. I have hired a coach for tomorrow so I may escort you home."

Elizabeth laid her spoon on the table. "Mr. Darcy, I thank you for your solicitude, but I could not possibly inconvenience you further."

"It is no inconvenience—"

Elizabeth continued speaking. "Furthermore, I cannot possibly arrive at Longbourn in your company without giving rise to speculation."

A fist squeezed Darcy's heart. Of course, *he* would not mind provoking such speculation since he still hoped to make her Mrs. Darcy. But he did not want her to marry him because of speculation any more than he wanted her to accept his hand from a sense of obligation.

Perhaps he should throw himself to the floor at her feet and beg. *It would have the advantage of surprise.* Instead he grasped the edge of the table in an iron grip and mustered a reasonable tone of voice, murmuring, "Elizabeth, you should consider—"

Her hand arose to stop the flood of words. "I thank you for your assistance, Mr. Darcy, but I am exhausted. At this moment I want nothing other than to see my family again."

Richard coughed and looked away, no doubt wishing he were somewhere else.

She wants her family; she does not want me.

The fist around his heart was crushing it. Somehow Darcy managed to expel a few words from his constricted throat. "Of course, if that is your wish. I...er...will send you in the carriage tomorrow."

She blinked in surprise. Did she really believe he would send her post when he had the means to make her journey safe and comfortable? "I thank you, sir," she said finally.

"It is my pleasure."

She arose from the table, and the men followed suit. "I find I am still weary, so I will retire for the night."

Once she had departed, Darcy turned to Richard, who had the air of a man who had been dragged unwillingly into a lovers' spat. "*You* should accompany her to Longbourn."

"Arriving with me would give rise to just as much speculation," Richard said mildly. "And the War Office expects me in London tomorrow."

Darcy slumped back in his chair, hating his cousin's logic.

Richard waved an unconcerned hand. "Send a maid with her; she will be fine." Darcy did not respond. "She may come around, Darce. She is not indifferent to you."

Darcy snorted. "Yes, I do not inspire indifference. Loathing, perhaps, or nausea. But not indifference."

"She will recognize her true feelings in time."

Darcy gave his cousin a level look. "She hated me before all of this. And then for a week I took advantage of her ignorance, lying to her again and again." *Perhaps I should strive for indifference.*

"You did it to save her life," Richard said. "Surely she understands that."

Darcy gripped his glass so tightly his knuckles turned white. "She did not love me—did not trust me—before. I have given her no reason to change her mind. Quite the opposite." He downed the contents of his glass in one gulp.

"Did you offer her your hand?" Richard asked.

"Of course! What do you take me for?" Darcy poured more gin into the glass. "She does not want it, Richard." He stared at the clear liquid, promising himself that he would get thoroughly foxed another time when he was at his leisure.

His cousin glanced at the doorway through which she had departed. "I am not certain about that."

Darcy raised an eyebrow. "Did you not hear what she said?"

"Aye, but I also heard what she did *not* say. She wishes to go back to Hertfordshire and see her family, which is perfectly understandable.

She did not, for instance, declare again that you are the last man in the world she would marry."

Darcy took a sip of the gin. "She already voiced that sentiment. It would be redundant."

"Or she thinks it is possible she might consider marrying you."

"Perhaps if I were the last man in the world." Darcy's lips twisted in a grimace.

A corner of Richard's mouth quirked upward. "Surely you would rank above Dreyfus."

Darcy could not prevent a chuckle from escaping. "Damn you, Cousin."

"Wait and see," Richard advised, slapping Darcy on the back. "She may come around."

Darcy hardly wanted a wife who would "come around," but additional debate would only continue the conversation, and he was weary of the subject. He downed the gin in one gulp. "You, my friend, may be optimistic if you wish, but I know what she has said to me." He set the glass on the table with a thud. "I have no reason for hope."

***

Darcy knew he should leave well enough alone, but Elizabeth would travel to Longbourn tomorrow while he departed for Pemberley. He might never have another opportunity for a private conversation with her, or, God forbid, he might never see her again. After a couple of glasses of gin with Richard, another conversation seemed like a grand idea.

After a brief visit to his room, Darcy took his candle down the corridor and knocked softly on Elizabeth's door, hoping she had not already fallen asleep.

"Come." Her voice was soft and low.

He opened the door slowly, peeking his head around the edge. Elizabeth sat by the window, her eyes growing wide when she saw him. "Mr. Darcy! I expected it to be Mary again." Fortunately, she still wore the muslin gown; the nightrail would have been too great a temptation. Her hair was down, falling in dark waves around her face.

"I beg a moment of your time."

"Of course." She set down the book she had been reading. *From where had she obtained a book?* "Please, have a seat." She gestured to the chair opposite hers.

Before settling into the chair, Darcy handed her a slip of paper. She examined it by the light of her lamp. "What is this?"

"The names and directions for my banker and my solicitor. If you should ever find yourself in any kind of need, please consider them to be resources."

She shook her head and laid the paper on the little table between their chairs. "I cannot accept this. You owe me nothing."

Darcy rolled his eyes. "I told you falsehoods about the most basic facts of your life."

"You had good reason, and I have forgiven you. You need not make amends."

"Even if you have no intention of using the information, please keep it—for my sake if not your own. It will grant me peace of mind."

She stared at the paper as one might a poisonous snake, but finally she took it in hand. "Very well."

Darcy sighed with relief.

"Did you want anything else?" The impatience in her words was belied by the compassion—near pity—in her eyes.

Yes, I would beg you to be my wife. Somehow—just barely—he managed to prevent the words from escaping.

"Mr. Darcy?"

He pulled himself from his reverie. "I had initially thought to make you a formal proposal of marriage."

Elizabeth's eyes widened, and she very nearly stood as though about to race from the room.

"But I do not want to make you an offer at an inn."

Elizabeth's shoulders relaxed. He forged ahead with the part of the plan that had initially caused him reservations, but he no longer had any pride left when it came to Elizabeth Bennet. She knew all his secrets; there could be no shame. "I will not make a formal offer of my hand now, but you need only say the word, and a proposal of marriage will be forthcoming."

Elizabeth sat very still.

"Not out of a feeling of obligation or guilt, but because I love you."

Her lips parted, but she said nothing.

Darcy kept his head up, not showing that he had hoped for a different response from her. Did she understand how sincere he was? He leaned forward in his chair, focusing all his attention on her. "You may write to me from anywhere and at any time, and I will come to you."

He held her eyes until she gave him a solemn nod. "I will remember."

"Good."

Biting her lower lip, she looked toward the window. "Be careful what you promise, sir!" Her voice shook despite the jovial tone. "Someday when you are two and fifty, I will write to you: 'now I am ready for my proposal'!"

He could not join her laughter. "If that is how long it takes, then I will wait," he said with a solemnity he hoped would convey his sincerity.

"But, Mr. Darcy—"

"I liked it when you called me William."

She nodded an acknowledgement. "Mr. Darcy, surely you will have a wife and six children by that age."

Darcy stared out of the window into the inn's courtyard. "I very much doubt I will ever find someone else I would consider marrying."

"But—"

"I do not need to provide an heir. The property is not entailed. Georgiana may inherit."

She shifted uneasily in her chair. "I see you have done much thinking on the subject."

"Since the minute I left Hunsford Parsonage," he said in a low voice. Elizabeth had no response, and her face was blank. He could not guess her thoughts. Did he sound desperate to her ears? Was she eager to escape his pathetic importuning?

"I have taken up enough of your time," he said, standing. "You should sleep in preparation for your journey tomorrow."

He strode purposefully for the door, intent on an immediate exit. But he could not deprive himself of one last glimpse of her, sitting by the window, her face illuminated by the golden glow of the candle. She rose to her feet, dark curls tumbling around her shoulders.

And he was lost.

No one could expect him to resist the power of those curls. *After all, I am only human.* He closed the distance between them, plunging his hands into the dark mass of hair and tilting her head back so she could receive his kiss.

"Elizabeth!" he moaned against her lips. They parted to admit his tongue just as her body molded itself to his. Elizabeth's mind might be divided in her opinion of him, but her body had made a firm decision. The marital bed with Elizabeth would be…exquisite. His hands roamed around her back and shoulders, traced the soft skin of her neck. For an instant he allowed himself a brief moment of hope.

But he quickly suppressed that feeling. This was farewell. He could taste it on her lips. Somehow he knew he would not see her again soon—if ever. He tried to savor the taste of her lips, the scent of her skin, the feel of her under his fingers—to memorize it and tattoo it upon his heart. He must stow away these memories to sustain him throughout the long, lonely months and years ahead.

Far too soon she stepped away from him, her chest heaving. "You must leave now."

Darcy nodded, temporarily incapable of speech. Releasing his hold on Elizabeth's shoulder was difficult…almost physically painful. He did not want to surrender this last point of contact with her.

Finally, he forced his hands down to his sides and edged toward the door. "Do not lose the paper. Anytime. Anywhere. I promise."

She gave him a bittersweet smile. "I will not. I will not forget, William."

Chapter Nineteen

Elizabeth's departure from the inn in the morning was rapid and somber. Colonel Fitzwilliam bid her adieu with promises to visit should he ever be in Hertfordshire. Then he stepped away to give Mr. Darcy some private time with her, but the master of Pemberley hid his feelings behind a mask of stone. Was he embarrassed about his revelations from the night before? He merely kissed her hand and wished her a pleasant journey before handing her into the carriage.

The journey itself was pleasant, with good weather and a well-sprung, comfortable carriage. Mr. Darcy had hired Mary from the inn to accompany Elizabeth, and she proved to be an excellent traveling companion. She kept Elizabeth entertained—and distracted—with amusing stories about the mishaps of her many brothers.

Elizabeth was excited to see her family again but could not help missing Mr. Darcy. His absence was a sudden emptiness that brought about an almost physical ache. Again and again she thought of things she would like to share with him. Turning to tell him, she would find Mary beside her instead. *It means nothing*, she told herself. *I am simply accustomed to his presence; I will grow accustomed to his absence.* A tightness in her chest belied these words.

Her pulse quickened when she spied the familiar sights of Meryton. She had been from home not even two months, but it felt far longer, a lifetime ago. Her life in Meryton could have been lived by a different person. She knew she looked like a different person. The inn's mirror had shown a woman who was thinner and more tanned than the one who had embarked on the cutter. Even her hair glinted with hints of red from her time in the sun.

Would the alterations disturb her family? What if they did not recognize her? *Now I am being fanciful! I have not changed so very much. Still, I am returning from the dead, and they are not prepared.*

Her stomach fluttered nervously. Elizabeth did not know what to expect—except their joy at her return. No, she also could predict with a moderate degree of confidence that her sudden reappearance would cause her mother to take to her bed and elicit pious platitudes from Mary. Oddly enough, she was even anticipating these eventualities with pleasure. Perhaps absence did make the heart grow fonder.

The carriage pulled to a halt in front of Longbourn. Elizabeth heard her sisters before she could see them.

"La! What a fancy carriage! I wonder whose it is?"

"Jane, did Mr. Bingley buy a carriage?"

"Whoever it is, I hope he is unmarried!"

From the carriage window, Elizabeth viewed her younger sisters spilling out of Longbourn's front door, giggling.

Jane and her parents followed at a more sedate pace.

Elizabeth waited until the entire family was present, clustered around the carriage, before opening the door and climbing out.

Her father staggered backward. Jane gasped. Lydia screamed, "Lizzy!"

"But you are dead," Mary said faintly.

Within seconds, Mrs. Bennet's shrieks drowned out all other sounds. "It's a ghost! Get away! Begone, foul spirit! Haunt us no more." She pulled Lydia with her as she backed toward the door.

Elizabeth had to laugh. "Mama, I am no more a ghost than you are."

"Do ghosts arrive in carriages?" Kitty asked.

Jane was the first to break their paralysis as she fairly flew into Elizabeth's arms. "You are alive! Alive after all!" With her arms around her sister's neck, the eldest Bennet daughter sobbed into her sister's shoulder.

"I am so sorry for what you had to suffer!" Elizabeth murmured into her sister's hair.

"I-It is q-quite all right," Jane sobbed. "N-No trouble at all." Elizabeth had to smile. *Same old Jane, wanting to ensure that nobody else was uncomfortable.*

"Lizzy." Elizabeth left Jane's arms for her father's. His eyes glistened behind his spectacles, and for a long moment he was too overcome for words. "Are you indeed well, my girl?" Stepping back, he examined her from head to toe.

"I am well," she assured him, squeezing his hand. "I was ill, but that is at an end."

Her father discreetly wiped one eye. "Therein lies a tale, I am sure."

When he released her, Elizabeth was immediately seized by Kitty and Lydia. "Now we can stop wearing black!" Lydia exclaimed gleefully. "It does make me look so pale."

"True!" Kitty's eyes shone. "Oh, but all our clothes were dyed."

Lydia's eyes opened wide. "Which means we all need new frocks!" She looked beseechingly at their father. "Do we not need new gowns to celebrate Elizabeth's return to us? It is only fitting."

Elizabeth exchanged a smile with Jane. Lydia was quick to turn any situation to her advantage, even her own sister's return from death.

Kitty bit her lower lip. "I don't suppose you want your yellow bonnet back?" Elizabeth merely looked at her. "I did not dye it yet, but I added some orange flowers—"

"Which are the most garish things I have ever seen, if you ask me," Lydia said tartly.

"They are not—!"

"Are too!"

Lydia and Kitty walked away, squabbling, which allowed Mary to embrace her older sister. She regarded Elizabeth solemnly. "The Lord giveth and the Lord taketh away."

Elizabeth blinked, unsure of an appropriate response. "Indeed."

Mary nodded soberly, and then their mother was pushing her out of the way. "Lizzy, is it really you?"

"Of course, Mama." Elizabeth held out her arms.

Her mother moved cautiously into the embrace, first squeezing one of Elizabeth's arms. "You seem real enough."

"I assure you I am quite real." Elizabeth finally wrapped her arms around her mother. "The report of my death was erroneous. I was never dead."

Tears flowed down Mrs. Bennet's face even as she dabbed futilely at them with a lace-edged handkerchief. "It *is* you, my darling daughter! You have been restored to us." She turned to her husband. "We have been very blessed."

"We have indeed," he agreed.

"This calls for a special celebration," Mrs. Bennet declared, releasing Elizabeth. "A ham! We shall have a ham in your honor, Lizzy!" Before Elizabeth could respond, she had turned on her heel and was rushing back into the house. "Hill! Hill! We require a ham!"

Her father took Elizabeth's arm to escort her into the house. "As you can see," he observed with a wry smile, "nothing much has changed during your absence."

On Elizabeth's other side, Jane asked, "Would you like some tea? You must be famished." *Dear Jane, ever watchful of others' needs.*

"Yes, indeed. And there is a maid from the Ramsgate inn."
Elizabeth turned to see the maid standing by the carriage. "Can you make
sure she receives food and a place to sleep tonight before she must
return?"

Jane nodded and hurried back to the carriage to collect the girl.

"Ramsgate?" her father exclaimed. "What on earth were you
about at Ramsgate?"

"It is a long story, Papa"—she patted her father's hand—"but if
you ply me with tea and biscuits, perhaps I can be persuaded to relate it."

Soon Elizabeth was ensconced in the yellow drawing room with a
cup of tea and a plate of biscuits before her. The entire family had
gathered around, eager to hear about her misadventures. The prospect of
an exciting tale—which they could be the first to share with the gossips of
Meryton—had even induced Kitty and Lydia to delay a trip into town for
bonnet ribbons.

In between bites of biscuits, Elizabeth told her story. She
described how Dreyfus had taken her from the ship as a hostage and then
hit her on the head before pushing her from the boat. She had clung to a
piece of driftwood until she passed out, but it must have kept her afloat
until she washed ashore at Saint-Malo.

When describing her time in the town, she dwelt on the Martins'
kind offices but gave few specifics about Mr. Darcy's role. It was a shame
she could not grant him a greater share of the credit, but if her family
knew of their sleeping arrangements, her father would be appalled, her
mother would demand an immediate engagement, and the younger Bennet
girls would spread the story about Meryton by dinnertime.

She did describe her amnesia and the encounter with Mr. Dreyfus
at the farmhouse. But even as she related how they were forced to flee to
Paris and stay with Mr. Darcy's old governess, she was careful not to
mention their shared beds or how she had believed herself to be his wife.
She also made light of the dangers they had encountered. Her travels were
shocking enough; there was no need to burden her family with potential
evils that had not befallen her.

Lydia and Kitty hung on her every word, thrilling at every new
story of danger. Apparently Elizabeth's life was better than the best novel
from the circulating library. Her mother, quite overcome by nerves, lay
prostrate on the fainting sofa, although she was quick to take credit for
sending Mr. Darcy to France. "He saw how I was suffering, and he knew
he had to avenge your death somehow."

Her father's grave expression suggested that he guessed some of the things she had avoided mentioning, but he asked for no details. She did emphasize that Mr. Darcy had been a perfect gentleman, but it did little to smooth out the worry lines around his eyes. Jane's sympathetic smiles suggested that at least one person understood some of the complexities of Elizabeth's situation.

Tea time soon gave way to dinner, including the promised ham. Did her mother even recall that Elizabeth did not care much for ham?

Elizabeth had missed Longbourn's hubbub and chatter; every second with her family filled her with a warm glow. However, not long after dinner, her energy began to flag. Jane noticed immediately. "Lizzy, perhaps it is time for bed."

Elizabeth put down her book and stood, suppressing a yawn. "I believe you are right."

Jane also rose to her feet. "I will retire as well."

As Elizabeth shuffled to the door, she passed her father's chair; he took her hand and pressed it to his heart. "It is a miracle to have you back with us, Lizzy." She gave him a quick kiss on the cheek before navigating out of the door and up the stairs.

Once in her nightrail, Elizabeth was quite grateful to sink into the softness of the bed she shared with Jane. The candle on Jane's side of the bed flickered and caused shadows to dance on the walls. Jane, not yet ready for sleep, sat beside her sister. "Mr. Darcy must be quite violently in love with you to have gone all the way to France simply to avenge you."

There was no point in denying the obvious truth. "Yes."

"He was devastated when he arrived at Longbourn and learned of your... He was quite as distressed as any of us. It was as if his entire world had ended."

Not having a good response, Elizabeth stared at the canopy over her bed, considering how terrible it was to cause pain for the people she cared about.

After a long silence, Jane spoke again. "You were much thrown together in France, I believe." Her voice did not hold even a hint of disapproval.

"Yes, it was inevitable."

"But he did not make you another offer of his hand?" Jane's brows drew together.

"Oh yes, he did," Elizabeth assured her. "Well, I suppose not quite. He would have, but…he knew I would not accept."

Jane's head turned sharply to Elizabeth. "You do not love him?"

Elizabeth let her head thump against the headboard. "I do not know my own heart. My feelings are so complicated…and my thoughts so muddled."

Jane took one of Elizabeth's hands and squeezed it. "I pray you, tell me."

So Elizabeth described Mr. Darcy's claim to be her husband and what he had revealed about his feelings. She omitted only their kisses and how they had shared a bed—although Jane surely guessed.

Jane was silent a long time when Elizabeth was finished. "What are your feelings for Mr. Darcy now?" she asked finally.

"I was very angry when I first discovered his deceit, but now I understand it better—how it happened, why he allowed it to continue. I have forgiven him…" Her voice trailed off.

Jane waited for Elizabeth to continue.

"It is odd. I should be angry. I *was* angry about his falsehoods. But at the same time, I cannot shake the habit of seeing myself as his wife. I suppose I grew accustomed to the idea."

"Was he a good husband?" Jane asked with a teasing smile.

"The best sort of husband." Elizabeth grinned, but her expression quickly sobered. "I miss that closeness. The informality. The warmth." She rubbed her forehead with one hand. "But it was all a lie." Mr. Darcy had grown more formal and distant once Elizabeth had remembered everything. The absence of that intimacy was like the gap of a missing tooth.

Jane was silent for a moment. "Well, the part about being married was a lie, but the way he felt about you was not."

No, but… "I do not wish to become his wife because it is familiar and comfortable."

"That is why you did not accept his offer?"

"Yes…and…I…must discover how I feel about him—even when I am not in his presence. When I do not think of him as a husband. Before France I disliked him so intensely, and now he wants me to tie myself to him for life. Sometimes I want that, but do I want it because I am simply accustomed to thinking of him that way?"

"Oh, Lizzy…"

"It is all a muddle, Jane. I do not know my own mind. When has that ever been true before? My wit has always been the one thing I could rely upon. I suppose I grew a little vain about it. My mind has been betraying me for weeks…and it continues. I cannot decide…I do not know what I think…and I cannot understand why I feel this way."

Jane stroked Elizabeth's hair with calming hands. "I am certain all you need is time. You will sort it all out given time."

"I wish I had your faith," Elizabeth murmured.

Jane enfolded her sister in her arms, pulling her close. Surrendering to Jane's caring warmth, Elizabeth allowed herself to cry.

Chapter Twenty

Life at Longbourn quickly returned to normal. Everyone in the neighborhood came to visit the Bennets to marvel at the daughter who had "returned from the dead," and Elizabeth was compelled to recount her story time and again. She was touched to learn how many people were genuinely joyful at her return. The tale was even written up in a London paper, although the article got most of the details wrong and made no mention of Mr. Darcy.

Elizabeth's father took her into his study the day after her arrival and demanded a fuller account of her travels. She shared many details, but she did not tell him about believing herself to be Mr. Darcy's wife or sharing his bed. Her father was quite troubled enough at understanding they had traveled together unchaperoned and expressed concern about Elizabeth's reputation should that part of the story become widely known. However, he did not suggest that they seek an offer of marriage from Mr. Darcy. Perhaps he believed she still disliked the man and would not care to marry him.

Elizabeth said as little as possible to her mother about Mr. Darcy; fortunately, Mrs. Bennet was too preoccupied with her family's fame to recognize the marital opportunities afforded by her daughter's misfortunes.

If Elizabeth became a little quieter after her return from France, few noticed, save Jane and her father, and they ascribed it to the demands of recovering from the traumatic experience. However, Elizabeth found that her thoughts were not occupied with France or her experiences there; instead they returned again and again to Mr. Darcy.

In the midst of needlework in the drawing room, she would suddenly muse about what he was doing at that moment. Was he thinking of her? Had he changed his mind about her? Or she would be walking along a lane and realize that she was imagining what it would be like to show the place to Mr. Darcy. Would she ever have such an opportunity?

Mr. Bingley had been in London on business, but he arrived at Longbourn a few weeks later, very happy to learn of her return. It was the work of mere days before he finally proposed to Jane, an offer he would have made earlier if the family had not been in mourning. Jane graciously accepted, and the family enjoyed a new source of happiness. Elizabeth, for her part, was pleased to share some of the family's attention with her sister.

Still, the happy event provoked an unanticipated sense of melancholy in Elizabeth. The news of her sister's engagement—presented at dinner—had been neither unexpected nor unwelcome, and yet Elizabeth could not escape a persistent sense of sadness.

After dinner she took a stroll in Longbourn's garden. In the early September weather, everything was yet very green, but Elizabeth found herself unable to enjoy the beauty. As she sat on a stone bench, she found her thoughts turning yet again to Mr. Darcy.

What was he doing at that moment? Perhaps he was dancing at a ball or entertaining guests at a dinner party. He might be enjoying the attentions of a woman who likely was prettier—and surely wealthier—than Elizabeth. What if her caution caused him to lose interest? He might decide he did not want a wife who was so inconstant.

Such thoughts made her eyes burn, and she gritted her teeth. *I will not weep over this!*

The slip of paper was never far from her mind; she had carefully preserved it in her reticule, although she had no intention of employing it. He had declared his feelings to be immutable, but how could he be sure? On his way home to Pemberley, he might have encountered a woman who completely erased Elizabeth from his mind.

Simply picturing such an event cut into Elizabeth like a knife.

The sound of gravel crunching caught her attention. Jane approached cautiously, as if stalking a wild animal that might bolt. Elizabeth was tempted to laugh; surely she did not appear quite so nervous.

Jane extended her own handkerchief to Elizabeth as she took a place beside her on the bench. Elizabeth took it gratefully and wiped her eyes. No tears had escaped down her cheeks, but her eyes were brimming.

"I would not have accepted Mr. Bingley's offer if I thought it would cause you pain, Lizzy," Jane said softly.

"Your engagement does not cause me pain—quite the opposite. I am very pleased you are marrying him, and I wish you happy."

"So these are tears of joy?" Jane teased gently.

"No." Elizabeth breathed out a laugh. "I...do not know precisely why I am sad. You would do best to ignore me."

"Do you miss Mr. Darcy?"

"Yes, of course. I do not believe I realized how much I missed him until I saw you with Mr. Bingley. You are so happy together!" Stupidly her voice broke over this declaration.

"I can understand why that would be distressing," Jane said with mock solemnity.

Elizabeth could not prevent a laugh from escaping. "How did you know you are in love with Mr. Bingley?" she asked.

Her sister bit her lip, staring at the shrubbery on the other side of the path. "Do you remember when we viewed the stars on the roof of Uncle Gardiner's house? He told us how we could determine which was the Polar Star because it was brighter than all the other stars?"

"Yes," Elizabeth responded cautiously.

"At first I did not understand because *all* the stars seemed so bright and beautiful, but after a minute I could see that one of them was indeed the brightest. That is how I feel about Charles. There are many handsome men. Many well-spoken, gentlemanly men. But when I look at Charles, he shines so much more brightly than all the others."

Elizabeth felt as if someone were shining a bright star directly into her eyes. "Ohhhh."

Jane's eyes were fixed on the shrubbery, but no doubt she was imagining her beloved. Finally, her sister brought her focus back to Elizabeth. "Do you love Mr. Darcy?"

"I do not know."

"Does he shine more brightly than all the other men you know?"

"Yes," Elizabeth said slowly. "He does. He certainly does. But can I trust that feeling? What if it is simply the result of gratitude or habit?"

Jane shrugged. "That is a risk. Perhaps you ought not to attempt it."

Elizabeth's hands tightened spasmodically, crushing Jane's handkerchief into a little ball. "No, you are wrong! I ought to attempt it!"

One side of Jane's mouth curved up in a smile, and Elizabeth understood that she had been tricked.

"Clever Jane," she laughed. "Sometimes you know me better than I know myself."

Jane took one of Elizabeth's hands and squeezed it affectionately. "You should visit Pemberley and speak with him."

"What will I say?"

"Lizzy, when are you ever at a loss for words? You will know when you are there."

***

"William!"

Darcy started guiltily at the sound of his name. "Hmm?" He turned to his sister.

"You have not eaten any of your dinner!"

He glanced down at his plate; in truth he had forgotten they were eating a meal. "That is not so, Georgiana. I ate a…" He searched the plate for an empty spot. "I had a piece of potato…I believe."

Georgiana rolled her eyes. "I do not know why you bother to come down to dinner. You only pick at your food and stare out of the window."

I am the worst brother who ever lived. "Dearest, I apologize. Was there something you wished to discuss?"

"I was discussing it. You were not attending to my words," she said tartly.

"I am sorry. What were you saying? Something about the letter from Adele?" Since returning from France, Darcy had sought a way to bring Adele and her family safely to England and away from the dangers in Paris.

Georgiana made a sour face. "I was describing my plans to elope with Billy, the gardener's son."

A moment of panic shot through Darcy before he realized that his sister was joking. "The gardener's son is named Robert."

His sister sat up straighter in her chair and laid down her fork. "You must simply go and retrieve her."

"Adele?"

She rolled her eyes. "No! Adele will be here soon, I am certain. I speak of the woman who has occupied all of your thoughts."

Darcy dropped his gaze to the table. Apparently his melancholy had been more noticeable than he believed.

"You ran off to France to avenge her death and discovered she is alive. What I do not understand is why you did not just bring her to Pemberley."

Darcy slumped in his chair. "She would not have me, Georgiana."

"She would not have you?" His sister's tone was reassuringly incredulous.

"It is understandable; I lied to her. She has cause to be unhappy with me."

"Do you love her?"

"This is not an appropriate subject to discuss with my sister."

"Good! You do." Georgiana gave him a sunny smile. "You know where she lives?"

"Of course, but—"

"You have granted her enough time to think. You should ride to her home tomorrow and renew your offer of marriage."

It was a tantalizing idea: ride to the door of Longbourn and sweep Elizabeth off her feet. Her mother would be excited—at least about Darcy's fortune—and her father would begrudgingly support the idea—most likely.

"The worst that would happen is that she would say no. It might be a little embarrassing," Georgiana said.

Indeed, but Darcy had already laid himself bare to Elizabeth. Did he have any shame left where she was concerned?

His sister shrugged philosophically. "But what is a little embarrassment compared to a lifetime of living alone?"

She was not wrong. But could Darcy really accept advice from a girl of not quite seventeen years? Should he?

Still, life at Pemberley was dull and colorless. He pushed through his days with the enthusiasm of an automaton, performing his duties with scrupulous precision and no passion. If he visited Bingley at Netherfield and happened to make a trip to Longbourn…who knows what he might find? Elizabeth might have changed her mind, or at least softened her opinion of him. Perhaps he might persuade her…

Or perhaps she might accept another man's offer of marriage.

No, he must reach her before then!

Abruptly, he was on his feet. "I will have Bowen pack some clothes for me."

He glanced at Georgiana for approval, but her attention had been drawn by movement outside the window. "There is a carriage in the drive."

The dining room windows overlooked the front of the house; Darcy peered through them, noting a scruffy black carriage pulling to a stop before the entrance. "I believe it is the rig the Inn at Lambton hires out for visitors."

"Who would be staying at the Inn and visiting us—?" Georgiana started to ask, but the room was already empty.

Darcy strode purposefully toward the front entrance, reminding himself that running would be undignified. He knew who he *hoped* the visitor would be, but of course, that hope was most likely in vain. It could be a friend visiting on a whim. Or a matter of business. But he had just been thinking of her… Hope propelled him into the front hall.

Jones, the butler, was opening the door.

Darcy had never seen a more beautiful sight. Her dress was rumpled and stained with mud at the hem. Her bonnet was crushed on one side where she most likely had leaned her head while sleeping. Wisps of hair curled around her face, and dark circles lurked under her eyes.

But she was at Pemberley.

"Elizabeth!" Giving her no chance to speak, Darcy crossed the hall in two strides and gathered her into his arms. The kiss was desperate and passionate, as he poured nearly four weeks' worth of absence and frustration into it.

By the time he released her, she was even more rumpled—and quite bemused. Georgiana, Jones, two footmen, and a maid were all staring at him in wonder. It was, to be fair, uncharacteristic behavior for the master of Pemberley.

He would be mortified if she had arrived for some other purpose. To see the sights of Derbyshire, for example. Or to borrow a volume of poetry they had discussed. Darcy rubbed the back of his neck as his face heated. "Um…Elizabeth…Bennet, may I introduce my sister, Georgiana Darcy?" He gestured vaguely as the two women exchanged curtsies, his sister with a broad grin on her face.

He needed to regain control of the situation. "Er…Elizabeth…Miss Bennet, what brings you to Pemberley?"

Georgiana giggled.

Elizabeth's eyes darted nervously about the entrance hall; it certainly was far grander than the one at Longbourn—or even Rosings. "You…ah…said…If I changed my mind…" Her eyes took note of the servants—"on a particular subject…I should tell you," she said slowly.

Darcy ran his fingers through his hair, regarding her in bemusement. "I expected you to write to me."

She gave him an arch smile. "Mr. Darcy, you know it would be improper for me to write to you."

"And showing up alone on my doorstep is not improper?" he asked with a returning grin.

She fidgeted under his scrutiny. "Perhaps I…came to visit your sister."

Georgiana giggled again.

Darcy frowned. "Did you travel post all this way alone?"

"I did."

"Elizabeth—"

"Mr. Darcy, I found that after my recent journey through France, traveling by post through the English countryside did not seem terribly dangerous."

The risks she had taken! "Elizabeth—" he said in a warning tone.

"Miss Bennet," Georgiana interrupted, "surely you did not travel all this way to receive a lecture from my brother about your safety." She gave her brother a quelling glance.

"No." Elizabeth grinned at his sister. *Already they are allied against me; I am in trouble.*

"So what were you hoping would arise out of today's visit?" Georgiana asked with a mischievous grin.

Elizabeth responded to Georgiana, but her eyes sought Darcy's. "A few weeks ago—upon our parting—your brother promised me that if I wished it…a certain offer would be forthcoming."

"And you wish it?" Georgiana asked.

Elizabeth's gaze still rested on Darcy. "Yes," she whispered.

Darcy did not hesitate; at any moment she might change her mind. He dropped to one knee before her. The servants gasped as one. "Miss Elizabeth Bennet, would you do me the very great honor of—"

Elizabeth did not allow him to finish. "Yes! Yes, I will marry you. Yes, I will be your wife. Yes, I will pledge myself to you forever."

Mere words could not come close to expressing Darcy's joy upon this occasion. The only thing he could do was sweep Elizabeth into his arms and give her a most passionate kiss.

Epilogue

"Enough kissing, Darcy; there will be time enough for that later!"
Bingley's voice held more than a hint of laughter.

Darcy pulled away from Elizabeth but did not release his grip on
her shoulders. "You are a fine one to talk," he muttered to Bingley.

Bingley blushed a furious red. "It was only the one time!" he
protested. "And we believed we were alone in the garden." He gestured to
the people milling about Longbourn's drawing room. "You, on the other
hand, are kissing in plain view of everyone at your own wedding
breakfast!"

Darcy raised an eyebrow. "I dare anyone to gainsay my right to
kiss my wife after my wedding ceremony. I believe we have earned it."

Bingley sighed. "I suppose so." After all, the news of Elizabeth's
miraculous return from the dead and Darcy's role in her rescue had not
only given them fame in Hertfordshire but also granted them some leeway
with their behavior that other couples might not enjoy. Darcy was
determined to push that tolerance to its limits—not for its own sake but
because he simply could not prevent himself from expressing his affection
for his wife.

Elizabeth laughed. "Let us leave off for now, William. I would
like to converse with some of the guests at my own wedding breakfast.
There will be time enough for kissing later," she teased in a low voice.

These words alone were enough to stir the blood in Darcy's veins
and make him long for nighttime.

He had been right to decline Mrs. Bennet's plea for a long
engagement. He had waited long enough for his bride, and a month was
all he had been willing to grant for the sake of wedding preparations.
Scarcely less eager, Bingley and Jane had taken advantage of Darcy's
impatience and decided to make it a double wedding.

Thus, Jane and Elizabeth Bennet were wed to the loves of their
lives within seconds of each other. Nothing could have made the sisters—
or their bridegrooms—happier.

Mrs. Bennet had spent the last month in a frenzy of preparation,
but now she seemed a bit overcome by the proceedings. Rather than
gadding about the breakfast to chat with guests, she had collapsed into a
chair and babbled tearfully about how fortunate she was that her daughters
had found such fine gentlemen to marry.

Darcy surveyed the room in satisfaction, watching the people he loved most in the world enjoy each other's company—or at least tolerate it. In one corner, Richard had been trapped by Kitty and Lydia as they vied for his attentions. He was the only man in regimentals, so naturally he drew their attention.

Darcy had learned to his satisfaction that Wickham had been cashiered out of the militia after abandoning his regiment in Brighton to escape some debts. His whereabouts remained unknown. Elizabeth had discovered that Lydia had harbored some partiality for Wickham, but Elizabeth's untimely "death" had required the youngest Bennet daughter to return to Longbourn, undoubtedly escaping further meddling from Wickham.

Then Darcy's eye was caught by a most welcome sight: Adele— her niece and nephew in tow—moving in his direction. They had only arrived in Hertfordshire the previous day and still showed signs of fatigue from their journey. Adele and Marie were clearly delighted to be in England, and even Bernard had lost some of his sour demeanor when he learned his aunt might permit him to join the English army. He felt destined to be a soldier, but Adele had forbidden him to fight for Napoleon.

Darcy also had written to Mr. Martin, inviting him to leave France and come to Pemberley. The older man was considering it. The town of Lambton needed a doctor, so Darcy hoped that the Martins would accept his offer.

Adele embraced Darcy and Elizabeth, who introduced the French visitors to Jane and Bingley. "You will be remaining in Britain?" Bingley asked with a wide smile.

"Yes," Adele responded. "For now we will live at Pemberley, but we cannot remain indefinitely."

Darcy shook his head. "I have told you I would love for you to stay, and I always say what I mean."

Adele considered this. "That is true, but if I live at Pemberley, I would wish to contribute to the household. Mrs. Reynolds hardly requires any assistance."

Darcy exchanged a look with Elizabeth that made the latter blush. "We are hoping we could soon offer you a suitable occupation."

Adele frowned in confusion, but Marie covered her mouth, her eyes dancing with merriment. Apparently Darcy needed to be more explicit. "Mrs. Darcy"—how he loved the sound of those words—"and I are hoping to have the nursery occupied within a year."

The older woman's eyes lit up. "Oh, *magnifique*! I would love to help raise another generation of Darcys. Someone must teach them proper French."

"As you say," Darcy agreed. He had seen Marie entertain some of the children at the wedding breakfast and had no doubt she would make an excellent governess when her aunt retired.

Adele clasped her hands to her bosom, surveying the crowd. "I cannot believe you are wed, Will! It seems like only a few days ago you were sliding down the banister and spilling ink over your father's papers."

"Oho!" Bingley chortled. "So he did get into scrapes just like other boys! I had always wondered."

Darcy rolled his eyes at his friend, but Adele's eyes twinkled. "Indeed, he did. I could tell you stories…"

As the Frenchwoman involved Jane and Bingley in tales of Darcy's childhood hijinks, he drew Elizabeth away. He had been sufficiently sociable for a while; now he wanted a bit of time with his bride.

He drew her to a corner of the room where a window overlooked the garden. "William," she laughingly protested, "we should talk to our guests."

"We will in a moment," he said, nuzzling her neck. "I just needed to take a moment to remember how fortunate I am that I traveled to France and that you survived the shipwreck. I could have lost you so easily."

She regarded him with serious eyes. "Even when you found me, I was still lost—at least for a while."

He shook his head. "Not truly lost. I always knew you belonged with me, even when you had forgotten me."

"I must have slipped into the role as your wife so easily because part of me always knew I was destined to be yours. My soul knew what my mind had forgotten."

"So you are saying you never truly forgot me in your heart?"

"Precisely." She gave him a wide, wicked grin. "You are truly unforgettable, Mr. Darcy."

The End

Thank you for purchasing this book. I know you have many entertainment options, and I appreciate your spending your time with my story.

Support from readers like you makes it possible for independent authors
like me to continue writing.

Reviews are a book's lifeblood. Please consider leaving a review where you purchased the book.

Learn more about me and my upcoming releases:

Sign up for my newsletter Dispatches from Pemberley

Website: www.victoriakincaid.com

Twitter: VictoriaKincaid @kincaidvic

Blog: https://kincaidvictoria.wordpress.com/

Facebook: https://www.facebook.com/kincaidvictoria

About Victoria Kincaid

The author of numerous best-selling *Pride and Prejudice* variations, historical romance writer Victoria Kincaid has a Ph.D. in English literature and runs a small business, er, household with two children, a hyperactive dog, an overly affectionate cat, and a husband who is not threatened by Mr. Darcy. They live near Washington DC, where the inhabitants occasionally stop talking about politics long enough to complain about the traffic.

On weekdays she is a freelance writer/editor who now specializes in IT marketing (it's more interesting than it sounds). In the past, some of her more…unusual writing subjects have included space toilets, taxi services, laser gynecology, bidets, orthopedic shoes, generating energy from onions, Ferrari rental car services, and vampire face lifts (she swears she is not making any of this up). A lifelong Austen fan, Victoria has read more Jane Austen variations and sequels than she can count – and confesses to an extreme partiality for the Colin Firth version of *Pride and Prejudice*.

Also by Victoria Kincaid:

President Darcy

A modern adaptation of *Pride and Prejudice*

Billionaire President William Darcy has it all: wealth, good friends, and the most powerful job in the world. Despite what his friends say, he is not lonely in the White House. He's not. And he has vowed not to date while he's in office. Nor is he interested in Elizabeth Bennet. Although she is pretty and funny and smart, her family is nouveau riche and unbearable. To make it worse, he encounters her everywhere in Washington D.C.—making it harder and harder to ignore her. Why can't he get Elizabeth Bennet out of his mind?

Elizabeth Bennet enjoys her job with the Red Cross and loves her family, despite their tendency to embarrass themselves. When they drag her to a White House state dinner, they cause her to make a unfavorable impression on the president, who labels her unattractive and uninteresting—words that are immediately broadcast on Twitter. Now the whole world knows the president dissed her. All Elizabeth wants is to avoid the man—who, let's admit it, is proud and difficult. For some reason he acts so friendly when they keep running into each other, but she just knows he's judging her.

Eventually circumstances force Darcy and Elizabeth to confront their true feelings for each other, with explosive results. But even if they can find common ground, Darcy is still the president—with limited privacy and unlimited responsibilities—and his enemies won't hesitate to use his feelings for Elizabeth to hurt his presidency.

Can President Darcy and Elizabeth Bennet find their way to happily ever after?

Darcy vs. Bennet

Elizabeth Bennet is drawn to a handsome, mysterious man she meets at a masquerade ball. However, she gives up all hope for a future with him when she learns he is the son of George Darcy, the man who ruined her father's life. Despite her father's demand that she avoid the younger Darcy, when he appears in Hertfordshire Elizabeth cannot stop thinking about him, or seeking him out, or welcoming his kisses....

Fitzwilliam Darcy has struggled to carve out a life independent from his father's vindictive temperament and domineering ways, although the elder Darcy still controls the purse strings. After meeting Elizabeth Bennet, Darcy cannot imagine marrying anyone else, even though his father despises her family. More than anything he wants to make her his wife, but doing so would mean sacrificing everything else....

Mr. Darcy to the Rescue

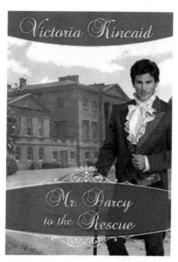

When the irritating Mr. Collins proposes marriage, Elizabeth Bennet is prepared to refuse him, but then she learns that her father is ill. If Mr. Bennet dies, Collins will inherit Longbourn and her family will have nowhere to go. Elizabeth accepts the proposal, telling herself she can be content as long as her family is secure. If only she weren't dreading the approaching wedding day…

Ever since leaving Hertfordshire, Mr. Darcy has been trying to forget his inconvenient attraction to Elizabeth. News of her betrothal forces him to realize how devastating it would be to lose her. He arrives at Longbourn intending to prevent the marriage but discovers Elizabeth's real opinion about his character. Then Darcy recognizes his true dilemma…

How can he rescue her when she doesn't want him to?

Darcy's Honor

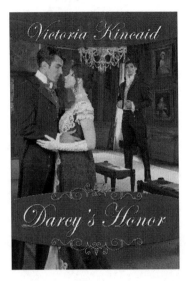

Elizabeth Bennet is relieved when the difficult Mr. Darcy leaves the area after the Netherfield Ball. But she soon runs afoul of Lord Henry, a Viscount who thinks to force her into marrying him by slandering her name and ruining her reputation. An outcast in Meryton, and even within her own family, Elizabeth has nobody to turn to and nowhere to go.

Darcy successfully resisted Elizabeth's charms during his visit to Hertfordshire, but when he learns of her imminent ruin, he decides he must propose to save her from disaster. However, Elizabeth is reluctant to tarnish Darcy's name by association…and the viscount still wants her…

Can Darcy save his honor while also marrying the woman he loves?

Christmas at Darcy House

Mr. Darcy hopes Christmastime will help him to forget the pair of fine eyes that he left behind in Hertfordshire. When Elizabeth Bennet appears unexpectedly in London, Darcy decides to keep his distance, resolved to withstand his attraction to her. But when he learns that Wickham is threatening to propose to Elizabeth, Darcy faces a crisis.

For her part, Elizabeth does not understand why the unpleasant master of Pemberley insists on dancing with her at the Christmas ball or how his eyes happen to seek her out so often. She enjoys Mr. Wickham's company and is flattered when he makes her an offer of marriage. On the other hand, Mr. Darcy's proposal is unexpected and unwelcome. But the more Elizabeth learns of Mr. Darcy, the more confused she becomes—as she prepares to make the most momentous decision of her life.

It's a Yuletide season of love and passion as your favorite characters enjoy Christmas at Darcy House!

Made in the USA
Middletown, DE
10 September 2018